SHUTTER

RAMONA EMERSON

Published by
Soho Press, Inc.
227 W 17th Street
New York, NY 10011

Library of Congress Cataloging-in-Publication Data

Names: Emerson, Ramona, author.
Title: Shutter / Ramona Emerson.
Description: New York : Soho Crime, [2022]
Identifiers: LCCN 2021061291

ISBN 978-1-64129-333-4
eISBN 978-1-64129-334-1

Subjects: LCSH: Navajo women—Fiction. | LCGFT: Detective and mystery
fiction | Thrillers (Fiction) | Ghost stories | Novels.
Classification: LCC PS3605.M485 S58 2022 | DDC 813/.6—dc23/eng/20211221
LC record available at https://lccn.loc.gov/2021061291

Printed in the United States of America

10 9 8 7 6 5 4 3 2 1

For Grandma, Minnie S. Emerson

CHAPTER ONE

Nikon D50 18-55mmDX

SOULS DON'T SCATTER like the rest of the body. They latch on for as long as they can, their legs pulled to the sky, fingertips white in desperation. Souls are grasping for us, for the ones they left behind, and for the truth only they can see. They are the best witnesses to their last breaths.

I stand in that bitter, cold wind with that ghost and take its picture.

Tonight, nothing was left. After two hours of metal on bone and flesh on asphalt, there were only yellow plastic forensic markers lined up like soldiers on the darkened freeway, all seventy-five of them marking the resting place of this soul, who was now merged with the blacktop, the blood and tissue part of its earth and chemicals. I watched the lead investigator lay another marker in the distance. Seventy-six.

Static crackled through the radio.

"We have OMI en route." Office of the Medical Investigator. "DB I-40 westbound at Louisiana walkover. A body on the highway. Respond. Photo One? Are you there?"

"Photo One. I'm here."

I knew then that I would be out here for hours. I clawed into my last pack of nicotine gum, pulling two pieces from the foil, and jerked myself into my paper suit and latex skin. Neither did anything to cut the cold. I ducked beneath the tape. We were always the first on the scene, the photographers. Next month would be sixty-six months for me. Five and a half years of taking pictures of dead people.

This person had been scattered—muscles and flesh torn by the push and pull of steel, by hot rubber and propulsion, speed and physics. The markers stretched out farther than I could see, a serpent of reflective yellow slithering into sky and tar. Too many people were on scene, mostly cops surveying the carnage, telling stories in huddles, pulled together by whispers.

I walked to marker one. Surrounded by the night sky, I took the first overall photo. I perched above; the wide angle lens was just wide enough. A galaxy of shimmering light set off every marker, every piece of flesh bound in yellow haze. The first ten pieces were small and unrecognizable, splinters of bone and chunks of tissue. By marker twenty-one, the pieces were bigger. A waxy, oily section of skin lay before me, the photo catching every detail of newly shaven legs, of the nick she gave herself probably that morning, of a faded tattoo saying "Forever." I could tell it was a leg by the ghostly white bone that protruded from the flesh. A femur. Twenty-two was a piece of ankle; twenty-three was a left foot with two toes missing—a snake and tree tattoo twisting out of the hole they left. When I found the toes about a foot away, they were still attached to each other by a thin rope of dry skin. Twenty-four.

The other leg was complete, torn low in the thigh. The kneecap faced north, scuffed to the bone, but the rest of the leg twisted south. The bones in the legs were cleanly snapped, the exposed flesh like outstretched hands. Every single bone in the right foot looked like it was broken. The pinky toe was missing. Marker thirty.

The hip bones were still intact, held together by the seams of the pants. About six inches of left leg remained, with no bone visible. My camera focused in on the partial tire track above the break. A breeze moved through and pushed the heavy iron scent of blood into my nose, a hint of decay catching in my throat.

The iliac crest overhung the torn flesh right above ripped, blood-soaked pants. Glittery sequins shimmered when I used my primary flash, shredded backbone pulling white into the camera frame. I used my slave flash and hot shoe attachment and tried the image again. On the rear viewfinder, I saw a twenty-dollar bill sticking out of the pocket. I hadn't noticed it on my first glance. Image count: 175.

I moved along the side of the road, approaching the shoulder in a grid, carefully measuring the length of each piece of debris and the distance between various fragments of the body. The liver, intestines, kidneys, and uterus had not fared well: the tissue flattened by tires and caked with debris. I found her heart at number thirty-four, in the grass away from the asphalt, as if an invisible angel had laid it in place. I had never seen a heart like this, so pristine I almost waited for it to beat. It was like a sacred heart of Jesus postcard.

By the time I got to number forty-seven, I had photographed half of her body, including most of her internal organs. But forty-seven was her torso. It measured about fifteen inches, according to my scale. The woman was petite. She had lots of detailed and beautiful tattoos, the stories behind them now silenced, the ink unchained. The skid marks, ten and a half feet long, lined up with her rib cage, jagged back roads that cut through the land-scape of her remains.

Around the edges of a frayed six inches of bicep, a tattered heather-gray T-shirt was rolled into a tight cylinder, cinching the skin. Two shimmering strips of nylon still rested lightly along her shoulder blade, the remnants of her bra. The rest of it was next to the torso, balled up and streaked with black tar. The scream of the charging flash orbited the night air. Image number 231.

A mist of condensation hung in the night sky. Even out in the cold, my hat and scarf were soaked with sweat. I peeled them away. I lifted my eyes to see how much was left. As I continued to shoot, I could hear the conversation between an investigator and a truck driver, the only driver who had bothered to stop.

"I didn't see anything out there. Just the thud. Just the thud like I've been telling you."

"I understand, sir. Where did the thud come from?"

"From the front left side, then way back on the left tires. I could feel the back ones roll over something, so I stopped."

"And then what did you do?"

"Jumped out of the cab." The man hesitated and grabbed the bill of his blue hat, the kind with the plastic mesh on the back. "Then I saw pieces, and I called it in."

Hundreds of cars had passed her, unknowingly carrying her flesh beyond the boundaries of the city. I was sure there would be pieces we would never find. It was only us now, five investigators, fifteen cops, and my camera, visible only by the turning, cherry-red lights of patrol cars. There was no moon out tonight; the sky was the color of indigo ink. I moved on. I was about halfway there and my fingertips were numb.

Number forty-eight began with pieces of arms and fingers. Her thumb was alone, the fingernail bit down to the nail bed, flecked with red polish. On the yellow line of the highway, we found her little toe, polished the same color as her fingernails. It was over twenty feet from the rest of her feet and legs. Image 456.

The largest piece of the skull was her jawbone, two bottom teeth missing, gums still bloody. Number sixty-eight. Even after the few hours she had spent on the road, her skin was soft. A delicate covering of fine hair lined the condyle of her jaw, the joint where the bones meet beneath the ear. It sat on the road at a forty-five-degree angle. There wasn't even a drop of blood on the skin. I pressed my finger to the shutter release and raised the viewfinder. My eye stung from the flash.

One of the scene investigators walked behind me with the medical examiner, Dr. Blaser, who carried a box of red biohazard bags under his arm. He reached out and touched my shoulder. I turned to see his awkward smile and his nod.

"Rita."

I returned the nod. They kept walking.

"So how long do you think she's been out there?" An officer scribbled on a report. Dr. Blaser stopped and looked at the sky.

"A couple of hours. When does the sun set again?"

My eavesdropping was interrupted by the shouts of officers chasing someone off the overpass. I watched as three onlookers ran into the shadows, followed by the beams of the officers' flashlights. I'd need to get up on that overpass to photograph anything that looked out of the ordinary. Officers in paper suits fanned their flashlights through fence lines and over handrails. I watched one lay down a marker. My feet began to ache. I needed to focus. It had been fifty-two hours since I last slept.

Her nasal bones and suborbital ridge were crushed into a chalky white puzzle immersed in crimson. Marker seventy-seven. The insides of the skull began to appear in various fragments, broken at the skeletal sutures. The yellow markers stood at attention: eighty-eight, eighty-nine, ninety. I photographed one of the eyeballs, free from its bone and muscle, lying between a crushed beer can and the remnants of broken windshield glass. Number ninety-three. The pieces of teeth were five inches from a pile of ash and cigarette butts—what remained of a two-day snowstorm. Some travelers along this highway had passed this way over two weeks ago and dumped their ashtray onto the road. It had frozen there, strangely protected from the elements by the melt and freeze of ice. Number ninety-eight.

I walked onto the overpass, a two-lane bridge with walk-ways on the sides. The cement moved beneath my feet as police directed traffic through one lane of the bridge. A small section of the walkway was cordoned off with yellow tape; a lonely yellow marker reflected in the passing headlights. Two detectives waited impatiently for me to photograph a purse that sat on the curbside. The fat, ugly one was Detective Martin Garcia. The other was his completely silent new partner, Detective Vargas. His long-time partner, Detective Armenta, had a heart attack last month and had officially retired. The marker: M2—Miscellaneous.

"We need to see if we can find some ID in this bag, Rita," Garcia said.

No one could touch anything until I took a picture of it. The two of them were antsy. Garcia's hands were on his hips; his greasy skin bounced back the rosy orange light of the bridge lanterns.

"Can you?" He brought an imaginary camera up to his face and pressed the button.

"Where's M1?"

"Over here. On the other side of the railing." He pulled sky-blue gloves over his fat, hairy hands.

I walked up to the railing, shining my flashlight down below.

A pair of red stiletto heels hung from a steel beam that jutted from the overpass, the ankle straps caught on the jagged edge. Garcia peered over with me.

"Guess she didn't like 'em, huh?"

Above the red stilettos, a technician covered the rails of the bridge in powdery black. A trail of smudges led to the black outline where they tried to lift prints. It was the last place our victim had touched the overpass. Two sets of finger groups, four fingers on each side, had gripped the metal in desperation. She had not wanted to jump. The two partial handprints showed a larger presence, someone with strong, thick hands and deep lines in their skin. The left print was smeared, but the right one was clear and showed that whoever had helped her to the edge had been wearing rubber gloves. Forensics pulled the tape anyway and transferred them to the evidence cards.

The flash lit up the bridge and filled the camera frame with the red shoes, size seven. I dangled myself over the railing, balancing with the weight of my boots. Flash. The viewfinder read 965 of 1,000 images.

Back at M2, I hovered above the bag and dropped my scale on the concrete. The bag was ten inches long and six inches across. The white leather was soft, worn, and scuffed underneath, the brown leather handles darkened with oil and dirt. The zipper was open. I raised the camera and framed the purse, the only witness here to what had really happened. On the right side of the bag, there was a shoe print pressed into the leather. It looked like a work boot. One of the investigators pulled a wallet from the bag and opened it, sending a tattered photograph to the ground. A young woman with long, full, and slightly curled hair, smiling, her right arm around the neck of another woman with a glowing white halo of hair. The young woman had an electric smile and wore a red tank top, a tattoo of a baby's face on the right side of her chest. I had seen that tattoo before—well, what was left of it. They found her driver's license and laid it on top of the wallet. I snapped a photo of the ID: Erma Singleton. Size 7 shoes. Thought it would last forever. I pressed the shutter down. Image number 1,000.

As I made my way off the bridge and back to the highway, the sky was turning from black to blue, the stars disappearing from bottom to top. The new light revealed the uneven strip of aged blood that skittered left, right, and in spirals on the highway— the path of her body's final movements. I changed memory cards. The light allowed me to frame the scene from above as it unfurled beneath the red shoes, the first splash of blood directly below the dangling, stained leather.

The Office of the Medical Investigator had collected and sealed nearly all the body. Only a few yellow evidence markers remained. The haggard-faced investigators were eager to crawl back to their homes and bury their heads beneath the pillows. I could only hope that I would be able to fall asleep when I got home.

I followed the blood and searched for anything we might have missed. The lingering smell of death was developing.

I saw it then. A small hunk of flesh hadn't been spotted by any officer or investigator. We all had walked this path before, more than two or three times, but we had missed it. The skin matched the color of the slightly reddened clay on the roadside, drawn into the earth, the pull of death's process.

"Over here!" I called.

I took a few pictures before they had a chance to contaminate the scene. The beams of the flashlights dropped, the hollow light fixed on my boots. A piece of face, the ear and the eye still intact, the lid partially open. The eye was green, turning iridescent as they watched.

"Can you go ahead and make a marker for this one, Officer?"

Nothing.

"Officer?"

"Oh. I'm sorry." Officer Branson was three days on the job. He laid down a yellow marker.

One hundred.

I took the picture. I had taken 1,015 pictures of over a hundred separate pieces of a human being and her belongings. I had five scrapes on my own hands and knees and one filthy white paper suit.

I sat in my car for fifteen minutes and labeled three photo cards and five pages of notes.

The pain started somewhere in my temple, I closed my eyes, hoping to escape it, but it stayed—the pain, and the heavy yellow light that was sitting in my front seat.

CHAPTER TWO

Exakta VX 1000

THESE LIGHTS HAVE been with me for as long as I can remember. And even now, I remember almost everything.

I was a quiet baby. My grandmother told stories about how I would stay silent for twenty-four-hour periods, depriving her and my mother, Anne, of sleep because they wondered if I was dead. But there I would be every morning, eyes wide, looking to the sky, where there was a ray of light only I could see. I didn't cry. I was just awake. All the time.

"I think something is wrong with her, Mom." My worried mother would watch me stare into space, letting out a giddy laugh.

"There is nothing wrong with her," my grandmother would say. "She's just talking to someone out there, and it's none of our business."

I remember my grandmother saying this. She looked over her shoulders all the time, trying to glimpse what I was staring at. Now I know there was nothing there.

For me, there was a collection of lights and smiling faces—high-pitched giggles and highlighted silhouettes. The lights played with me like parents play with their newborns. They would pull close to me, enough that I could smell their sweetness. I learned to love them and the honey drops on their whispers. They never hurt me or brought darkness to me, so I always smiled back.

As an infant, I watched my mother sneak over my cradle railings at night, her creaking camera shutter snapping pictures of me while I lay awake. Her eyes were a distant abstraction of brown fragments through the elongated viewfinder. I remember her Exakta with the left-handed shutter button, her chipped fingernails, her deep-set brown eyes, just like mine—I remember all of us sitting under the golden light of my mother's bedroom and marveling, awake.

I felt the expanse between us as my mother would take frame after frame, pulling the camera away from her face only to look at me like a specimen, a jagged piece of a puzzle that she couldn't finish. My mother was beautiful. She was too young to be my mother. Her face was soft and naive, with the easy, gentle hint of an unrecognized future. When she held me, I was afraid of falling. Her arms were small, bony, and inexperienced, rocking from side to side unsteadily, drawing me closer and looking at me with blurry, watering eyes. When I was hungry, she fed me. But her gaze moved past me and into a future that I could not be a part of.

How obvious it was that poor Anne had no idea what she was doing with a baby. The conception had been a hurried affair, and I was a haunting reminder of Anne's bad decisions. After two and a half drinks and a two-block walk back to her small, cold college apartment, she had finally surrendered to my father, a boy named Abel who had pestered her for months with smiles and dimples. She'd tried to take his picture, but he always refused. She pressed the button anyway, collecting photographs of fragmented faces, eyes and lips segmented by his intruding hand in frame.

The morning after she finally gave in, Abel kissed her and said he would be back; she never saw him again. Never in class, never on the street. Her friends remembered him with curly hair and light eyes. But Anne remembered his black hair, straight and shiny, and his eyes, dark brown and mysterious. He had a small mole right above his left cheekbone.

Anne has never forgiven me for coming into her life and yanking the brake on her future in the most unforgiving way. Here she was again, living with her mother, me at her breast, my eyes wide open. And what of Abel, this ghost that was my father? She screamed his name as she packed to return home, me in her stomach. She would shout his name in desperation as she walked alone outside my grandmother's house. And for this I was sorry.

Three years after she had come home to the reservation, on the anniversary, she left us. The house was quiet except for the slow stir of coffee in the kitchen. My grandma sat in the blue of morning, the cresting sun hauling light from her white cabinets. She lifted me on her knee and smiled. We both knew that it was better this way. Grandma's arms were strong and able and experienced. I knew she wouldn't drop me.

That was all I saw of my mother for a few years, except for a picture that my grandmother had pinned to her bedroom wall. My mother, wearing a light pink sweater, stood in the rain, her moist hair forming into ringlets. She grinned with her eyes straight ahead. When I made my way into my grandma's room and stared at the photograph, Mom's eyes followed me. I would run from left to right, right to left, and her eyes turned with me. Sometimes I would just sit and talk to the picture, imagining our conversations.

After Mom left, my grandma took me to the medicine man, and he sang for me. His hands were strong and thick but soft. When we came into his house, he spun me in circles. He blew smoke and said prayers; his bone whistle echoed in my head for hours. I finally started to sleep, an hour here and there, eventually in blocks of three and four.

I learned early that no amount of prayer or smoke or love was ever going to change the fact that these lights wanted to talk to me. Even at three years old, I knew it was something that deeply terrified my grandma and our medicine man. It was something that I was going to have to hide from them.

As I got older, I taught myself how to look beyond the ghosts and mute their voices. I learned to listen to the world in ways no one could imagine. My ears focused on the sounds in Grandma's house: the creaking door hinges, the high-pitched scream of Grandma's tea kettle, the tick of her scarecrow clock. I integrated their voices with these sounds, with the songs of birds at my grandma's bedroom window, the constant drone of Highway 666 to our east, and the whispers of the wind coming through the valley beside the Chuska Mountains. I learned to listen for wild horses running in the wash below the house and the herds of sheep grazing in the valley. Anything to keep the sight and sound of ghosts from taking over my every waking moment.

But no matter how strong I think I am, this thing—call it a gift or a curse—is still a part of me, just like my veins, heart, and hands. It is attached. It is a part of my voice and vision—this visually enhanced speakerphone from some other place. I can't turn it off.

CHAPTER THREE

Nikon D50 18-55mmDX
Revisited

I DIDN'T KNOW how long the detective had been tapping on my window. Droplets of water covered my windshield.

"Are you okay in there?" I watched his lips move, only half hearing the words. I rolled down the window.

"I'm fine. Long night."

"Shall I get one of the guys to drive you home? You look tired."

My head throbbed. "I'll be fine. Just needed some rest." I turned the key, surprised that I'd fallen asleep at the scene. I could see my breath. My skin felt thin and brittle in the morning sun. The office was only a few miles from here—I could bag things up there and move on home to bury myself in some blankets.

The APD crime lab building was shaped like a giant adobe cube. The small, square windows floating six feet above the ground let light in for about two hours a day during the steely gray Albuquerque winter. The building sat between I-25 and the Rio Grande, flanked on one side by a city recycling plant and, on the other, an emissions testing center. Sometimes, in the morning, if you were there early enough, you could smell the sweet dough and heated yeast of the bakery on the corner, but only if the wind blew in the right direction.

The photo and video offices were empty, with one last fluorescent light in the corner blinking toward extinction. Duplicated DVDs and CDs sat out, waiting for cases. I pulled the cards from my camera and began the download, the computer spinning in time and my brain along with it. The download bar ticked slowly. I hoped it would finish before my boss, Samuels, arrived. With only 35 percent of it downloaded at 8:26 A.M., I wasn't going to make it. The thought hadn't finished before the front doorbell began to chime.

"Rita! Are you in here?" Samuels's horrible voice boomed through the building.

I stood up in my cubicle with 45 percent of the job downloaded. "Right here."

"I hear you guys had quite a mess last night. I thought you all would be there for a few more hours."

Samuels breathed heavily as he moved toward me, his forehead glistening with sweat even in the frigid morning air. Spearmint gum, Windex, and pipe tobacco. The man's smell reminded me of the parking arcade in the Old Town Hotel, where the bums slept in the elevator's glass enclosure. Last time I was there, one of the bums was dead, his eyes still looking toward the opening and closing elevator doors as tourists walked past him all night, some tossing pennies into his empty coffee cup. No one knew he was dead until security poked him with a stick. He was as stiff as the concrete he rested on, sitting up with knees bent. I thought of him as Samuels approached, his smell following. I breathed through my mouth.

"I just got here. I thought I would download before I went home. I need to get some sleep."

"You're on call for the next two days. You know that, right?"

"I'm already working on my days off. Can't anyone else take pictures? There are ten people in this office who can."

"You can always go work at the bakery. I hear they're hiring." Samuels closed his office door. I dug my nails into my chair.

I knew the drill. Car accidents, petty crimes, property crimes took place every day, every night. Samuels sent out one of the scene investigators to snap a few photos, take a few measurements, help put things in bags. But I was there in case there was something that couldn't be messed up, where protocol had to be followed, where not one detail could be overlooked. In the five years since I had been with the Crime Scene Unit, I had developed a reputation as an asset, seeing things through my lens that analysts sometimes missed. Samuels knew I wanted the overtime, that I couldn't say no. The man depended on me like the oxygen, sugar, and tobacco that coursed through his muddled veins.

Samuels's white beard was a drugstore Santa's, his stark, white hair stained putrid hues of yellow and brown from years of smoking out of the same mahogany Calabash pipe—a naked woman entwined in a web of vines and flowers. His fat fingers displayed a huge maze of blackened veins where the brown resin of his pipe had dug deep into the smallest crevice. His desk, however, was miraculously clean and organized: well-filed documents filled yellow correspondence folders alphabetically and by topic. His photography was the finest example of forensic images—never out of focus, always to specifications.

He reminded me often about his credentials, his licenses, his degrees, and his years of experience. He never ceased pointing out my inadequacies, accusing me of lacking a true eye, or of soft focus on one of the sharpest photos I had ever taken. I didn't know whether it was his ego or his lectures that got under my skin, but I knew I was irritated, mostly by the fact that when I took that image home and blew it up hundreds of times its size, I finally saw my soft focus. Samuels had seen it through his thick, acetate glasses, stained ochre by his pudgy finger pushing on the bridge of the frame. He was the best and was willing to hire me with no experience. And I was doing what I loved—taking pictures. What more could I ask?

My training had gone quickly. Two years before I moved to the crime lab, Samuels took me to my first job—"A sensitive issue," he'd explained. His clients had brought a case against a youth home where their son had been living for two days. On day two, he'd had "an accident" and ended up in the morgue.

"The police department sent two blind officers to this investigation." Samuels scoffed.

The youth house had been closed since the incident, but the building had been sold and renovations were set to take place. The defendants were relying on the police photos of the incident, about six wide shots of the bedroom. Before the scene was destroyed, the boy's parents wanted photos that could prove his death had been no accident but the result of a severe beating, something the facility denied.

Samuels had instructed me to hide a camera in my coat and to follow along. I knew only the basics and the protocol from books and classes. He made small talk with the security guard until he paused and stared at me, eyes bulging. I knew that had to be my cue. I interrupted their conversation.

"Excuse me," I said, "but do you have a restroom I could use?"

"Upstairs, left."

I could hear their conversation continue as I stepped quickly up the stairs and into the hallway. The crime scene was immediately to my right. I ducked quietly under the yellow tape and began to shoot. There were three separate groupings of blood splatter that were about eighteen inches in diameter and seven or eight large, fist-sized holes in the porcelain-white walls. The rug was dotted with several pools of blood, the biggest seven inches in diameter. I laid a crinkled dollar bill on the floor for a size reference. It was something I had seen in a movie. I snapped away for a good two minutes, then stopped by the bathroom on my way out to flush the toilet for authenticity. They were still talking when I came down. We said our goodbyes and walked out the door.

Samuels hired me full-time the next day. I worked for his office for two years before we both moved to the crime lab.

SAMUELS HAD WORKED on these kinds of cases for over thirty years as a private investigator and as an evidence specialist—they were his bread and butter.

In the years before the Albuquerque Crime Lab hired Samuels, the whole police department had faced millions in lawsuit settlements and federal investigations. They were in desperate need of turning over a new leaf. When Samuels was offered the chief investigator job, he jumped at the opportunity to build on his retirement and closed his business. He was here to make sure the crime lab cleaned up its act. In the past five years, Samuels had kept it on an upward climb, even if the same could not be said for the police department as a whole.

The hiss and smell of Samuels's terrible coffee brought me back into reality. I could see myself reflected in the blackness of the screen—my dark hair and eyes accentuated by the deep, tan circles that cradled my lids. I was using my eyebrows to keep my eyes open. The hazy light of my migraine was returning.

The chair in the corner of my cubicle turned with a long

creak. Erma Singleton—the poor woman who lay in pieces on the highway—rocked in it, one leg over the other, red nail-polished toes glinting. I just stared at her ghost, my skin prickly from her heat. I couldn't do much else.

"What happened?" Erma whispered.

"I'm sorry," I replied.

"Who are you talking to?" Samuels barked, walking up with his arms full of files. The empty chair spun next to me.

"No one," I said.

CHAPTER FOUR

Paper and a Box

THE YEAR I turned five, Grandma taught me how to build a camera. It was also the first year that my grandpa began to visit me. At first, I didn't know it was him. My grandma, so heart-broken over his death, never kept a picture of him in our house.

Grandma could make anything out of nothing, and that is how we lived together in her little house. We had running water and electricity, which was a lot out there on the reservation. My grandma had built her house with her own hands, with concrete and nails and tar paper shingles. Grandma loved to tell stories about how all those Navajo women in the community would stare at her like she was crazy as she hammered away on the shingles of her roof and brought stones for her fireplace when the light had fallen low in the sky. The women had watched as Grandma yelled at the young men from the hardware store who'd done work on the house one weekend while she was away. She recounted the events over and over because I begged her to.

"Those fools put my garage on the wrong side!" she'd say, making me roll around in laughter. "Who needs to look out of their kitchen window into their garage? Not me!"

In protest, my grandmother never put a permanent floor in the garage. It always sat there with the same dirt floor that it began with.

"One day, Rita, I'm moving my garage to the other side. You'll see," she would say. She would tickle my stomach, and I would run away, the fresh laughter still working through my body. I wanted that garage on the right side, too, just because that was what Grandma wanted, even though I knew she could never afford to move it.

On the reservation, nestled deep within the red canyons and forgotten communities, tattered trailers and the skeletons of long-abandoned hogans stood like teeth. Hot sand ran into every crack and hole when the winds blew. Now, only shells remained, tied together with thinly stretched chicken wire and bare logs. Grandma had picked a good spot for her home site, hidden to shelter her house from the relentless west-to-east winds. Her home was a beacon of modern living nestled between territories preserved in times gone by. The mountains were at her front door, which faced north, and a dry riverbed made up the backyard. She liked to grow corn and squash, lettuce, and radishes. She sat out in the summer sun with me and her saltshaker, and we would eat fresh radishes from the ground, washed free of dirt with the cool water from her green hose.

Grandma and I used to take long walks into the dry riverbeds behind her house, looking for the long, green Navajo tea stalks that peeked out of the sand. Before gathering the stalks, Grandma would pray in Navajo and sprinkle her yellow corn pollen on them—we had to thank the tea before we could use it.

"Don't take the whole thing. Don't take it from the root. If you do, they won't be able to keep growing all summer," she lectured.

Her hands were full of the light-green stalks, their yellow flowers rising like unruly wires through her fingers.

I pulled gently at the plant, leaving a healthy six-inch stalk behind. Eventually, I rolled the stems inside my dirty T-shirt. We walked for a couple of hours before deciding to turn back, our legs sore from trudging in the deep sand. Grandma rolled her empty cloth flour bags around her neck to keep her cool. As we made our way up the final hills, our pockets and shirts filled with tea, I could see beads of sweat on Grandma's face. Her face was red with labor.

"Never get old," she said. "Do you hear?"

"Okay, Grandma."

Once home, we bent the tea into bundles and wrapped them with string. Grandma left the bundles out on the table to dry for a couple of days, then moved them to her copper tea canister. When she finally let me drink tea with her in the evenings, she would stare at me with a smile and shake of her head as I filled my tea with sugar cubes and milk from the can. Eventually, I convinced her to let me have morning coffee with her, sharing the off-white milk, sugar, and coffee concoction at the kitchen table.

On the day before I turned five, Grandma and I drove deep into the woods toward the Chuska Mountains on the other side of Tohatchi, where the blue spruce and aspen trees hissed only feet above the trail road. Our pickup shook and rattled along the way. Grandma had loaded us up with a shovel, a shabby gunny sack, a tattered cotton sheet, and a black box. I knew the sheet and gunny sack meant we were going up to the piñon trees to get nuts to roast and sell. A good gunny sack–full could make Grandma a little money here and there. I loved piñon nuts freshly roasted from the oven. When Grandma roasted and salted the piñon, the house filled with the smell of warmed pine sap.

We found a good spot near the creek and made our way up.

When we came across a tall, stout piñon tree, its cones full of brown berries, I worked myself up the branches and shook the tree with all the strength I had in my arms and legs. Grandma spread her white cotton sheet below and sat, quietly sorting through the pine needles to find the nuts.

"In the Navajo way," she explained, "you aren't supposed to shake the branches like you did just now." My feet braced my weight above the needles and branches. "When the piñon is ready, it will fall to the ground by itself. You're being impatient." She shook her head. "Doing it like that calls the bears to you. But they would have to get through me. Bears know better than to bother your grandma—the meat's too tough."

I pulled myself down out of the trees and sat at Grandma's side. We picked piñon until the sun was about to set and our gunny sack strained from the nuts pulsing inside.

When we got back to the truck, Grandma heaved our gunny sack into the cab and caught her breath. Then she grabbed the black box she'd brought, poking a small hole with a pen and covering it with black tape.

"What is that, Grandma?"

"I am going to make us a camera out of this box." She turned to me and smiled. "It's been a long time since I've tried this, so let's hope it works."

I watched her in silence as she pulled out a dark blanket, draping it over herself and the box. I could hear a rustle and scrape under the wool.

"Grandma. What are you doing?"

She emerged from the blanket with pieces of pine needles in her hair.

"I had to put some paper in the camera." She pushed me into the last beam of sunlight. "I'm going to take your picture."

"With what, Grandma?"

"With this box. Now, be quiet and watch. Stand right there." She waved her hand to the right and I moved with it. "Right there."

I watched her pull the sticky tape from the makeshift camera. "Stay still."

A bright light came from behind my grandma's head. Standing in the yellow haze, I saw the gray shadow of a man, thin and refined in a white cotton shirt, the sleeves rolled up to his forearms. I didn't know if I'd seen him before, but something about his presence was familiar. He smiled deeply as he looked at Grandma, then began walking toward me. I felt the surge of his energy when he came to a stop to my left. He left heat in the corners of my eyes. I turned back to the camera and didn't even breathe for a good ten seconds.

"That's it." She fastened the tape back to the hole and put the black box back into the truck cab. The cloudy form trailed her, then flew away into the late afternoon shade.

"You took a picture? Already? When can we see it?"

"Soon, Rita."

I watched Grandma's box all the way home and wondered how it could possibly be a camera. It looked like a discarded card-board box from our garage, painted up with tar.

We arrived thirty minutes later and unloaded the loot from the piñon trees. My grandma carried the black box in and walked straight into the closet, emerging with a black plastic bag.

"We'll take this into town tomorrow," she said, resting the black plastic bag on the table with her *Reader's Digest*. "Don't open it, because it will ruin the picture."

I stared at the untouchable bag. I wondered if the man would be in the picture with me. I hoped he would. He had a nice smile, with a perfect dimple on one cheek.

IT TOOK US thirty minutes to drive to Gallup the next day. The white light of midmorning made the sagebrush on the side of the road glisten. Herds of sheep dotted the landscape between the dirt road and cattle guards. On the way in and out of town, Grandma and I would count the hills. There were nine hills there and nine hills back.

We pulled into a space in front of Mullarky's Photo Shop, right off Route 66. I could hear the whistle of the trains that moved through the city, some clanging on the long and oily track line. Mullarky's was across from the tracks in an abandoned bank building from the early 1900s. It had a fake but regal façade with old Kodak signs and neon lights. When you walked in, the door rang like an aged church bell.

Mr. Mullarky was a white man with bright eyes and deep lines falling from the sides of his face. He wore a lot of turquoise on his wrists, more than I had ever seen any Navajo wear.

"Hello, Mrs. Todacheene. It's been so long since we've seen you in our shop." The man was still holding Grandma's hand. I wanted him to let it go.

"Hello, Tom." She freed her hand from his grasp. "I have something I need developed. I took Rita's picture yesterday with a box camera and wanted to see if it worked. I haven't tried this in a while." She slid the black bag onto the counter.

"Well, just hold on a bit. This won't take long at all." He moved his body between the glass cases and went to the back room. I wondered about what the Mullarky man did behind that black curtain. I tried to follow but was tethered by Grandma's lingering stare.

Instead, I wandered around Mullarky's shop with my mouth open. The west wall was bent into a soft corner, much like the storefront. The wall was covered in small rectangles, forming a grid of color. The green boxes right in the middle fanned out to the yellows, the whites, and the reds. The yellow rectangles said KODAK in bright red letters and stood in rows all the way to the end of the building.

"Grandma. What's in here?" I pointed to the colorful boxes.

"That's film," she explained. "That's what you put in the camera to take a picture."

Up on the walls, there were dozens of pictures of Gallup in another time: the train station, Navajos in velveteen and moccasins, Indians in warbonnets and outfits I had only seen in the movies. There were classic cars like the ones in fifties movies, some filled with Navajos, their hair in short crew cuts, with letterman jackets and their jeans rolled up in tight cuffs.

Glowing iridescent lights shone from Mr. Mullarky's glass boxes. There were seven display cases in all, each packed full of cameras of different ages, colors, sizes, and shapes. Their silver edges gleamed, their black-and-brown leather casings shimmering right alongside the colorful price tags. The prices were outrageous. My face and hands pressed against the glass panes, etching cold silhouettes.

Mr. Mullarky came out of the back room with a perfectly square piece of white paper that hung heavy and wet in his hands. I ran to Grandma, eager to see what was there.

"It looks like it came out perfectly; there's just a bit of light that must have snuck in there."

He laid the paper on the glass counter and held the corners back to stop the picture from curling. It was me and my blank look, standing next to that juniper bush out by the piñon trees.

The print created a perfect circle of image on the white paper. Just to my left, above my shoulder, was the light. I wanted to tell Grandma about the man I had seen just before the picture was taken, but I knew better than to say it in front of Mr. Mullarky.

"Sometimes that happens, you know," Mr. Mullarky said. "Maybe some light snuck in from the side. Looks like sunset. That can be tricky."

"Well, at least it came out. Not bad for me, though, Tom. I haven't done this in years."

"Hold on." Mr. Mullarky walked to the back and returned with the black plastic sleeve. "I've put some more paper in there for you. Maybe you two can try it again. I put that print in there for you too—the one of Nelson." Nelson was my grandpa, but he died long before I was born.

Grandma and Mr. Mullarky shared an aching smile before they said their goodbyes. I investigated the front window display. ON SALE: POLAROID SX-70 LAND CAMERA—GET YOUR PICTURES NOW. My grandma walked up from behind me and tugged at my shirt. She shook the plastic sack and smiled.

"We have an instant camera."

As we drove back in the quiet, I wanted so desperately to tell Grandma about what happened to her picture. I wanted to tell her about the man, how he smiled at her and at me, and about the love I felt radiating from his heat. I was scared that she might think I was crazy. The yellow of the setting sun reminded me of the warmth of those ten seconds when I stared into Grandma's black camera and held my breath. I fell asleep.

When I woke up, I was alone in the truck. I saw my grandma holding the door with her elbow, her arms full of paper sacks. I got out and helped her unload. Grandma only let me get the small bags that weren't too heavy. By the third trip, I was sweaty. She sent me out one last time to get the sleeve.

"Do you have any peaches in any of those bags?" a voice spoke out.

The warmth of his light began to build on my face. It was the man, but he was formless—a portion of a face beside my grandma's coyote fence. Startled, I ran inside, my heart racing, my throat dry and sticky. I slammed the front door behind me to catch my breath.

"What's the matter?" Grandma said. "Your face is red. Are you okay?" She pushed me to the table and took the black sleeve from me. "Sit down." She poured some apple juice into a glass and put it in front of me. "Drink."

I swallowed the liquid without taking a breath. My chest heaved and my heart ached. Grandma pulled one of her cloth flour bags out and soaked it in cold water, then wrapped it around my neck. I was starting to feel better when two crimson lines poured from my nose and dotted the table.

"Goodness," Grandma said, moving the dripping rag to my face. "I think we had a little bit too much fun today, she'awéé'." She pulled me in close and touched my forehead.

I still felt the heat on my face, the warmth that had bled through. Grandma rose and put a pot of water on the stove with two bundles of Navajo tea. The room filled with the smell as I rolled my basketball under the kitchen table with my foot.

Grandma cleaned her hands on her apron and moved to the table. I watched her take a picture about the size of my hands from the black bag. She smiled as she sat.

"I just love this picture," she said. "I haven't seen any photos of your grandpa in years. That trunk of mine is way too heavy to lift." She took off her glasses and rubbed the red marks left on her nose. Her shoulders shook, so I walked to her and put my little hands on her back. I turned to see the picture framed between her thumbs: his hair was cut short, and his cheekbones were high and handsome. He wore a cotton button-up shirt and pleated slacks; his army coat hung on his arm. He was smiling deeply, a dimple on his cheek.

"Grandma." I pointed to the picture. "Grandma, that's the man who made the light on your picture."

"What do you mean?"

"I saw him yesterday."

Time stopped. Grandma's gaze was strong and bottomless. I felt her hands shake as she held onto me, looking into my eyes.

I sensed her panic, love, and longing all at once in that moment. The yellow light filled the room again—I saw the man behind her, his body forming only when he neared her. He was still young and smiling. The light reflected on half of Grandma's face made her look younger than any picture I had ever seen of her.

"Rita! Don't lie to me." She shook me to attention. "When did this happen? When I took your picture?"

"Grandma," I said. "It's happening right now."

CHAPTER FIVE

Sony Cyber-shot DSC-F828
II Digital Camera

DOWNTOWN VILLAGE WAS one of the oldest apartment buildings in Albuquerque, rising five stories above the street below. The first four floors housed six small apartments, each door just like the one next to it. On the lower levels, the paint was still the hollow green of a hospital emergency room. It remained that way in part because all the elderly people who had settled there since the 1960s detested change—each existing in their small apartments, watching the walls of their rooms outlive their husbands and wives. The long-standing ladies of Downtown Village were sweet, lively, and almost completely deaf.

My apartment was on the fifth floor—a small floor with only two units, forming the pinnacle of the building. Years before, Mrs. Santillanes, my eighty-seven-year-old next-door neighbor, had put a gloomy green bulb into the hallway socket, giving everyone who visited a dreary complexion.

Inside my apartment, I switched on the lamp and unwrapped myself in its gentle glow. I had surrounded myself with visions of my childhood: the gray-green hue of blooming sagebrush and the red sand of the bluffs surrounding Grandma's house filled my walls. In the living room, a giant photograph of my grandmother covering her eyes sat next to another huge photograph of the local trading post and the beautiful mountain that stood outside her door. Photos of the four sacred mountains decorated each wall. In this space, I was almost home.

Ten hours had passed since I had left the scene on the freeway. I didn't even have the strength to take off my shoes before I lay down on the half-made bed and drifted off to sleep.

7:49 P.M.

I slept only four hours, awakening to the screensaver on my computer—a distant beach I had never been to—and slid my hand over to my mouse. I could feel my camera watching me as I nestled in bed, commanding me to back up files. I rose. I pulled the chip from its chamber and pushed it into the port of my computer. The screen brightened the whole room as the photos loaded, the blue bar measuring time with every slow tick. I emptied what was left of a forgotten cup of coffee as the first images began to pop up. The familiar uneasiness of the scene welled in my stomach.

My final photo materialized. A lifeless eye stared into the frame, and I stared back. I could see every detail of Erma's skin, young and flawless save for the darkened blood around the edges. I sat back and studied the fragment of her face.

"What happened?"

I jumped. Erma was sitting on my couch, her shoulders rounded and her gaze on the floor. I recognized the sequins from her blouse and the denim of her jeans, but her skin looked cold and waxy. I was thankful she wasn't sitting there in the condition she was in on the freeway.

"I don't know," I replied. The room rolled with cold, like a sheet of frost.

"I can't remember anything. It's like it's all been erased."

"They're investigating—"

"I need to get home," Erma yelled, cutting me off. It made my heart race. "Where am I?"

Erma's ghost pushed past me and stared at the image of her face on my computer. She turned to me, and a rush of panic tingled through my skin as her scream pierced the room.

"My baby is at home." She paced, spreading her cold into my living room. "You have to help me get back to my baby. Do you hear me? You have to help me."

"I take photographs. I'm not sure what I can do."

Erma moved closer. "Help me get back to my baby, or I'll make your life a living hell." Her desperation echoed through my body until my head nearly splintered. She shared her fear with me and fed me her despair. I wondered how long I could wait to tell her that she was never going back.

CHAPTER SIX

Nikon FE

AFTER THE EPISODE in the kitchen with my grandpa's ghost, Grandma stood vigil in my bedroom, unaware that Grandpa's spirit was lighting up the room brightly, like God's flashlight in my face. I didn't sleep all night.

Instead, Grandpa's light told me stories about Grandma—his first sight of her, young and strong, his longing for her now. In that room, he knew she still longed for him. There had never been another man in her life since Grandpa died all those years ago. She truly belonged to him forever. But Grandma didn't see him, and she didn't hear him either. She just cried and cried, until she eventually lay down with me in my little bed and went to sleep. I stayed awake and talked to Grandpa, answering his questions about my mother and about the lives we now lived.

"So, did your mom finish school?" Grandpa asked.

"She is still in school. She is studying in the city. It's a three-hour drive to visit." I was full of information. "And I can read and do all kinds of things, like count the miles all the way."

"And Grandma takes you there?" He smiled.

"She did. Two times. But it costs a lot of money to go, so we just stay here." I saw his hand and reached over to touch it. My hand went straight through his shallow skin. "Why don't you just go see her?"

"I've gone to see her a lot of times, but she doesn't know I'm there. She doesn't see me like you do. Besides, it isn't nice to pry." Grandpa's ghost rolled up his sleeve. "Look at what me being here has done to your grandma. I don't want to make her sad anymore." His spirit flickered. "I couldn't live without her all these years."

"You're still gonna come see me, though, right?" I was starting to worry about him leaving, already missing the warmth of his light.

"Ch'įįdii. That is what they call it. All that bad stuff that is left after a person passes on. That can make you sick. I could be making you sick."

"I've been seeing them a long time, Grandpa. I'm not sick."

I could see him thinking, knowing that his own spirit was here and had no intention of ever causing me harm. "There are going to be some spirits on this side that don't have good intentions. They will want to use your gift to do their bidding."

"What's bidding?" I asked.

"It means they'll use you to get what they want done. I don't know how you are able to do what you do, but you must learn to control who you let in here." His finger pointed to my head. "It's like a light switch. You must know when to turn it off. If you don't, they will keep coming, and we could lose you, Rita. We could lose you to those ghosts." He looked down at my nose just as I felt the trickle of a nosebleed on my lips. The room began to brighten as the sun crested the mountain. His light faded as the morning sun slipped past my curtains.

GRANDMA HAD ME loaded in the car and headed to the clinic before we even had a chance to eat breakfast. She was frantic as she told the young doctor about my hallucinations. The doctor tried his best to calm her, sitting her in the waiting room with the rest of the Navajos.

Going to the clinic always meant waiting at least two hours. I quickly began to realize it was probably the worst place I could be. Ghost lights of all sizes and shapes moved in and out of hallways, passing through doors and sitting beside people hacking and coughing in the waiting room. A TV soap opera played in the distance—another love lost. I thought about what Grandpa's ghost said and pulled myself closer to Grandma.

I noticed a little girl in the corner—a most defined light. She stood atop one of the joined plastic chairs, her arms around the neck of a young, crying woman dressed in black, her hair in front of her face. She held a piece of Kleenex in one hand and an empty orange bottle in the other. The little girl hopped from chair to chair, then into the woman's lap. The woman never budged. I looked at everyone in the waiting room. No one heard her cries but me.

When a voice came over the intercom calling for the woman, she stood and walked through an open door at the end of the hallway, the little weeping girl followed behind, grasping for the woman's hand. Even behind closed doors, I could still hear the cries.

Near the fire exit, a tattered Navajo man sat asleep in the chair, his legs outstretched and his ankles intertwined. The acrid smell of poison poured from his skin and wheezing mouth as he breathed in and out between snores. Next to him, an elderly man yelled in his ear in Navajo. The tattered Navajo man heard nothing—he just sat there and snored. The elder looked toward me. I stared right back.

The Navajo ghost knew that I could see him, that I could hear him. His light hovered near me. I could see his gentle face desperately trying to convey something to me, but he spoke in Navajo, and I only understood a few words here and there. He pointed at the drunk man asleep in the chair and scolded him with everything he had. The more upset he got, the hotter he became, until I felt myself moving away from him, wrapping my grandma's arm with mine. I tried to look away.

Seven other lights came and joined him, pointing and talking in a jumbled mess of Navajo, English, and other languages I couldn't understand. Some tried to pull at my hands and arms to no avail; their forms would just fall through. I wasn't afraid of it—the light. I could feel their desperation.

The nurse called my name just when the heat was beginning to be too much. Grandma held my head close to her chest. My forehead pulsed with raw heat; my body was weak and tired; my eyes burned with light as we walked into the exam room.

The doctor poked me with needles, taking small plastic tubes of my red insides out into the world. They put things in my mouth and hit my knees with rubber mallets. They asked me questions; they looked in my ears, measured me, and found nothing. There was nothing on this earth that had tainted me or infected me. I was normal.

The exam room began to glow as a kind-looking woman took form behind the doctor. She was motherly and friendly and talked to me when Grandma and the doctor looked at my X-ray outside the room.

"Today is my boy's birthday. I love to come and be with him on his day. I know he can't see me, but you can. How can you do that?"

I shrugged.

"Well, it's quite a gift."

"It gives me a headache," I replied. Her form disappeared as they came back in.

"We found nothing wrong with her, ma'am," he explained. "She probably just had a little too much sun." He tousled my hair and smiled. "Keep her inside. Lots of water and cold compresses."

I nodded and smiled.

"Happy birthday," I said.

He smiled and turned to look at me. "Thank you. How did you know it was my birthday?"

"Your mom told me."

THE RIDE HOME was quiet. I could see Grandma looking at me. She kept squeezing my hand and pulling me toward her. She was terrified, thin tears coming out of the corners of her eyes.

It began to rain in huge sheets—the droplets creating lakes of chocolate milk in between the dirt and the asphalt. I pressed my head against the icy glass and watched the rain dance for me, pulling and pushing through drops and gathering momentum toward the bottom. The heat of fever came in heavy rushes, like sandbags being dumped on my body.

Grandma pulled into the driveway of St. Mary's Church, skidding the gravel out with the truck's tires. The white chapel had a turquoise doorway and a long, steep stairway that led up to the entrance. She parked and carried me into the double doors. Her arms gripped me like a baby as she dipped her fingers into the holy water and walked to the front pew. The lacquered wood floor of the church creaked and swayed with each step.

My nose filled with the sweet and burning smell of incense and the hot air of lit candles. She laid me in the front of the altar and kneeled, her hands pressed together, her eyes closed, her face raised to the sky.

I could hear the rain on the roof of the church, a sacred dance of angels tapping on the shingles. I could hear the overlapping voices over the rain and thunder—the words of the ghosts that still lingered in the church. My grandmother prayed and prayed. She asked my grandpa to give me peace, to spread the word. She asked all the ghosts to leave me to my childhood and to the future I had not lived.

WHEN I AWOKE the next morning, a dull pain remained behind my eyes. One spirit remained. Grandpa. I waited until I heard the running of water in the kitchen before speaking.

"Grandpa. I think Grandma thinks I'm crazy."

"No, she doesn't. She's just worried about you. That's all. And she should be." Grandpa paused. "Remember what I told you. Just like there are bad people out there in the real world, there are bad people in this world too. If you let them get too close to you, then they can grab you."

"You mean they can take me? Like a dead person?" I asked.

"Maybe. Or they can make you crazy."

"But they are invisible people, Grandpa. Like you. They can't touch me." I reached out for his hand. "See, I can't touch you, so you can't touch me."

"No. I can't touch you," Grandpa answered. "But there are spirits that are much more powerful than your grandpa."

"Who are you talking to?" Grandma asked. I hadn't even noticed that she had turned off the water. When I turned back around, Grandpa was gone.

CHAPTER SEVEN

Nikon DSLR—NIK3PRO
Night Vision Module

At 3:25 a.m., the phone rang. I sat and listened to it ring four times, then answered it without a greeting.

"Rita. Rita? Are you awake?" Samuels sounded desperate. "We've got a Popsicle downtown." He waited. "Rita. Rita?"

"I've got it. Where?"

"Down on Third Street. It's kind of in your neighborhood. That's why I called you. Angie's working the scene and she was hoping you could help her out."

My apartment was freezing. I couldn't muster a response.

"I promise to leave you alone for a day if you go out to this one."

"On my way."

I staggered to my closet, taking out the only clean shirt I had, white as bone, lonely and uneven on the hanger. I pulled my arms through the sleeves, put on my work shoes and whatever warm clothes I could find, and stepped into the hallway.

As I walked down the stairs and through the building's narrow, dusty corridors, the sound of an argument was already pouring out of the floor below. Mr. Taylor mumbled through crumbling doughnuts and coffee, lecturing the couple next door about their odd hours. I nodded as I trudged past, noticing his sweaty T-shirt and musty robe.

"And you too, Kodachrome," he bellowed. "Don't you ever sleep?"

I kept moving.

I made my way in and out of alleyways and between the crackled buildings. The scene was only three or four blocks from my apartment, near the stretch of homeless shelters and food distribution centers. I brought a couple of cameras, flashes, and lights with me, and I could feel their weight. Fake luminarias and Christmas lights lined the adobe walls along the downtown offices, waiting for the snow.

Albuquerque cold never really means snow. It only means the deep, dry freeze of the high desert. That, mixed with sixty-mile-per-hour winds and the occasional flash rainstorm, characterizes Albuquerque's winter woes. They call it the "snow hole."

My body shivered inside long underwear and three jackets.

When I made the turn on Third Street, I saw the patrol cars—one sitting with the lights turning, sending ropes of red onto the wet road. Officers sat in their cars, heaters on, watching me walk by through the holes of condensation in their windows. The Crime Scene Specialist Unit had already arrived and were just beginning to pull their toolboxes from the vans.

"Hey, Rita," Angie called out. Sergeant Seivers was one of the senior CSS field agents, now only a few months from retiring. She had three kids, twin girls and her eighteen-year-old son, all wrapping up high school in the next couple of years, so she was getting ready to move to California with her husband. "I know you went home to sleep, but I couldn't wait to see you."

"No rest for the wicked, I guess."

"Girl, I don't know when you have time to be wicked." She laughed a contagious laugh, and I caught myself smiling. Angie was one of those women who could be your sister and your mom all at the same time. She'd hugged me the first time she met me, always brought extra sandwiches in her lunch box, and stocked caffeinated sodas in her mini fridge. She knew when I didn't sleep. She could tell when I was hurting. Just the motherly type. She was also my supervisor.

Angie was one of the first women to make sergeant, with her master's in science and specializations in everything from ballistics to laboratory forensics. I learned all I could about investigating and reading a scene from her. I was going to miss her.

"So, what's going on?" I wanted to get this going and get out of there. My eyes burned, and my body hummed as I shivered.

"A couple was walking home from up on Second Street, by that billiards place. They saw this poor gentleman lying here under the bench. I guess they noticed he wasn't breathing because there was no steam coming out of his nose." We made our way over to the body lying in the street. "I thought I would bring you down and see if you could see something I'm missing."

For months now, there had been a rash of violence against the people that lived on the streets of Albuquerque—with Native people taking some of the worst punishment. Of course, life on the streets was dangerous for everyone, but recently we had seen an escalation of the callous prejudices and hatreds that came with the history of this city. It had only been a year since we were on the scene of the murders of Cornelius and Otto Tsosie, two semi-homeless construction workers who had fallen asleep in an alley down by the university. Before they could see their next morning, two teenagers had crushed their heads with cinderblocks only three blocks from where we were standing. The hate on these streets lived and breathed.

Freezing to death on the streets wasn't any better, although they say if alcohol is involved, it could help to numb the pain—it thins the blood and speeds the process along. You could still catch a hint of alcohol on this man, but only the ME would know how much. He lay there in a semi-fetal position, as if he'd pulled himself tightly together, only the grip of death finally allowing him to relax. He was dressed in a timeworn marine jacket, government issue, with the name tag torn off, only a T-shirt beneath that. He looked like he could be Navajo or a Native of some kind. His cheekbones were riddled with scars—long scrapes and puncture holes—and so were his hands.

There was a stark and unnerving silence, just the sound of our breath crystalizing in the air and distant radio calls from Angie's unit. It was fifteen degrees outside tonight.

"Well," Angie said finally, "I'll talk to the medical examiner. I don't know if he died here or was dropped here. I think we need to make sure."

She was right. We needed to know.

I grabbed my camera out of my bag, hanging the strap around my neck, and began to look around. Angie pulled some evidence markers out of her toolbox and walked with me, filling out the scene diagram and making notes. I took the first picture about fifteen feet out. We were outside a former office building that now housed a divorce lawyer and a Chinese massage parlor. The bench the man lay beneath sat under a small Chinese oak, planted there recently in the city's attempt at revitalizing downtown.

I had ten establishing shots from every angle. Angie placed the yellow markers on the ground as I snapped the photographs. An empty vodka bottle rested flat on its back, the remaining liquid unfrozen. Marker number one. His wallet was right behind him, as if it had fallen out of his pocket. Number two. There was about $2.50 in change around his left hand. Number three. His right hand was balled into a fist around his stomach; we could tell it was holding something tight. A dark blue bandanna, with a ring of sweat and dust around its edges, lay about five feet from him. Number four. His boot heel was scuffed badly—as if he had been dragged backward, his foot scraping on the ground. We were surrounded by concrete; there was no way to tell if the scraping had happened here. The other boot was two feet, seven inches from his bare foot, and he wore no socks. Number five.

We pulled out a rolled piece of paper from his right hand that turned out to be a photograph: a young man sitting in a white chair under a tree with a little girl on his lap. The girl wore a light-yellow dress with flowers along its cuff. *Michelle Atcitty, age three* was written in blue ink on the back. But we found nothing in the wallet that let us know who he was. He had two bus passes, a business card from the urgent care clinic down at the shelter, and three dollars. That was all.

I continued to take photographs of the man. He wore a tarnished turquoise ring on his roughened left hand. He had handsome features, but he was weathered, his skin a dark red, the maroon of wind and alcohol. His face was frozen by the winter moisture, his lips arched into a disturbing grin. I snapped seventy-seven images onto the card, the body documented for environment and measurement. I stepped up one more time and focused closely on his face. The shutter opened and closed.

"Háadish nits'éé' łee' sitą́?" His eyes moved, turning to look at me. He had asked me in Navajo where I was from, or where my umbilical cord was buried. It was one of the only Navajo phrases I could remember.

My camera fell to my ribcage, the leather strap pinching my neck. I stood and stared.

"Tohatchi naashá," I answered.

Angie stood in the blustery air, talking to the ME and sipping her coffee. "You okay over there?" she shouted.

I stared again at the dead man lying on the sidewalk. His sickening gray-blue eyes were frozen in place. I wondered if he heard me.

CHAPTER EIGHT

Polaroid Land
Camera 1000SE

THE YEAR I started kindergarten, a blue car pulled into Grandma's driveway and dropped off my cousin Gloria and her suitcase. She wore her hair down—that hair of hers that never tangled, that was always where it needed to be—and was tall and thin and had a steady smile. She had been left with Grandma for the same reason I had: our mothers could not take care of us. My mother was at school somewhere, but Gloria's mother, Ruth, was nowhere to be found. She walked the streets in town, one hour away, with a spiritless and injured group of Indians. She loved to drink and would sometimes go months before she came home for a few days, stole money, and left once again. Gloria was sixteen when she came to live with us. It was the best thing that could have happened to us.

One day, after Gloria had been at Grandma's house for a couple of weeks, I came home from kindergarten with a swollen and scraped cheek, my pride hurt from a schoolyard scuffle.

"Who did that to you?" Gloria pulled me closer, examining the wound.

"Just some boy at school."

"You need to point him out to me. Understand?" She moved us toward the bathroom, her hands guiding my shoulder. The pain kept me silent. Gloria pulled Grandma's iodine from the top shelf, along with a bright white tuft of cotton. The brown liquid seeped into my open skin and stung me through to the bone. Just thinking of that kid's rotten face sent the smell of iodine to my brain.

During lunch the next day, Gloria found me in the playground as I hung upside down like a bat on the monkey bars.

"Where is he?" She was smoking a cigarette and chewing bright pink gum at the same time.

I pulled myself upright and identified the boy, Felix, who stood with his friends, pushing the smaller kids from the moving and swaying seats. He was seven and older than all of us—a fact he never let us forget.

When Gloria walked over to the group, they scattered, leaving Felix alone in the shadow of my cousin as her cigarette smoke loomed above his head. He stood defiant, his feet cemented to the moving sand. She punched him in the eye before he had a chance to say a word. He lay on the sand in shock, holding his cheek and covering his tears.

"Next time you'll think twice about hitting little girls," she warned. "I'll be watching you."

With that, she jumped over the chain-link fence and ran into the hills, one chubby, huffing security guard trying to give chase.

She waited for me every day when I got off the bus. We would play basketball in the setting sun. Sometimes she would spin me in circles—fast enough that my feet would hover above the swirling earth while her hands held on like smooth and gentle clasps—until I couldn't breathe from laughing so hard.

One afternoon, Gloria and her friend Bertha were waiting for me at the bus stop. Bertha was taller than Gloria and twice as big. She wore lots of makeup and had a devil tattoo on her arm, but she was quick with a smile. As I walked off the bus, a huge flash of light came toward me. I rubbed my eyes, then saw the camera spit out a sheet from its mouth. Bertha grabbed the sheet and shook it in her hand like a one-winged bird.

"Grandma told me that you're into cameras and stuff, so I told Bertha to bring hers over." Gloria pulled on the camera strap. "Show her."

It was amazing. Just a few seconds ago Bertha had taken my picture, and now, here was proof. I was smiling in the photograph, the bus driver obscured, a boy waving through the window. I rubbed my fingers on the edge of the photo, wondering if the color would come off in my hands.

"Let her try it," Gloria demanded.

"Okay, okay." Bertha handed the camera to me. "Don't drop it though. It's my mom's. She'd kill me."

Gloria grabbed Bertha around the shoulder and smiled.

"Take the picture, kiddo."

I put my eye to the viewfinder and pressed the button, feeling the electric gears moving inside. The photo came out a white square on a white surface, shapes and colors coming to life with the burst of light and air. Gloria and Bertha both looked so happy and bright in the picture; their hands pressed into each other's arms.

IT WAS ONLY seven months before the older kids found Gloria and pulled her from me. She began to go to school less and less, coming home with the boys my grandma always complained about. By early summer, I was alone in an empty house. I watched television by myself until Grandma came home from work.

I always tiptoed to Gloria's bed when I heard her come in late at night, after Grandma was asleep. Her room smelled of cigarettes and sour juice.

"Where did you go, Gloria?" I'd ask.

"Places I never want you to go."

On my sixth birthday, Gloria didn't come home. Two days later, she finally did, but only to grab a jacket and a handful of crackers from the kitchen while Grandma was still at work.

"Where are you going, Gloria?" I sat in the kitchen watching her.

"We're just heading out to a friend's house out in Coyote Canyon. I should be back tonight." Gloria scanned the fridge.

"Grandma was worried when you didn't come home."

"I stayed at Bertha's. Her mom's car wasn't working, so I got stuck out there." Gloria opened the front door to leave.

"Take me too," I begged. I could see someone sitting in a red junkyard truck waiting for her. Sparkling, furry dice hung from the mirror. "Who's that?"

"We're going up to the top of the mesa. I'll be back late. So you better stay here." Gloria walked out and I ran after her, jumping into the back of the truck.

"I'm going." I wrapped my arms around the spare tire in the back.

Gloria just stared at me, then shouted to the guy in the driver's seat. "Move over. I'm driving."

Up on the mesa, in the Chuska Housing Project, government homes stood like stones above the community of

Tohatchi. They were all the same—four walls and a roof and nothing more. Many of them were abandoned, their sparse yards overgrown with tumbleweeds and empty dog houses.

Gloria pulled into a deserted driveway and parked. We were at the house at the end of the road, where the back-yard overlooked the Chuska Mountains. Aside from the graffiti all over the house, it was still in one piece, the door and windows intact. Gloria and her boyfriend sat on the tailgate and smoked and passed a can between them while I went to look at all the stuff inside. There was a busted television, wire hangers, and outdated calendars. There was even a radio sitting in the kitchen among some broken plates. I turned the knob and a scratchy radio signal came through. The light from the setting sun made the whole house look orange, and when I put my hand in the air, I made an impressive shadow.

The sound of a door being slammed forced my attention. I ran to the window and watched my cousin walk away, hand in hand with her boyfriend, into the windy mesa. I felt my heart thump frantically in my chest. She had left me alone there with the desperate drip of a faucet in a white sink, the disturbing melody of "Lost in Love" by Air Supply filling the air. My small hand turned the knob on the front door. It was locked from the outside. I cried. At six years old, I could not help it. I was paralyzed by fear, by the thought of my grandmother never finding me. The start of the engine made me scream. Gloria drove away from the house, from me, in that red pickup truck.

My cousin never did come back for me. After a couple of hours, the lights of a truck lit the tattered government house from the outside in. After hours of fear and desperation, my little face had become swollen. Trails of dry tears ran parallel to wet new ones, the palm color of terror traced on my skin. I strained to see who was there. The lights were so bright and my eyes so sensitive that I could not make out the figure that came through the dry landscape.

They tugged at the door handle and knocked. I could not move. I covered my ears as the knocks turned into kicks and strikes. The door swung open, bathing the room in dusty silver light. My grandmother stood there calling my name, but I still could not move. God only knows how she knew where to find me. I never asked, and she never said.

I had been there for about five hours, from what I was told. For me, it had felt like years. I really believed that I would never leave, that I would be stuck inside that lonely house for the rest of my days.

I remembered the ride back to my grandmother's house. She held me tightly to her. I could hear the beat of her heart and could smell lilac and ivory soap mixed with the smoky scent of cooking oil. She stroked my head and dabbed my swollen eyes with a damp cloth and hummed a Navajo song as the truck engine hummed its own tune through town. I watched small dots on the ceiling of the truck cab move in and out of focus.

Grandma slowed when the reflecting red and blue lights of a police car took turns dancing on the pickup's ragged hood. I sat up. Two policemen slowly waved vehicles through a path of broken glass and mangled steel. It was then that I saw it: the red truck. The furry dice were still hanging from the rear-view mirror. It looked like it had rolled a few times, coming to rest on its blown tires, Gloria's boyfriend still upright in the front seat.

Grandma's truck squealed to a stop amid the burned scent of melted tar. She gasped and sobbed, trying to shield my eyes from what I had already seen. Gloria sat lifeless, trapped in the mangled red metal. I would never forget her face that night. She seemed surprised that she was dead. Her eyes were open and looking at us. My grandmother grabbed a blanket from the back of her seat and went to her, covering her body and face as the police tried to pull her away.

WE PICKED OUT a light-blue coffin for Gloria and had her dressed in her favorite outfit—a T-shirt and jeans. I could still see the cut on her head as it rose into her hairline.

When the funeral service was over, everyone walked past her and looked down at her body. Grandma and I were the last ones to see her before they closed the casket. I didn't want to see her like that. That wasn't her. I finally cried.

"Hey, kiddo," a voice said. "Don't do that. Don't cry."

I pulled my hand out of Grandma's hand and turned to look. Nothing. I knew that was Gloria's voice. I looked at her while the box closed. She was as still as a frozen lake. Grandma grabbed my hand again and led me out into the gloomy echo of the church. My little heart ached.

When we got home, people sat around in silence and put food inside their mouths. Father Henry sat with my grandma at the table. They talked about everything except Gloria. I hid underneath the table, watching as everyone's shiny shoes shuffled by, and the Navajo ladies, with their knee-highs rolled down around their ankles, came and sat with Grandma and talked Navajo.

"Kiddo?" Gloria's ghost said. She was beautiful, just as I remembered her that day, with her jeans and her T-shirt and red bands around the collar and sleeves. I reached out and tried to hug her, but I went right through.

"Gloria. It's you. You're home," I said.

"Shhhhh," she said. "They can hear you."

I looked up to see the Navajo ladies peeking beneath the tablecloth. My auntie Ruth, Gloria's mom, tugged me out and looked me straight in the eye.

"Gloria is gone, Rita," she explained. "She's dead."

"No. She's not," I answered. "She just doesn't want to talk to you." I pulled away and ran out the door.

I sat on the edge of a rock behind my grandma's house and cried. I begged Gloria to follow me, but she didn't.

When I went back into the kitchen, I could see the eyes fixed on me and hear the whispers from the hallways. They must have all thought I was crazy. Those people would never look at me the same again.

I walked into Grandma's room and hid in her closet, where the dark was safely scented like Grandma's clothes. It didn't take long for Gloria to join me. Her light was warm, but it flickered like a dying flashlight.

"They don't believe that I can see you, Gloria," I said. "They all think I'm crazy."

"Or that you're a witch. You know how Navajos are," Gloria answered. Her reply crackled like a bad phone connection. "They're all out there waiting to see what you do next so they can go home and gossip about it."

"That means that you can't come back." I started to cry. "I don't want you to go, but you have to keep going. Otherwise, Grandma will always be sad just like when Grandpa died. She will always cry after you."

"Okay, kiddo," she answered, and just like that, the light was gone.

When Gloria left, she took all the others with her. From that point on, I never again saw any lights in my grandma's house. It would always be the one place where they weren't allowed.

CHAPTER NINE

Canon EOS 5D

I SAT INSIDE Angie's van and closed my eyes. My body ached with insomnia. Angie got into the van just as fatigue tears rolled down my cheeks. "Honey, when is the last time you slept?" She pulled some baby wipes from her purse and placed them in my hands. "Wipe your eyes."

The burn finally began to subside as I pushed against the sockets of my eyes, rubbing the stinging tears from my face. "It's been a while," I said.

"We're all done here anyway. I'm driving you home."

Angie started the van, buckled herself, and pushed the vents to storm force. The engine was running, the air hot and thick. I couldn't help but roll down the window. A small group of officers chuckled around their coffee, looking my way and shaking their heads. Typical.

"Don't worry about those guys." Angie patted my leg. "There's a reason they are all still on patrol."

Buildings passed us in whirs of color as we moved from shadow to shadow in the early morning hours. Only occasional squares of light splashed on the street from open bakeries. The rest of the city was asleep in their homes or hotels, on their office couches, and in their cardboard beds in the doorways of buildings.

"You know." Angie nudged my arm to pull my mind from the street. "This is why I'm getting out of all this while I can. I used to be able to deal with these crazy, stressful hours, but those days are gone, honey. I'm too old. And it's only getting worse. You know that, right?"

"I do." I was uncomfortable. Her words made me think of my grandmother growing old by herself in that house between the mountains. I felt the nausea of guilt.

"You need to get out while you still have half your mind intact," Angie said. I could feel her stare on my face.

"After I save a little more . . ."

"You've been saying that for the last five years. Haven't you saved enough? I mean, you're always at work. You never go any-where."

She was right. I never went anywhere.

"Rita, you're a good kid, and you take great pictures. That's got to count for something. Go shoot something besides dead bodies."

We pulled up to my building as the sun's heat began to swing heavy. Angie grabbed my hand, depositing five pills.

"Don't take all of those at once. Just one now to get you to sleep, then save the rest for when you're having trouble." Her eyes narrowed. "One, Rita."

"One," I promised.

The apartment building's halls were eerily quiet, with only the faint hums of oxygen tanks and refrigerators on the bottom floors. My shuffling feet created the simplest of melodies in the echo. The dark-green light of my floor moved closer and closer until I was bathed in it—then my wide-awake neighbor opened her door.

"*Mija*, come in here. Come in here now!" Mrs. Santillanes pulled my arms through her threshold and handed me a dark mason jar. "Drink this. All of it. Your soul needs it, *mija*."

Her hands were chilled and soft as the folds of her skin rubbed my face. I couldn't even speak. Instead, I turned toward my apartment and let the momentum of my movement get me through the door. I pulled one pill from my pocket and drank down Mrs. Santillanes's mixture like it was chocolate syrup. Sleep spread its warm coils through me, pulling my body down to my couch cushions.

The deep sleep did not stop my mind from working. The gears still churned, blood and memories pooling like channel lakes of faces and words. All of it was stopped by Erma Singleton's screams.

In my dream, I sat perched on the branch of a tree that stretched over the constant roar of the freeway traffic. I watched a car park next to the embankment before the bridge. Erma was shrieking at the top of her lungs until a dull thud stopped the noise. A huge man emerged from the back door of the sedan, looking left to right in the darkness. He pulled the woman out of the backseat and threw her over his shoulder like a duffle bag. I jumped from my perch above and landed only feet from the two of them. As usual, they couldn't see me. This was a one-way mirror.

Erma came back to life and fought like I've never seen anyone fight. She swung at the giant for a good minute, tugging hair and scratching skin before he hefted her over the edge. She held the railings so hard that I could see the tendons in her wrists—Dr. Blaser, the medical examiner, once told me those tendons were called the palmaris longus.

The man watched Erma fall into the lanes of traffic. He chewed his gum as a truck rolled over one of her legs, only pressing on his brakes for a second, then moving on. The giant turned and walked back to the sedan. I rushed to see who was sitting in the front seat. I couldn't make out much, except that there were three men inside. Three big men, but I managed to hear a voice.

"I told you to keep her out of this. This. *This* is on you."

There, in the darkness, I could see the crime scene just as it was before we arrived, preserved in the silence. Erma's ghost pulled itself back over the side of the bridge and looked straight at me.

"Time to wake up," she said.

CHAPTER TEN

Pinhole

EVEN THOUGH GRANDMA and I tried to get back to normal, there was nothing but darkness for months. My aunt Ruth had tried to move into the house to help Grandma, but Grandma didn't want her there. She was angry. Whenever she looked at Ruth, all Grandma could do was remember Gloria.

The lights that I saw now were strangers. They were at the post office checking their boxes or walking along the side of the road when Grandma and I drove to town. They were everywhere, just like the real people were, everywhere but at home.

When I went back to school, the kids were afraid of me. I'm not sure what they had heard, but I felt more alone than ever. Without Gloria to back me up, I wondered what would happen to me out on the schoolyard when no teachers were watching. But no one bothered me. They feared me. I spent almost all my time there by myself. Until the day I met Judith.

I was washing my hands at the sink, lathering up powdered pink soap when I saw Judith in the mirror for the first time, staring at me from the door. When I turned, she was gone. I looked back to the mirror, where she had moved closer. Her head drooped to the side like a puppy. She looked like she was in first grade, like me, and wore a gray dress with a white collar and brown shoes. Her face was colorless and her hair a dark black. A blue bow wrapped her braids. We stared at each other through the mirror until she spoke.

"Can you play with me?" Her voice was shaky and full of echoes.

I didn't know what to say.

"Yes." I barely finished the word before she appeared in front of me, no longer trapped inside that mirror in the bathroom.

We played almost every day after that, swinging together and hanging upside down on the monkey bars. We laughed and talked each day during recess. Eventually, I tried to take her picture, bringing Grandma's black box to show and tell. Judith stood in front of the class facing me, a faint smile on her face when I pulled off the tape. No one believed it was a camera. No one but Judith.

I noticed that the other children had started to stare. One of my classmates walked over to me and Judith during recess. "My auntie says that you talk to dead people," she said, food dried around the corners of her mouth. "Are you talking to someone dead now?"

"Maybe," I said.

"What are you talking about?"

Judith looked at me in silence and placed her finger over her lips.

"Nothing," I said and watched my classmate walk back out into the sand.

After recess, the teachers had us line up single file and march into our classroom. Five girls, including myself and Judith, decided to go to the bathroom before going down the hallway.

I finished quickly and headed toward the door, but Judith pulled me back.

"Don't let them out," Judith hissed.

"What do you mean?"

She started to laugh, a high, haunted laugh that spread through me as I shut off the lights in the bathroom. The girls, still sitting in the stalls, began to scream at the top of their lungs. I ran out and listened as stalls slammed open and closed and their little feet raced to the door. I held it shut as the girls cried and screamed inside. All Judith and I could do was laugh.

"Stop that right now, Rita." Our teacher, Mrs. Smith, ran toward me and pried my fingers from the door handle. Judith's laugh had become my own, echoing through the walls. When the door opened, the three girls rushed into the arms of Mrs. Smith, their faces wet and red. I was sent straight to the principal's office. I was in trouble, and Judith was nowhere to be found.

I hated seeing Grandma walk into the principal's office. She was tired—I could see it on her face, and I could feel it when she moved closer, sitting next to me in front of the principal's looming wooden desk. They began to talk about me, about my difficult behavior, my isolation, my obsession with talking to myself, and now, this episode in the girls' bathroom. I drowned it out and focused my energy on looking for Judith. It took only a few seconds for me to wish her into the room.

Judith stood quietly in the corner, perched beside the window, her appearance a misty haze.

"You got me in trouble, Judith," I scolded. "You should be sitting here with me. This was your idea."

Judith roared with laughter, her head pulled back, her neck elongated like a chain of bone. Even though she was a girl, I felt a timelessness to her evil.

"Who are you talking to, Rita?" Grandma's voice broke through it.

Judith crept up behind Principal Bennett and rested her fingers over her pursed lips, her stare becoming harder.

"I'm so sorry to trouble you with this, Mrs. Todacheene, but Rita needs to learn that this is inappropriate behavior and will not be tolerated. I'm already getting calls from the parents of some of these girls. We've had to send them home early; they were so terrified."

"Do you hear this, Rita?" Grandma raised her voice.

I looked at the ground. I had not wanted to hurt anyone. Thinking of the terror of the poor girls in the bathroom made my guts sink like a rock.

"I'm sorry, Grandma," I said. I was sorry. Mostly that I had hurt my grandma. She had already been through so much, and here I was, making it even harder. "I'll stop talking to her."

"Who are you talking to, Rita?" Principal Bennett chimed in.

"Judith," I said.

"Is she your imaginary friend, Rita?" Principal Bennett looked at Grandma, who wasn't smiling. She knew. Grandma stared at me with that look of fear I couldn't stand.

"She's not imaginary," I said. I watched Judith move slowly to Mr. Bennett's door. Grandma and Mr. Bennett watched in silence as it crept open on its own. I closed my eyes and pushed Judith's energy from me like blowing out a candle. Judith slammed the door shut. Grandma and Principal Bennett jumped in their seats and turned to look at me.

"She's gone," I said.

When Grandma and I got home, I opened my camera box in the front yard and watched the photograph I took of Judith and the class turn black, the edges coiling away from the tape.

CHAPTER ELEVEN

Canon EOS 5D Mark III
(Low Light)

IT STILL FELT like Erma was in the room as I pulled on yesterday's clothes and went down to my car. I sat there shivering until the heater rattled and creaked its way to life, then I headed out into the morning, toward I-25.

It was almost midday when I arrived back at the overpass where Erma was thrown over. There had to be a good reason why Erma had latched herself to me.

I knew now what I didn't know as a kid: my grandpa had been right. Some ghosts never even realize that I have this thing. The ones who know I can see and hear them are rarely strong enough to push themselves in. If they do, I dispatch them quickly. But some manage to break through. Those are the ones that want something to happen. They need something from you.

It is a feeling you get, like a ball in your stomach or that heartbeat that comes when you look over the edge of a cliff. Sometimes they fill you with prickly heat or smother you with cold until your muscles cramp. When I was younger and unable to control the channels that the voices navigated, their presence would give me nosebleeds and the most tremendous pressure in my head. They preyed on my youth and my naiveté because they knew I hadn't learned to set boundaries.

The one thing I couldn't do was ignore them. That was impossible. It was best to keep yourself healthy and strong because the voices knew to take advantage when you were sick or weak. Even small bouts of insomnia or the flu could trigger the switch. The dead would be waiting in line, glaring up at the neon sign outside my psyche.

The power never worked liked you wanted it to. Earlier on in my time at the department, I had tried to find out leads on cold cases to see if the ghosts of the unsolved murders in the city had to get something off their chests. Back in 2003, the remains of eleven women were found west of town, up on the mesa that overlooked the city. I visited the site several times, just waiting for the ghost of one of the women who was buried in the mass grave to come and talk to me. I visited for years. Not one came.

The killer was dubbed the "West Mesa Collector" but was never captured by the police. There were two suspects in the case: one, the major suspect—living only two or three miles from where the women were found—was killed by the boyfriend of the girl he had just raped, murdered, and rolled into a piece of carpet. The other was a serial rapist police knew to be stalking prostitutes along Central Avenue. He received a life sentence for other crimes, but he was never pinned to this one.

What this work proved to me was that people were evil. The things I saw day after day were unthinkable, and the people who did these things sometimes still walked the streets. It was hard when you knew the truth but had no way to share it, no way to lead the police officers straight to a killer's door. If I told the department what I could do, they would surely fire me, maybe lock me up in the nearest mental hospital. My years on the job would be written off, as I would be. Any would-be psychics, or "psychic detectives," are quickly dismissed by the departments, accused of retrofitting facts and calling them visions.

My "visions" couldn't be defined as "post-cognition"—like the psychics you see on television, who can "feel" the past. I didn't feel their past. I felt their presence. I just relied on them to tell me what I needed to know. I had no control over who knocked on the door.

Erma was powerful. She gave me back the headaches of my youth and the bright lights buried in my memories. She was able to pry into my weaknesses unlike any other being I had encountered. My mind was buzzing and looking to be anywhere else but the final moments of Erma Singleton. But there I was, standing on the overpass where she took her last breaths, watching the approaching cars rise between the lanes. Erma's fear and dread became my own. I began to feel the pressure building in my head.

The busy sounds of the overpass were swallowed by a child's cries. In my mind, I could see Erma Singleton picking the little girl up and twirling her around. From the other room, a voice:

"You're going to be late."

"I know, Mom," Erma answered. She carried the girl into the other room, and I followed them. Erma kissed her mother on the cheek. "Thanks," she said. She pulled her leather purse to her shoulder. "I'll be right back, baby." Erma blew a kiss to the little girl and pulled the door shut—a slam that startled me into reality.

I had never done that before, let something draw me that close. I felt Erma as if I had been dropped into her own spirit. Even there on the overpass, I could smell her daughter's skin and the toast burning in the kitchen.

I took one more look over the overpass, the morning light

turning dark, the wind rising up to my face. I still felt Erma at my back, as well as an urgency that raged hot.

"Help me!" I heard Erma's screams getting louder and louder as I watched her fighting the giant. "Help me." Her voice was in my ear. "Help me, now."

It was my ringing cell phone that broke me from my meditation. "Rita here."

"We're having a busy morning. Are you on call?" Samuels rustled papers in the background. "Dammit, I can't find the schedule."

"I don't know. What day is it?" My watch read 6:49 A.M. The sun was finally warming up the city. Erma still had my stomach in a ball and my mind at a tilt. I was disoriented and hyperaware all at once.

"Someone filled the old Imperial Motel with holes. First reports in call it a drive-by. I think the lady is still alive, so it's not a fatality yet. But from what I understand, she's not doing well. Detective Garcia is heading it."

Garcia again. After thirty years on the force, the man had absolutely no emotion or empathy. He was on just about all the fatality calls that I was on, and we didn't get along right from the beginning. His way of breaking the ice with me had been to tell me his one Navajo joke.

"So, these two East Coast hookers decided to move out to California. They're driving through New Mexico and stop at a little trading post." Garcia was already chuckling. "There were two Indian women sitting out on the front porch—the four women started to talk, you know, like women do. One Indian woman says, 'Well, I'm a Navajo and she is an Arapaho.' The one hooker said, 'No shit. Well, I'm a New York ho and she a Chicago ho.'" He had roared with laughter. When I didn't laugh, he muttered under his breath, "Women."

Once, when I was only a few months on the job, I watched Garcia take some money off a guy they had in custody. Police had found the body of a woman who had been raped and bludgeoned in her apartment. She had been decomposing there for at least two days while her killer sat in the living room and watched the television. When the police arrived after the woman's mother filed a missing person report, the killer was sitting there, eating a bowl of cereal next to her body.

They emptied his pockets: a pack of cigarettes, a lighter, a knife, and a wad of money an inch thick. I snapped photos in the apartment, but I kept an eye on Garcia. After they bagged the woman and put her in the OMI van, Garcia stuffed the money and knife into his pockets. The smokes he shook until one slender stick came out of the pack. He used the guy's lighter too. Then he got in the car. I'll never forget that.

7:21 A.M., IMPERIAL MOTEL—FIRST AND CENTRAL AVENUE: DRIVE-BY SHOOTING.

I walked to the perimeter, happy to see that there were no bodies lying beneath white sheets. Garcia lumbered toward me, his industrial strength cologne cutting through the cold air. The last time I'd seen him was on the overpass above Erma's dismembered body, his round, pocked face shining with sweat. Now he looked blue from the early morning light, choking for air above the straining button of his collar.

"So, where's the boss? He didn't tell me he was sending you."

"Sorry to disappoint," I replied. "You know he has better things to do than to spend his morning with you." An enema would have been better than spending any morning with this man.

He threw me a bright blue set of rubber gloves. "So, are you waiting for an invitation or what?"

"What happened here?" I said, ignoring him.

A young officer spoke up. "From what we can tell, it looks like it might be some gang activity. We have no leads, but shots were fired from a vehicle moving west to east, and we don't think our victim was the target. The vic is in her early twenties. She's probably going to make it, but she sure was a bleeder."

The photos began outside. We counted and photographed over three hundred pieces of evidence in two hours—including the 130 brass shells that were scattered between the thick yellow lines in the hotel parking lot, where a trail ran over thirteen feet long before stopping abruptly, leaving a black skid mark. It must have sounded like a war zone, but that was what this town was becoming. I photographed a scene like this every month or so. Usually, it was a kid involved in a gang thing or a drug thing, sometimes just an unlucky soul in the wrong place at the wrong time. None of it ever ended well. There was always a car wash somewhere in the city raising money for a young man or woman's funeral. That, and the plotting of revenge in someone's basement.

The fact that she was a bleeder was an understatement. I could taste the blood in my mouth the second I came into the room. There were already scene investigators counting projectiles, property, dropping evidence markers. I took out my camera and my adhesive tape and began to take pictures. So far, I counted over fifty evidence markers, and I could see more as I moved further into the scene.

First, the establishing shot—the overview—then the corners. The flashes illuminated the seven pools of blood on the floors, now hardened shells of glistening black. Along the walls, I could see the young woman's path from the floor to the nightstand, a ten-inch streak of blood that I marked with an evidence ruler;

her bloody fingerprints moving up toward the phone; the bloody nine and one of her call. A pair of wings emerged from the wall behind the bed, the imprint of her bloody shoulder blades. As I flashed image 88, I realized the victim must have sat here for a while, spilling the life from her body. The blood on the bed measured a circumference of ten inches, moving three to four inches down into the side of the mattress. From this viewpoint, I could see her glancing out the shattered window to what must have been her view of the approaching police and ambulance. Images 97 through 102 were her perspective, the blue light of morning silhouetting the officers passing in the shattered glass. It was a miracle she was alive.

I snapped over thirty photos of her belongings, scattered around the timeworn orange carpet. Over by the door, I photographed a set of luggage leaking thin, uneven stuffing from holes left by escaping bullets. Many of the projectiles were embedded in the walls and in the cheap wooden bed frames and dressers. The handles of the luggage were bloody, as were some clothes lying next to an empty briefcase. Photo 145 was of the briefcase with its yellow crime scene marker, "M" for miscellaneous. When I moved toward it, I could see there was a scatter of white dusting the corner, but the drugs were gone except for what had escaped through a bullet hole.

I took a photograph and called one of the officers. "Hey, did you guys see this over here?"

Garcia looked my way, his face pressed against his phone. One officer dropped another yellow marker on the site: N-1— narcotics. I pressed my finger down, sending a flash around the room. I could smell Garcia approaching, hear his breathing right behind me. He eyed the new evidence, never dropping the phone from his ear.

"May be more than just a drive-by, Detective Garcia," I said. He ignored me.

There were bloody footprints, about one hundred bullet holes, bloody shoe prints, razor blades, casings, cigarette butts, shredded photographs, mirrors and straws, shattered beer bottles, and countless other things that weren't even distinguishable. Four hundred thirty photographs later, I walked out of that lonely hotel room trying to clear my throat of the heavy iron taste. An investigator stopped me, pulling at my coat.

"Ms. Todacheene, right?" He extended his hand.

"Yes. Rita." His grip was firm and his hand, warm.

"I am Lieutenant Declan from Internal Affairs." He handed me a card and pointed toward the scene. "Gang activity?"

Declan was a little over six feet tall and had dark hair and a serious face. He wore a nice suit, but not too nice—just enough to say he had taste, but not enough to make him look full of himself.

"Internal Affairs?" I asked. "Are you lost?" Like clockwork, my phone rang. OFFICE. I silenced it. "I'm sorry, but I have another scene to go to. I hope you'll excuse me." I turned away, but he grabbed my shoulder.

"Do you think she's going to be okay? The victim, I mean." He continued to follow me.

As I put my bag and gear into the car, I saw her: the victim, thin and confused, still dressed in her nightgown. I knew the answer then.

"We've been trying to talk to her for weeks. She only replied to us yesterday morning." Declan turned to see what I was looking at.

"I don't think she's going to make it, sir," I replied. The poor woman was sitting shotgun next to me before I had a chance to blink. Her ghost was in shock, pulling at her blood-soaked, holey nightgown.

"How do you know?" He leaned against my car.

"I just know." My phone began to ring again. I had to take it.

"We've got another one over here. You close?" I could hear Samuels chewing gum.

"What is it?" I kept my eye on Declan's suit; he kept his eye on me.

"Rollover fatality involving a police officer. Eastbound I-40 at the interchange. About five minutes from where you are now."

"I'm en route." I hung up and looked at Declan, this time meeting his eyes. "Sorry I couldn't have been more help." He was still staring at me as I pulled away from the scene.

"Does this mean I'm dead? Just like that?" the woman's ghost asked.

"I'm afraid so." I weaved in and out of traffic.

"I wasn't ready," she said, then disintegrated into my passenger seat.

7:45 A.M., I-40 WESTBOUND AT THE INTERCHANGE: FATAL ACCIDENT INVOLVING AN OFFICER

I drove onto the scene about five minutes later and grabbed a hardened granola bar from my glove compartment. A small red sedan was on its roof, most of the top half of the car crushed into the dust, hay, and debris that usually sat in roadway medians. The police had already covered the left side of the vehicle with a white sheet. The front end was mangled, the metal pushed up into the leaking engine. The smell of hot oil and antifreeze was fresh. The approaching traffic had almost come to a standstill as death-curious drivers wove through the bits of car on the asphalt.

I spotted a few familiar faces, shook their hands, and asked about the scene. It looked like the victim—another woman— had become distracted and veered off the road at a high rate of speed. But they were unsure how the other vehicle—a city vehicle, an off-duty officer—had been involved.

My first shot was taken from the back bumper of the idling ambulance, as high as I could get from the still-hectic scene. Judging from the marks left on the road, she had traveled quite a distance after the initial loss of control. I lowered myself from the ambulance and walked slowly up the road to look at the tracks, then snapped a few more establishing shots of the scene. A deep, black skid mark was shaved into the asphalt on the left side of the road. The metal of the rims had sparked against the black surface, leaving a huge gouge. I snapped a photo. From that point, the car had to have flown into the median at seventy to eighty miles an hour, flipping and landing on its roof. The woman had no chance. She must have died on impact while desperately trying to gain control.

The driver of the city vehicle had only minor injuries: a cut above his eye and a grid of cuts and punctures from glass. We took pictures of him on the scene. Detective Burns from the Vice Unit in Albuquerque was a fifteen-year veteran of the force whom I'd only met three or four times. He seemed perturbed that I was taking pictures of him and asked me repeatedly about the driver of the red sedan.

"Is she alive?" he kept asking.

"Sir, I don't know. I'm just taking pictures. Turn please." His hands had several scars and bruises around his knuckles. When I had him show me his arms, he had two parallel, healing cuts right up the cuff of his sleeves, one on each arm. He turned them over, embarrassed. I pretended not to see them.

"What happened to your knuckles? That didn't happen today?" I kept shooting pictures. I could feel him looking at me, but he never did answer. By the time I was done, they were already pulling him away to the ER.

Detective Burns's car was pretty banged up in the back, like he had been rear-ended violently. The front looked pristine. On the right side, the mirror was torn off and there was red paint on the door. I pulled out some tape and framed the red flecks. It was weird that they were on that side, especially if he was rear-ended. How would that happen? It wouldn't.

I must have snapped upward of one hundred photos before I made my way toward the red sedan. The coroner had been there fifteen minutes and was getting antsy, chain-smoking beside the highway. The officers had built a small box barrier around the car with white sheets; the door hung open, a female body pouring from its insides. Her torso had been crushed under the car's weight and her legs pinned beneath the dashboard. Her arms were visibly broken. One delicate hand gripped the wheel. The body leaned to the left, resting uncomfortably against the front seat. I began to snap pictures of her, hoping there was no small child out there wondering where their mother was. I knew that someone out there loved this woman. Now her vessel was empty and silent, still buckled into reality.

I looked into the viewfinder of my camera and framed her body. The afternoon light had come in from the opposite window and created a strange halo around her head. Small trails of blood had soaked her light brown hair into a hard, thin sheath, turning it a dark and thick black. It had also created a murky and permanent seal to her eyes, glued shut by the once-vital fluid. I snapped a flutter of eight or ten photos until the sounds of fists hitting the hood pulled at my attention.

"Did you see that fucker cut me off? Okay, maybe I cut him off in town, but I didn't mean to, you know what I mean? Well, he followed me here, racing up on me, flipping me off." She kicked the dirt, unaware that she was no longer a physical presence. As she moved closer, she stopped to look at herself—the self belted in the car. Then she looked at me and saw me looking at her.

She immediately came toward me like a rush of hot wind, her feet not touching the ground. Her face was so close to mine that I could feel her heat and rage. I hadn't let anyone, dead or alive, that close to me in months. I tried to pretend that I didn't notice her, but I couldn't help but step back. Her presence was powerful. I caught my foot on the edge of the asphalt and fell to the ground, dropping the camera into the dirt.

"Are you okay?" said a young officer. "What happened?" He extended his hand to help me off the ground.

The victim stood there looking at me, her chest heaving in panic. "You can see me, can't you?"

I tried to pretend I didn't hear her.

"Hey, are you okay?" the young officer asked again.

"I'm sorry. Yes. I'm fine," I lied. "I'm just tired—punchy. I guess I didn't see that ridge there." By then, the investigators, the other officers and even the tow guy had begun to stare at me.

"Hope all the pictures are okay." An officer handed me my camera. He stared at me strangely and feigned a smile. I grabbed the dusty strap and looked at the back of my camera. It still worked; I could see that the photos were there.

"They're fine," I stammered.

The heat rushed toward me again. She was there, in my face, trying to make eye contact. I tried my best to stare straight ahead, as if there were a full and unlimited portal to the world right at her head's center. Her voice was loud and powerful.

"I know you can see me. I know you can. Tell them. Tell them what happened. Tell him that this guy won't take no for an answer. We dated for, like, five months, and I broke it off a month ago. And he won't leave me alone. He wanted me to die." She screamed at me with such a force that I know I must have jumped, startled from what everyone else saw as silence.

I turned to see the young officer staring at me, waiting to see what I was going to do next. "Officer, I think I've taken enough. Thanks for your help." I walked away from the scene, pulling up the collar on my coat. The ghost trailed right behind me.

"Did you hear what I said to you? Listen, lady, I know you can hear me. I know you can see me standing right here in front of you. Why won't you tell them? Why won't you tell them what I said?" She followed me all the way, forcing me to look her in the eyes. I walked through her four times before I made it to my car, where I closed the door and sat in silence. I could see her standing at my window through the corner of my eye, but I didn't make eye contact. She bent down to stare at me and banged on my window. The coroner walked by too, following me with his eyes, a look of concern on his face.

"What do you want me to tell them?" I started the engine. "That this woman's ghost is telling me the officer ran her off the road?"

She seemed surprised that I responded, then continued to bang at my windows. "Please tell them. I don't care what you do, just tell them what I said. Talk to me again. Tell me you hear me."

"I hear you, ma'am," I said. "It will all be in my report and in the photographs." I pulled away as fast as I could. When I looked in the mirror, she was gone. I prayed that she would stay away.

My phone buzzed on the seat. Voicemail. I pulled over on the side of the road and looked through the photographs. The call could wait. The thirty-eighth image confirmed exactly what the woman said—the scrape of red paint flecks along the left panels and doors of the officer's vehicle. Just like he'd run a red vehicle off the road.

The phone buzzed again. The voicemail. I had to listen.

"Rita, I know you're on scene right now, but you're going to need to hang in there a few more hours . . ."

I hung up without letting the message finish as four or five patrol cars whirred past me, their lights ablaze. The phone jumped in my lap. OFFICE. I didn't know where those cars were headed, but I knew I was probably going to be following them.

CHAPTER TWELVE

My Camera Box

GRANDMA DIDN'T BELIEVE me when I said that Judith was gone. I could see it in her face. We drove home without a word, and we stayed that way for the rest of the night. There were times when you could talk to Grandma and get her to smile, and there were other times when you could see and feel that she needed to be left alone. I sat at the table and watched Grandma make gravy and corn on the stove. It was my favorite. The house was quiet that night. We wiped our faces and brushed our teeth in the heat of silence.

When I woke the next day, Grandma was already at the table having coffee. She smiled and pulled me toward her.

"Rita," she said, pressing into my arms, "you have to help me."

I nodded. I would do anything she asked of me.

"I'm going to have to take a trip and I can't really tell you about it yet, but I will. Do you understand?" I shook my head and smiled. Grandma hugged me so hard I felt like my bones might snap.

My time with Judith had finally broken Grandma. Her insides were in a panic. She felt alone and trapped. She wanted me to stay with her, but she knew she had to get me out.

"Mr. Bitsilly is going to watch you over the weekend. I want you to help him with whatever he needs. If he asks you to do something, you need to do what he asks." She continued to squeeze my arms. "Don't worry. I'll be back to get you."

"Did I do something bad?" I felt a lump rise in my throat. I hadn't meant to hurt Grandma when I was talking to Judith. I was lonely. That was all. Now I was going to have to spend the whole weekend with the medicine man.

"No, she'awéé'." She hugged me again. "You are doing your best." She touched her camera box, which was sitting on the table. "I'm going to leave this with you. It's yours now." She put the black plastic envelope in the box and grabbed the sides of my face. As she embraced me, I could feel a bounce in her shoulder as she cried.

She dropped me, the box, and my little suitcase off before the noon sun burned the land yellow. Mr. Bitsilly and I watched Grandma's truck turn onto the highway and drive into the distance. Mr. Bitsilly smiled wide. "C'mon. I made some lime Kool-Aid."

The screen door slammed behind him, wood against wood. I watched over rooftops and through tree branches until Grandma's truck was completely out of sight. As I moved inside, I saw Mr. Bitsilly's grandson sitting on the worn couch, his face shiny and wet and his feet hanging bare over the edge of the cushion. I sat next to him and watched cartoons as the summer heat began to build through the house.

"What's in the box?" He pointed to the camera box on my lap.

"Nothing yet," I answered.

Mr. Bitsilly needed lots of help. It was only the three of us: Mr. Bitsilly, his always-quiet ten-year-old grandson, Travis, and me. By the time the sun was setting, we had helped him stack a healthy pile of wood along the front of his hogan and filled all four of his water tanks over at the well. We watched the sunset, deep with orange and red over the valley in Tohatchi, with plastic mugs of green Kool-Aid in our grips.

Late that night, we heard the cries of a woman outside the front door of Mr. Bitsilly's house. His shoes shuffled toward the door in the darkness as Travis and I rose from our blankets. The woman was hysterical, her breath skipping as she spoke rapid Navajo. We sat silently on the couch as Mr. Bitsilly put his arm around the woman and led her into the hogan.

The two of us tiptoed to the doorway and spied. Her name was Rosemary Nez, that much I understood. She cried hard. I had no idea what was going on in the conversation. I just watched their faces and knew their words were full of sadness and evil.

"Do you know what they're saying?" I whispered.

Travis looked disgusted. "Her son is missing." He moved close to my ear. "He's been doing drugs and drinking, and he hasn't come home in a few days."

The woman gripped Mr. Bitsilly's hands and continued.

"She wants my grandpa to pray for him. She is saying she has nothing to give him."

"Travis!" Mr. Bitsilly's call made us both jump. Travis rushed through the door in his pajamas. "You two go get me some wood." We did as we were told, then watched him build a fire. We sat on the porch and listened to Mr. Bitsilly sing into the sky. There was a stark white moon out that lit up the land for miles. The heat had finally gone to sleep, and nothing moved but the sound of his prayers.

Travis broke the silence. "How come you can't talk Navajo?"

"I just never learned how."

"Doesn't your grandma talk Navajo to you?" He looked at me out of the corner of his eye.

"Not all the time. Not like your grandpa talks to you. You're lucky." In the distance, I could see only a shadow, a movement deep in the rabbitbrush, but I was certain it wasn't an animal. It stopped and listened. Mr. Bitsilly's voice lingered through the canyon.

"I hope that Grandpa's singing helps to find her son."

Travis walked back into the house. I had no idea what the woman's son looked like, but someone was standing in the darkness. I ran back into the house and closed the door.

"Are you okay?" Travis said. The television flashed on his face.

"I just need to come inside," I explained, and joined him in the living room, watching the silent images flicker.

There was a violent bang, shaking the windows and sending Travis and me running into the kitchen. It sounded like someone had thrown a brick at the door.

"Are you two okay?" Mr. Bitsilly came into the room.

We couldn't talk or move, only stared at the door waiting for the next thump to ring out, but nothing happened. Mr. Bitsilly opened it wide. Nothing. We looked out into the darkness with Rosemary Nez by our side, tears streaming down her face. Mr. Bitsilly sent us to our beds on the couch. A short while later, I heard Mr. Bitsilly take Rosemary to her car, then trudge back up his porch steps. When he stopped to look at us, I pretended to sleep. He shuffled to his room and the whole house went black, helping me to close my eyes and rest.

In the morning, I woke before anyone else, and I knew that Mrs. Nez's son was dead. I dreamed about him all night. I dreamed about his car and the sound of laughter. It had been an accident. He and two girls had gone up to the cliffs above Chuska

Lake and drank until they could barely stand. As the two girls slept off their drink in the backseat, Deswood Nez made his way to the edge to look out onto the darkened water. Then he slipped. His body flipped and turned on the rocks and trees below until he came to a stop at the bottom, a hundred feet from his car and his companions. When the two girls woke up the next morning and found Deswood gone, they figured he had walked home. They did the same. He was still lying down there, a slight smile on his face.

I walked outside into the crisp air before the highway began to move, before all the reservation dogs began to howl and chatter about their nights beneath the scarce, barren streetlights. I lingered across the street from Mr. Bitsilly's house, looking out into the bushes and grass that lined the field, feeling the pull of the leaves on my fingers.

"Rita," Mr. Bitsilly called out. "What are you doing over there? Get back over here."

I ran back to see Mr. Bitsilly get down on one knee and look straight into my eyes.

"Rita, you can't just run off like that without telling me where you are going." He squeezed my hand. "I promised your grandma that I would take care of you." We walked hand in hand to the steps and sat down.

"I think I saw him, Mr. Bitsilly," I said. I pointed out into the field. "His shadow was standing out there last night while you were singing."

"Whose shadow?" I could feel his blood coursing through his fingers as he held on to my hand.

"Mrs. Nez's son. He's dead, you know."

Mr. Bitsilly released my hand. "You don't know that, Rita." Mr. Bitsilly stared out into the empty field. "You shouldn't say that kind of thing."

"It's true," I said. "He visited my dreams last night and told me right where he is."

"Rita." Mr. Bitsilly was angry now. "You can't lie about this. Mrs. Nez is so worried about her son. How would you feel if your grandma went missing? Wouldn't you want to find her?"

"I'm not lying." I began to cry. The thought of missing my grandma filled me with anxiety. "He fell. He fell right by the lake. He is still there."

I could feel Mr. Bitsilly shaking. He stood up and took my hand once again, walking us into the house, into the kitchen, where he grabbed the phone and dialed.

Travis couldn't stop staring at me as Mr. Bitsilly called the police over to the house. We sat waiting for them in the kitchen, silent except for the occasional *pop* from the coffee pot. When they pulled into the driveway, they spoke to Mr. Bitsilly from their cruiser windows. I strained to hear what they were talking about.

"It's true what they say about you, isn't it?" Travis said.

I didn't answer.

"People say that you see ghosts and things. Is that true?" Travis kept at it. "It doesn't scare me, you know. You have some kind of special gift, like Grandpa. You just know things."

I stayed silent. It was only my second day away from my grandma and I couldn't stop thinking of her leaving me here— like my mom left me, like Gloria left me—to live out my days with Mr. Bitsilly and his grandson. I was terrified.

Mr. Bitsilly came into the room and sat down with me and Travis. "The police are going down to the lake to look for Deswood," he said. "They will let us know what they find after they talk to Mrs. Nez." He never took his eyes off me, but it wasn't the look of mistrust. He was worried about me. "Do you promise me that you're telling me the truth, Rita?"

I could feel tears on my face. I couldn't control them.

"You need to rest." He rose to his feet and led me to the couch. "If you're worried about your grandma, I'm sure she is fine. She will be back here tomorrow, you'll see."

I lay down on the couch and watched the flicker of the television, but sleep wouldn't come to offer its comfort. Instead, I cried after my grandma. I knew that it wasn't good to cry after people, but it came like a flood.

Mr. Bitsilly and Travis sat and watched television with me, but no one spoke. After Travis drifted off to sleep, Mr. Bitsilly sat on the floor by me, next to his boots.

"Did your grandma tell you where she was going?"

"No," I said. "But I don't think she can take care of me anymore."

He looked surprised at my answer. "Why do you think that, Rita?"

"Because I can feel it."

"I guess you're right, in a way. Your grandma went to help your mother settle into a place for the both of you. It's time that your mother took responsibility for you."

I couldn't say a word.

"We will always be here for you, Rita." He looked in my eyes. "This place will always be here for you—a safe place." Mr. Bitsilly stopped. "The two of us are connected. I think you were just meant to do something more."

We sat in silence as Johnny Carson pushed through his curtain. Mr. Bitsilly was right. Maybe we didn't see things in the same way or use our gifts in the same way, but there was a bigger connection between us, as if we sometimes shared the same eye.

On the day my grandma was set to return from her travels, I went into Mr. Bitsilly's closet and taped some photo paper into

Grandma's box camera. I told Mr. Bitsilly and Travis that I was going to take their picture, but they didn't believe me.

"You're going to take our picture with that box?" Travis asked. "That's crazy!" Reluctantly, the two of them sat on the porch with Travis on the bottom step between his grandfather's knees. I pointed the small hole at them.

"Watch," I said and pulled the tape from the front of the box. They chuckled. "Don't move," I said. "Stay very still." They looked perfect—Mr. Bitsilly in his big overalls and well-worn moccasins and Travis in holey jeans, his skinny brown legs popping out. I pushed the tape back into place and ran back to Mr. Bitsilly's closet.

When I came out, the police were in the driveway. Travis and I watched the officer advance toward us. He was coming to tell us what I already knew.

"Yá'át'ééh, Mr. Bitsilly," the officer said. He took off his hat and wiped his brow. "I just came by to let you know that we found Deswood Nez yesterday. We wanted to thank you for your help."

"I'm sorry to hear that he has left us," Mr. Bitsilly said and shook his head. "Thank you for coming by to tell us." We all watched the young officer walk back to his car and pull away. Travis and Mr. Bitsilly looked at me. There was nothing else said.

CHAPTER THIRTEEN

Nikon D200 AF-S DX Zoom-NIKKOR
17-55mm f/2.8G IF-ED Lens

4:34 P.M., 11271 JUNIPER HILLS— POSSIBLE MURDER/SUICIDE

THE SCENE HAD been secured by the time I had arrived. I left my car as close as I could, parking with the yellow tape up against my hood. I wasn't looking forward to what we would find inside. The radio scratched through. "Mobile unit in route. Eastbound on Tramway from I-25." I rested my bag on my shoulder and walked under the tape.

The house was beautiful. It was one of those homes that sat perched on top of the mountain, their mirrored glass sending prisms down to the rest of us. Photo one was of the outside, photo two the house number, and three the entire foyer just as I saw it, with high, wide ceilings and white and periwinkle accents. As I walked into the front door, I could smell the faint hint of gunfire and potpourri. Silver frames covered every available piece of wall on the right side: baby pictures, soccer games, family get-togethers, a young couple standing next to each other. The man was recognizable immediately.

Judge Harrison Winters was a nice enough man. I had met him a few times at police fundraisers and when I had to testify in court. He always seemed as uninterested as I was to be at those events. About a month earlier, they'd caught the judge high as a kite and passed out on the freeway with a very young woman. They found a huge amount of cocaine in the car and two open bottles of eighteen-year-old scotch. The girl—a sixteen-year-old prostitute—had been reported missing in Arizona. He was toast.

I took three more steps inside and saw Judge Winters's wife lying on the floor, a deep and blackened hole right in the center of her head. Her face was surprised, her eyes wide open, and her lips purple under the uneven lipstick still left on top. The wound measured about two inches in the widest areas—a starlight tear and burn telling us that the gun must have been right up to her head. We found and photographed P-1. The slug had passed through a wet sponge, bounced off the counter, and embedded itself in the wall behind the sink. There was an oval spray of blood on the window above the sink and on the ceiling. Her head was in a pool of black, the blood dried around her face. I took sixty-four pictures in the front room: Mrs. Winters, the blood-spattered mail in her hand, the bloody handprints on some paperwork on the table. Even her dog was dead, bloody and mangled by the sink. I photographed the shell casings, three in all, shimmering next to two or three breadcrumbs and a collection of wiry dog hairs. A .45.

The living room was untouched and spotless. Every glass and coaster was in its place, the television still on but the volume muted. Detective Massey sat at the head of the stairs, taking off his gloves. Massey was still a youngster, maybe three or four years on the force, and he had already made detective. An impressive feat.

"Hey, Massey." I extended my hand. "You get a look upstairs yet?"

"Yes," Massey said, and nothing else. Whatever was up there was horrible. I walked up the steps, snapping pictures as I went. Photo eighty-seven was of a bloody handprint at the top of the stairs. The fingers were fat and strong, the lines perfectly distinguishable. Photo eighty-nine was of another handprint at the door of the nursery. Just as I stepped inside, I heard the baby's keening cry, the kind babies use after they get a shot or hit their heads. But there was no baby in that room—at least not one that was alive. Another officer stood at the door and turned when he saw me, refusing to even look me in the eye. The crying continued, louder and louder, as I walked to the crib in the corner. The giraffe sheets were covered in blood, as was most of the bedding and stuffed animals around the crib. The gunshot had gone right through the little girl at the base of her neck and out through the bottom of the crib. Photos ninety through one hundred fifty captured the scene in the room, the blankets, the wound, and the blood that had pooled beneath the crib. I took every photo with a lump at my throat. When OMI came to take her body, we photographed her face. The bullet had passed through her right cheek, leaving a bloom of skin and blood right below her eye. We all watched in silence as they took her little body away. Her crying remained, a dull whine.

I found the boy in his room, hiding in the closet, shot through the top of his head. He had fallen stiffly onto the toy-covered floor, his face in dirty clothes. I photographed him as he was: the blood spatter on the winter coats, his posters surrounding the portal of his closet door. I estimated he could not be more than ten years old. He was an uncanny reflection of his mother in the kitchen. Even their wounds were the same. I guessed he had probably heard what was happening downstairs and hidden, only to be found and shot. I photographed the boy and his room for over an hour. The space, despite three of us drawing diagrams, making reports, and taking pictures, was silent.

I felt a tug at my coat. The boy. I couldn't help but look him straight in the eyes.

"He's not here. The one that shot us." He looked at me, devoid of emotion. "He went in there and shot my dad too. I heard it. Come on. Let me show you." He pulled my arm so hard, I thought people might notice. I couldn't believe I could feel him.

"Rita? Are you okay?" It was Angie. When I looked over at her I felt the sensation of tears burning my cheek.

"Yes. I'm fine. Just a long day. A long, long day."

"Do you need a break?" She squinted at me.

I felt a push of air at my arm—the boy's ceaselessness.

"No. I need to finish up here. What time is it anyway?"

"It's seven. What time did you get here?" Angie kept writing in her report.

"About four thirty. Just one more room." I walked toward Winters's home office.

Detectives Garcia and Vargas stepped past Angie and me at the doorway. They reviewed the diagram while Garcia scribbled on his report.

"So sad to see it happen this way." Garcia shook his head. "I never would have expected a murder-suicide from Judge Winters." He moved around the desk and stared at the back of Judge Winters's open head wound.

Judge Winters sat at his desk, his eyes cloudy and fixed on the ceiling. There was some slight stippling and blackening around the wound, with a thick line of blood trickling from the hole in his temple; the exit wound was on his cheek. On the wall behind him, tissue, hair, and skin covered his juris doctor and other diplomas. His hands hung at his sides and his .45 lay on the floor beside him. We found the slug embedded in the carpet under his desk. Image 285 was the wide shot of the room, and image 315 was Judge Winters's desk, covered with unspent .45 shells.

As I pulled the camera up to my face, the little boy appeared at the left of my frame, his finger pointing toward the doorway.

"That's the one who was here."

I turned around to see Garcia and his partner still scratching out the report, joined by half the evidence team.

I felt an undulation of rage behind me and turned to see Judge Winters's dead, scowling face staring at me. The force of his hate hit me hard, like a ball to the face—the orange flash and sting.

"See, Dad! See. She can see us."

I stared at Judge Winters, dead and angry.

"Get out of my house!" he shouted. He moved right through my body, filling me with a sickness I'd never experienced before. I could feel his death.

I stumbled out of the office and down the stairwell, knocking a framed photo off the wall at the bottom. The glass shattered from the corner, breaking the frame into two even pieces.

"Rita!" Angie reached for me. "What's wrong, Rita? Are you okay?"

In the photo, the police chief and the mayor stood on one side of Judge Winters, and Detective Garcia and another man dressed in a tailored suit stood on the other—all smiles and arms over shoulders.

"Help me." Erma's cold breath coiled around my neck, stiffening my neck and jaw and vibrating my skin. "I'm not leaving until you help me."

My nose felt hot, and my lips pulsed as I felt the trickle on my lip. Blood. Then blackness.

CHAPTER FOURTEEN

Kodak Ektralite 10

AT MY SEVENTH birthday party, I saved the oblong box from Grandma to unwrap last. Maybe it was a watch, like something in silver and turquoise. I ripped the tape and paper back to find *it*.

The Kodak Instamatic X-35F came in a bright yellow box with a roll of Instamatic film and a long, shimmering box of prisms—the flash. When I opened it, the instructions fell on my lap; I began to read them immediately, forgetting my birthday guests. The camera was a rectangle in brown and black, the back of it opening like a car door swinging wide. I opened the film packaging, inhaling the strong aroma of fresh plastic and stale factory air, and snapped the cartridge into place. The shutter button was on the front of the camera, on the right side of the lens. I peered through the viewfinder and watched as everyone—Grandma and Mom, Aunt Ruth, Travis, Mr. Bitsilly, and our neighbor Mrs. Bitsie and her dog—looked back at me, their faces wavy in the lens. I pressed the button.

"Rita is my favorite photographer," Mr. Bitsilly said. Everyone laughed.

With the taste of cake and frosting still on my tongue, I

walked the distance around my grandmother's house looking for snapshots with my camera. The late summer afternoon provided a flood of marigold and magenta onto the otherwise dry, sandy ground of the reservation. Tohatchi framed everything in a sharp contrast of shades and color, of time and of atmosphere. The yellow blooms of Navajo tea stood stiffly, swaying along my grandmother's fence line. I focused on my grandmother's perfect white house alongside the moving tea stalks and snapped another photo.

From that point on, I took pictures of everything and everyone. It got to the point that my grandmother had to limit me to one roll per week.

"You are going to put your family into bankruptcy," Grandma would say.

At first, I felt punished by my one-roll limit, but soon I realized that this was the ultimate way to wait for the perfect shot. My early photographs consisted of my usual reservation encounters—picking corn with my cousins, my grandma at her sewing machine, some men butchering a sheep, boiling fry bread in a hot black skillet. Eventually, I began to venture farther into the cliffs and canyons behind my grandmother's house. The Chuska mountain range became the backdrop to hundreds of photographs as I searched and found Cheii the horned toad, Miss Bitsie's wandering cows, and a few rusted cars from the '50s and '60s. I finally climbed to the top of a crested bluff near the highway and saw a dozen photographs emerging down below. I ran down the hill, the cuffs of my pants capturing sand by the handful.

I came to a halt by the highway. A black cat—dead only a few hours. He hadn't started to smell or get stiff. I could not even see blood until I moved closer. I looked up the road, spotting a dark snake of black where the car had tried to swerve. I stood over the cat and snapped the picture, the first in a roll of twenty-four. Make that twenty-three, now.

I caught his full and strong body—his fur a deep black, darker than the highway, darker than anything I had ever seen. His eyes were open and looked straight forward. I rested my head on the hot asphalt and caught his gaze, the highway rising behind him: twenty-three, twenty-two, twenty-one. His tail had been flattened, his glossy fur matted and frayed at the edges of his injury. The camera flashed. Twenty, nineteen, eighteen. A dented brown pickup truck passed by, the inhabitants slowing down and watching me. I caught their faces. Seventeen, sixteen. Only fifteen left.

A delicate rain began to fall, neutralizing the heat of sand and asphalt, spreading a gilded and transcendent hue over the land. I stared at the cat again. His sharp, pearly fangs peered out from his open mouth. Click. Fourteen, thirteen. I darted across the desolate highway and framed the cat again, this time in the beam of light from the approaching storm.

Click.

WHEN MY GRANDMOTHER came back from town with a developed roll of film, I buzzed with excitement. I never knew whether the photos would come out until I could hold that waxy envelope in my hands and slip my finger beneath the fold to pull the sticky gum apart.

This time, my palms began to sweat as my grandma got out of the truck. She was not happy. She slammed the door, then grabbed my face and stared into my eyes.

"Dooda," Grandma said. "*No!*" She dumped the photos on her kitchen table and glared at me. The envelope had already been opened. "Now we have to call the medicine man."

Photo fourteen sat on top. I could make out the dead cat's white fangs.

From the kitchen, I could hear Grandma on the phone. She talked to Mr. Bitsilly in Navajo, but they were talking about me, this much I knew. I also knew the visit to Mr. Bitsilly's would be a waste of time. I loved Mr. Bitsilly, but his singing never made anything different.

That night, we sat on the dirt floor of Mr. Bitsilly's hogan, listening to his raspy voice as he sang into the night air. Trails of sweet sagebrush smoke arose from the floor, escaping through the hole in the ceiling. He blew his hot breath through the bone pipe, pressing my hair back, and continued to pray and sing for me. My grandmother soon joined him in song. I wanted so badly to understand what they were saying, but my grandmother didn't want me to know. She had once told me that my language would only get me in trouble. Suddenly, without any warning, Mr. Bitsilly rubbed his chin on my forehead so hard that it hurt. The pipe echoed in my ears and Mr. Bitsilly spit bone, hair, and blood into his handkerchief.

After a long day there in the hogan, I didn't feel any different. I could feel the love and concern coming from the prayers, from the songs, but nothing had changed. I knew they still looked at me, wanting to know why I had this connection to dead things. For Mr. Bitsilly and Grandma, that connection was the most dangerous thing possible. They were scared of the sickness that death could bring.

After we left the hogan, we went back into Mr. Bitsilly's house, where I sat at the table with an overly sweet vanilla cookie while they lectured me about my pictures.

"Death is something that you need to leave alone, Rita. Don't touch dead things; don't look at dead things." Mr. Bitsilly glared at me out of the corner of his eye. "And don't talk to dead things."

"And don't take pictures of dead things," my grandmother added.

"You've been doing so good." Mr. Bitsilly looked at Grandma. "All we're saying is that if you keep inviting dead things into your life, it could open the door. You never know what path a spirit has taken until they are in your head. Don't let them know that there is a door. Don't let them know that you are the key."

They talked to me about what death leaves behind—the spirit, the essence. They cautioned me about the evil that lives in that spirit, like a cancer, a presence of terminal energy. Mr. Bitsilly warned me over and over until it scared me. This must have been what Grandpa told me about.

After the conversation, I escaped to the living room, where the lone bulb lit up all of Mr. Bitsilly's football posters. Grandma followed me. Mr. Bitsilly saw us look at the posters and the red-and-white frames decorating his walls and blushed.

"The Cardinals are my team," he admitted. "But they never win."

ON THE RIDE back home, I watched as my grandmother's tádídíín bag—her medicine pouch filled with corn pollen—and her crucifix dangled in the light of the late afternoon. She sat quietly, her rough hands grasping the steering wheel. I loved my grandmother. She didn't look or act like any grandmother I had ever met. When I went to friends' homes or saw other grandparents at school, they were always what you would expect a Navajo grandmother to look like. Other grandmas dressed in velveteen and wore their hair in buns tied with wool, like in every book I'd seen about the Navajo people. They had sheep and lived in hogans. But not my grandmother.

My grandmother wore her hair short and curled. Later, when it became sprinkled with gray, she would sometimes dye it the shiniest jet black. Her hands were worn, but she took great care to keep them clean, her nails cut short and sanded perfectly. She made her own clothes from bolts of light cotton—dresses or nice pants and a blouse, closed with silver pins. She'd learned how to sew in boarding school in Phoenix. Both she and my grandfather had gone to boarding school. One day, while we were peeling potatoes at the kitchen table, she had told me all about it.

"The city was full of cars and people. Everything moved so fast. But in Phoenix, at the boarding school, they taught me how to cook, to sew, how to take care of children. I learned how to read and write. I learned to act like a white person. But I also learned about other things. Like how to build things, how to use a camera. I learned what it was like outside of the reservation. That is important. If you never leave, you never know how good your life can be. Sometimes, I think it was a good thing that they took me away to school. Otherwise, I would be living in a hogan in the middle of nowhere with my sheep. I would rather be here with you."

Grandma had a way of explaining things. I never interrupted her. I just let her talk. She had lived through a lot, each line in her face giving us a map of years and experience. She was incredibly strong.

As we drove home from Mr. Bitsilly's house in the rain that day, my grandmother said, "When my mother died, I was only a little girl. Maybe five or six years old. She had a terrible cough for months. When she was hot with fever, she coughed blood. My grandfather knew she was about to die. He explained to me in Navajo that she was going out to die, then two young men, covered in ash and smudged with pine sap, came in and carried my pale mother out of the hogan. She smiled at me as she left and held on to my braid, right up to the tip, then let it fall. I ran to the window and watched them take her to a fire they had lit in the distance. I stood there for hours. My little feet ached, but I didn't care; I didn't want my mother to leave. I cried after her. My father took me aside and scolded me. Crying after someone when they're dead is the worst thing anyone could do because it keeps them here in this world. They wouldn't want to pass on. My father feared death like he feared no other thing on this earth.

"But what always confused me was that death was so evil. It was as if when we died, we went to hell. I didn't want my mom to go there, so I cried and cried to keep her here. I watched in the moonlight as my mom parted this world in the summer night. Every once in a while, the lightning from the storm lit up the canyon, and I could see the two strangers picked to guide my mother to death. As family, we were not allowed to be a part of her passing.

"I remember when she died, as the sunrise bled into our door, the two men came into the hogan and washed the ash from their bodies. My father told us we were not to ever speak my mother's name again. But late at night, my sister and I would talk about her as our father, your great-grandfather, slept. All of this is just something we believe—that death is evil, that it carries despair . . . or at least, that's what we were taught to believe. That sickness my mother had killed a lot of our people, and I think it made us scared of death forever. I don't even know what to believe anymore." Grandma shook her head.

We eased into our muddied, rutted driveway, our tires rumbling in deep tracks, as the moon was high in the sky. I could not help but think about the story my grandmother had just told. How cruel life could be, and death, a crueler and more evil experience. I didn't like how Navajos thought of death, like a first-class ticket to hell, and even at that young age, I wondered about all of it. What was real? Who was telling me the truth?

I LOVED BEING there in my grandmother's house. The familiarity of the green checkered curtains blowing gently in the breeze of early summer, the still-warm tortillas sandwiched between the handmade potholders. We would talk and talk about everything while country songs drawled from the speakers of her clock radio. Every day was like this with my grandmother. This was where I wanted to be forever, where I belonged, free from the press of civilization.

Grandma had other plans. She prepared me for what was to come. It was time for me to move in with my mom. Grandma explained that I would return each June through August to be here among the tall, blooming stalks of Indian tea, to witness the invitations to late-night singing beckoning from spray-painted roadway signs, and to spend the cool nights on the porch with my grandmother.

But Grandma encouraged me to stay with my mother. "This is not where I want you to end up," she would say. "There is nothing here for you."

"But you're here."

"I will always be here," she would reply. "You will not. I don't want you ending up like Gloria."

I didn't trust that my mother could take care of me. After all, she had left me here and moved on with her life. She rarely visited. It was like Grandma had to remind her that I existed, and in doing that, Grandma had to remind my mother about her bad decisions.

That night, my dream was touched by a freezing fear. I saw myself get up off the couch, my bare feet touching the stony linoleum. I walked to Grandma's door and pressed my face against the stained wood to check that she was still breathing—something that I had done since I had learned about the miracle of the beating heart. Grandma had read me a book about the heart's chambers and the electricity of our own bodies—miraculous, but also, something that could stop with little warning. My grandmother's mortality was something I feared more than the approach of my own death.

In my dream, I could not hear her breathing. I let myself in. There she was, lying in her bed, not breathing. I grabbed her limp body and desperately tried to shake the life back into her veins, but she was gone. My body began to fade, my strength failing, my arms disappearing into nothing. Pieces of my teeth began to fall into my lap, and as I used my tongue to feel where they were coming from, I only pushed them out faster and faster. As I disintegrated into nothing, I jolted from my sleep. My grandmother sat at my feet, staring at me like she had watched the whole thing unfold on a movie screen.

She grabbed my hand and led us out into the morning. She took a softened satchel from the pocket of her light cotton dress. She spilled some of the bright yellow powder into my hand and into hers as she prayed softly in Navajo. She prayed for me, for my mother, and for our future. We sprinkled the yellow corn pollen in our hair and in our mouths and distributed what was left into the air. She looked at me, smiled, and turned to walk back toward the house. I stayed behind and watched the last of the floating prayer catch the beams of the rising sun.

CHAPTER FIFTEEN

Canon 5D—In Two Pieces

HOSPITALS SMELL LIKE alcohol pads and Band-Aids. That's how I knew where I was.

"Hey, look, I think she's waking up. I think she can hear us."

"Lady, can you hear us? Can you hear what we are saying to you?"

I didn't know where the voices were coming from, and I didn't care to find out. A rubber-gloved hand pulled at the skin beneath my left eye, a flashlight stinging. I sat straight up in the hospital bed.

"Hold on, young lady. You're going to have to lie back and relax. We're running a few tests—making sure everything is okay up there." The doctor chuckled and poked at my forehead.

"I told you, Rita." Angie spoke up from the chair in the corner. "I think this job is getting the best of you."

"Or you need to get to work!" Erma's ghost sat next to Angie. "I can hold this door all day." A bright light rose behind her as I watched shadows move through and around her.

I tried to shake off Erma and the whitened, sick haze in the room. Lights bubbled and circled around Erma and Angie.

Features emerged, like faces silhouetted through clean white sheets on a clothesline. They pressed in and out and talked in a million hushed voices. I had to get far away from Erma and this place as soon as possible. When there are one or two of them, their voices are manageable. But a hospital full of lost souls had their eyes on me now, knowing I could hear them thanks to Erma. I felt their deaths, just like the Winters scene, and it was getting worse.

"Rita, are you okay?" Angie pressed. "What's the matter with your eyes?"

"Can she see us?" a little ghost asked. "I heard that she could see us."

"Oh, she can see you just fine," Erma offered. "She can hear you too."

I looked down at the little girl; she was a shell of white light. Something about children's voices always forced me to look.

"She looked at me!" She raised a finger to my face.

"She can see. She can." The ghost of a man in an orange construction vest pushed the little girl aside. "Help us. Please, help us."

I stood, feeling the stings of the wires, tubes, and cables still attached to me. I headed toward the hallway, pulling all of it with me.

"Rita, don't." Angie tried to stop me, but I pushed her back as hard as I could. I couldn't even hear her voice anymore among the voices of a million ghosts going on at once.

"Please, you need to let my daughter know that I left the key for the box in my desk." The construction worker's ghost was once again in my face.

"Do you know where my mom is? I've been waiting for her a long time." The little girl tried to pull at my fingers.

A woman spoke in Spanish. "*Hija, ayudame. Por favor.*" I felt her heat on my arms. "*Por favor.*"

A teenager—still in her hospital gown and with cuts on her arms—tried to snatch my hair. "Are you a doctor? Can you give me something, you know, for the pain?" Her voice was indifferent and raspy, her heat the smell of a freshly struck match.

There were hundreds of them. They all spoke at once, in different languages, in different tempos and volumes, and tried their best to get my attention. One man's ghost pushed all the others aside. It looked like he had taken a gunshot to his face—half of it was gone; his left eye hung loosely in its socket.

"Tell my wife it was an accident. I never would have done this to myself. Never. The gun. It just dropped. Fell on the ground. Please." I couldn't take my eyes off him.

"Rita, look at me. Rita!" Angie pressed her fingers into my face. "What is the matter, Rita? What's going on?"

"They're all here, Angie," I answered. "You should never have brought me here. Get me out of here. Get me out of here now."

"It doesn't matter how far or hard you run, Rita." Erma stood at Angie's side. "We will find you."

The pressure in my head was unrivaled. My nose started to bleed again, the warmth spreading over my lips, my chin, and my neck. The ghosts felt my own life force and tugged on it like a rotten tooth. In a surge of panic, I yanked at the wires attached to my body.

"Oh my God, Rita." Angie pulled a towel from a side table and handed it to me. "Your nose. You must stay here. There could be something seriously wrong with you."

"If we all hold on to her, she won't be able to say no." The construction worker was determined. "Everyone. Hold on to her." And they did. I felt all their bony and cold fingers on my face, my back, my hair. Their force wrenched me so hard I thought my arms would be jerked from their sockets, that every hair would be plucked from my follicles. The pain was a descending pulsation. It was the pain of death, the ache of decay, the voices Grandma and Mr. Bitsilly warned me about—the darkness that stays. Erma was doing this to me. They had never been able to touch me before.

"Get me out of here, Angie," I pleaded. "Angie, please."

Angie grabbed a blanket from the bed and wrapped it around my shoulders. She held me up the best she could, her strong hands beneath my arms, and led me out of the examination room. The ghosts writhed and screamed at me in the corridor, desperate to come close to me, to feel one last pulse of life in their dead existence. I couldn't keep my head up anymore. I wrapped myself into that blanket and into Angie, feeling her pulse, strong and steady. My own barely beating heart was a thin, deliberate pulse marked by the running of blood from my nose and arm.

"Please, help me find my mom." The little girl yanked the blanket so hard that it flew from my shoulders and onto the floor. I watched her light morph to black, her face contorted by darkness. "Find my mother, now!"

The living inhabitants of the ER sat staring at us blankly, their injuries fresh and their bodies alive.

"Excuse me." The doctor was running toward us. "Where are you going?"

The automatic door flew open and blasted Angie and me with air and the beginnings of a light snow. We moved as fast as we could into the crime-scene van parked outside. Once inside, I looked to the rear to make sure none of the others were in there with us. It was empty of ghosts, but there was my camera.

My camera was broken in two—the lens free from the body and dented along the ribbed edges of the lens threads.

"What happened?" I asked, holding two pieces.

"Everyone on scene at Judge Winters's house saw you stagger down the steps and land flat on your face and on top of your camera." Angie looked at me out of the corner of her eye as she pulled out into the street. "So, are you going to tell me what happened in there? And don't try to tell me nothing happened. I've never seen you so scared. Never."

I had no idea that the county hospital was so full of souls. It was a testament to my own weakness.

"I don't know what to tell you, Angie." I felt alone and terrified. All this time, I thought I was in control, but now I found myself drowning, looking for the surface. "I'm haunted."

"What do you mean you're haunted?" Angie stopped at the light. "You need to quit this job, Rita. You've finally gone off the deep end."

"I . . . I can see . . . ghosts sometimes." I could feel my arm pulsing where I'd torn the IV out. I pressed my coat into the wound. "I don't know how else to explain it. I used to be able to control it, but now they know. It's Erma."

Angie was quiet. Quiet in the worst of ways. I didn't know what else to say, only adding to the suppression of sound.

"I think you should quit," she said at last. "Or maybe I should let Samuels know what's going on. I'm sure he wouldn't want you out on the field with these hallucinations."

"They're not hallucinations," I shouted. "They've been talking to me for years. Ever since I was a little girl."

"Maybe we should schedule an appointment with the department shrink." Angie pulled up to the front of my building. "I'm going to go talk to Samuels in the morning. I think you've been overworked the last few weeks. How many scenes have you been on in the last couple of days? I'm going to recommend at least a week off and monitored counseling with the department psychologist." She paused. "You know the work we do isn't easy. We see the worst of people. It is okay to say you need help. It's okay to admit that you're having a problem."

"Thanks for the ride, Angie." I grabbed my broken camera. I was tired of trying to explain myself and Angie was obviously not on the fast track to believing me.

"Rita? You need to go to the shrink," Angie shouted at me through the glass. "I won't tell Samuels about the hospital, okay?"

I didn't care what she told him. And for the first time in a long time, I didn't care if I ever went to work again. Somehow, I had let the whole thing get away from me. I was desolate and lonely, standing outside with a broken camera, wrapped in my muddy work coat with bloody tissues sticking out of my nostrils. Something had to change.

My body tripped and staggered like a drunk, the empty halls of my building echoing with every step. I looked up to see my floor in darkness. Mrs. Santillanes was sitting in the shadows, as quiet as a cotton ball.

"Hello, Mrs. Santillanes. I hope I didn't wake you." I took the last two steps, my legs stinging with muscle burn.

"Rita?" Mrs. Santillanes looked at me like I was a wounded dog. "Are you all right?" She pointed to my jacket. My sleeve had a broad semicircle of blood in the crook of the arm. She pulled me inside her apartment.

I had never been in Mrs. Santillanes's apartment long enough to see everything. I noticed the photographs right away. On the walls along the front hallway, Mrs. Santillanes had photographs framed in order of date. A color photo of her and some young children, a black-and-white photo of a very elegant woman and a child, and another photograph—a tintype—of a beautiful but mysterious woman. All their eyes were the same.

"You like the tintype?" Mrs. Santillanes stared at the image. "It's my *abuela*. She used to work at the drug store on Atrisco, handing out remedies to whoever came in." She straightened the picture. "She was a tough lady. They used to call her a witch because she knew more than she should." Mrs. Santillanes shuffled toward the kitchen and banged the back of one of her kitchen chairs. "Sit down."

I could not stop looking at her kitchen. In each corner of the room, there were small shelves that held wrapped bundles of dried leaves and vines alongside small statues of the Virgin Mary and Jesus. There were crucifixes on every wall and every shelf, sitting on tables, counters, and surfaces, even drawn on a small chalkboard alongside one of Mrs. Santillanes's grocery lists. When I turned to see out of her small kitchen window, Jesus met my stare, his frozen eyes in perpetual tears.

"Take that jacket off," Mrs. Santillanes ordered.

When I removed my jacket, I could feel the sticky adhesive of skin and blood. There was no way that night would ever be washed out of it.

Mrs. Santillanes straightened my arm. "That looks terrible. Look at that bruise. How did you get this?" She stared at the hole in my arm.

"I was at the hospital last night . . . well, this morning." The sun was finally heaving itself over the horizon. "I had to leave quickly."

She cleaned the skin with peroxide, sealed it up with gauze and a strip of electric tape.

"I'm sorry about the tape. It's all I have," she said.

"Thank you, Mrs. Santillanes." The lesion in my arm had stopped pulsing.

"What is this?" She pointed. I turned to see some blood on my side.

"Pull up your shirt. Let me see your back." She turned on the light, lifted my shirt over my ribs, and immediately began making the sign of the cross. "Oh, *hija*. Look at your back." She walked me over to her mirror in the foyer and showed me what she was referring to. "*Mira*. Who did this to you?" There were at least twenty or thirty small and large bruises and two sets of handprints right above my elbow.

"I'll be fine," I said, and pulled my shirt down. She crossed herself again.

I could see that she was shaken as she began to take jars down from the cabinets and mix, pour, and stir. She poured some tea into two small cups and brought them over to the table.

"Is this some of your special tea? Something to put me to sleep?" I absorbed the warmth of steam in my nostrils.

"No. That's just Lipton." She slammed four small jars on the table. "You need to put these in the corners of your bedroom so that you can get some sleep. If anything bothers you, you must ignore it." I didn't ask any questions. She pulled an egg from her apron and begin to rub me with it, going over my head and down my arms and legs. She moved to her cupboard, then pulled out a glass and filled it with water from a canister on her table. She cracked the egg into the water, and I watched the yolk sink to the bottom. "Take this and put it under your bed too. Whoever has their eye on you will let you go."

I walked into my apartment and went straight to the bedroom, placing Mrs. Santillanes's mixtures in the corners of the room and the glass of egg under the bed. Old superstitions, I was sure, but I was at the edge of sanity.

Erma was already there, sitting on the edge of the bed, watching me. "I'm dead, Rita."

"I swear I will get on it, Erma. Just give me a chance to rest," I begged.

CHAPTER SIXTEEN

The City—
Kodak Instamatic X-45

THE DAY I left Grandma's house, Grandma and I both pretended that it was not happening. I fed the dogs and gave them water. I sat with Grandma on the floor beside her rocking chair and watched one of her soap operas with her. We bagged piñon nuts and put bundles of dried tea into plastic containers. We packed my clothes and my pictures, but I left my Ektralite camera there on her dresser. That would be what I used when I came home.

We both cried when I said goodbye, even though Grandma told me not to.

"You're not supposed to cry when someone leaves you. It puts the bad spirits into your journey," Grandma said, tears falling down her cheeks.

Grandma stood outside in the late summer heat, one of those wet flour bags around her neck, her face shiny with tears and sweat. I cried the whole way back to my mom's house.

AS I ACCLIMATED myself to the new realities of city life, I still longed for the hot, dry days of Tohatchi. I walked the sidewalks of my mother's neighborhood, taking pictures with my mother's Instamatic. There was a bad-tempered drunk at the end of the block who I snuck up on one fall afternoon. The folds of his eyelids were heavy and created a tapestry of skin on his eye sockets. Something about the way the light hit the old man made him look like a tired seraph, his wings tucked behind his blanket of newspaper. When he heard the shutter of my camera, he jumped from his bench and knocked me back into the street—his laughter permeating our surroundings as he helped me off the ground.

"You owe me a pack of smokes for that picture, you know," he grunted.

He was the best part about that first neighborhood.

It was good to be with my mother again, but I preferred being on the reservation. I missed my grandma—her words, her voice. There was a permanence at Grandma's house that I didn't get here with my mother.

My mother didn't say much. She was a vagabond, an artist in the purest sense of the word, who was forced into jobs behind desks, filing colored folders and writing on chalkboards. She constantly fantasized, her eyes gazing into dreams—that same stare I remembered. By the time I made it to live with Mom, though, I could take care of myself. I didn't need to worry about my mother's unsteady hand at parenting when I knew how to navigate the world.

One day, her passion for her art left like a boyfriend who claimed he still loved her. On a Tuesday, she gave me her Canon AE-1 and all her lenses.

"Why are you giving this to me, Mom?" I was completely lost. This was the dream she had chased, for which she had left me with Grandma.

"I'm giving it up," she'd answered. "I've outgrown it and I have a new position at the school, running the arts program. I won't have the time anymore." She moved my hair out of my eyes as I looked down at the bag. "You're getting better, so you need a better camera anyway."

After my mom got the job, we moved from our apartment to our first house, in a new development on the outskirts of Santa Fe marketed to the surge of retirees and big-city transplants. The town was filled with hippies and middle-aged yuppies trying to find either themselves or their next buzz. We only lived there for a few months.

My mother and I then moved into her boyfriend's house, which had a huge cottonwood tree in the backyard. The walls were thick and natural, made with straw-filled adobe bricks. All the windows and doorways were rounded like a hobbit's abode, the air cool and crisp. It was right by a Spanish-style church and small, improvised altars were scattered throughout the alleyway behind the adobe. In the evenings, the small altars illuminated the alleyways with sprinkles of ruby-red light from the candle jars.

My mom and her boyfriend were engaged within two months. My mom was the photographer and poet, and he was the writer. They seemed perfect for each other. Both were meticulous and intense. Both folded their clothes into eight-inch cubes and rolled their socks in impeccable rows in the dresser drawers.

At first, he wouldn't tell me his name and wanted me to call him "Dad." I chose to call him "my mom's boyfriend." He tied a yellow rope around one of the cottonwood's highest branches and made a sturdy swing for me, still trying to win me over. It never worked.

After they got married, we moved to the center of town. The

house was surrounded by a deep and vibrant smell of honey-suckle bushes and orange trumpet vines. A long, gated driveway led to a small guest house in the back. Couples moved in and out of there all the time, their arrival announced by a new beater car in the parking spot. I would spend my childhood perched atop the pitched roof and at the very edges of the crab apple tree that stretched out over the neighbor's yard. I watched the young immigrant family who lived next door, occasionally talking to the two children that lived in the back room. The honeysuckle bushes constantly pulsed with the sounds of insects and feral cats, each eking out a living in the backyard.

Walton was my stepfather's name. Walton Hughes. He was a white man who wore perfectly pressed T-shirts and jeans, thick wool socks, and old brown leather boots. This was his uniform and he never deviated from it. He carried a small fingernail clipper in his pocket and would pull it out when he was outside. He kept those nails cut within millimeters of the skin—short, clean, and almost painful. He smelled like vitamins and roots and ate nothing but peanut butter and tofu cakes. He was a writer. That's what he told everyone. But really, he was the manager of a small publishing house in town that published hippie cookbooks, natural food almanacs, and household remedy collections. I tried to ask him about what he was writing, but he never seemed to know.

"Can I read it?" I'd asked once.

"Well, it's kind of an adult story about adult things." He kept typing. "I'll ask your mother if you can read it."

"What is it about? Hippies, sex, and drugs?" I knew all about that. My mom had no filter when I asked questions.

"Well, I'm still finding the story." He kept typing.

"When you find it, please let me know," I said.

I know it was irritating to have me around. I was some other guy's kid. A pain in the ass. I was a constant reminder of their responsibilities, of the fact that they had to get jobs. They were artists who wanted to live as artists. I never saw her take pictures anymore.

When they got married, my grandma came in a fancy cream dress and shiny shoes. Her hair was perfect. At nine, I was the official wedding photographer. I was most proud of a photo I took of Mom and Grandma. They sat on a bench in the backyard, lit up by late spring sun. They both seemed so happy. I almost wished Grandpa's ghost had made the trip. Grandma seemed to like my mom's choice. He was friendly and had an easy smile. He also had a job. My grandma approved.

She pulled me aside at the wedding and kissed me on the cheek.

"I guess your mom is doing okay, isn't she?" Grandma squeezed my hand.

"Yeah, Grandma, she's doing okay," I lied. "I still want to come home though."

"This is your home now, Rita." She turned and watched my mom and her new husband. "But if he ever lays a hand on her, you let me know." Grandma's eyes narrowed.

"Okay," I said.

My mother and Walton were married for six years, and the last five were pure hell. They fought all the time, often turning violent toward each other. During one fight, Walton had broken one of my mom's cameras in a jealous rage. My mom returned the favor by throwing his typewriter into the street.

Toward the end of their journey, they had a fight that rivaled all others. By the time I got home, the quarrel had already begun, so I didn't get the full picture, but they were both screaming at the top of their lungs. I heard something about "that woman," then I heard the cabinets open. I walked in just in time to see my mother hurling coffee mugs at Walton's head. The first two missed, but the third one hit with a fine, mild *thump* on the forehead. He grabbed his face and checked his hands for blood. When he saw the crimson on his fingers, he began to grab dishes from the shelf and hurl them at my mother. The plates hit her in the back and sides and fell to the floor in countless sharpened splinters. That is when they saw me.

I stood there with my backpack on my shoulder, my mouth open in shock. My mom took Walton's distraction as an opportunity and heaved the giant skillet off the stove. She hit him over the head with such force that the man fell flat on my mom's new rug, a look of astonishment on his face.

"Get him off that rug. I don't want him bleeding on it." She raised her shirt to show the beginnings of bruises on her sides. Her hands were cut; her face was red.

I did as I was told and pulled on Walton's arms, unable to move his dead weight. His body was limp, his feet trapped under his folded body. He had a cut above his eye and a big lump on top of his head. His T-shirt was dirty and torn, and his hair was stiff. I pulled my Instamatic from my bag and snapped his picture—just as he was, bloody and beaten on the carpet. I snapped another picture of the kitchen, which was littered with broken plates and dried tomato seeds on the ceiling. This was not the first time this had happened, but it was the worst.

Walton moved out two days later, and my mom filed for divorce. I saw him once at a vitamin store in the mall. He still smelled like vitamins and didn't even say one word to me.

CHAPTER SEVENTEEN

Canon EOS 350D Rebel XT

I WOKE UP to the dull croak of my cell phone, stuffed under a pillow with the Ziploc bag and my broken camera right beside it. I pulled the card and lens out and transferred them over to another camera, a Canon EOS 350D Rebel XT, and scrolled through the images until I reached the last one, Judge Winters's gunshot wound. I had bought the 350D to encourage myself to do more photography of the things I loved—something other than death. The fact that it was still in plastic said everything.

My phone rang again. I didn't answer. I lay in bed and absorbed the quiet of my empty apartment, the reflections of all my photographs of home sending sunbursts throughout the room. I pulled the 350D to my eye and framed myself in the mirror. At last, it was just me. Alone. And hungry.

The refrigerator was empty as usual, but I was so relieved. There were no ghosts. The voices from yesterday were gone. No Erma. Having Mrs. Santillanes next door was soothing, but I knew that I needed something stronger than jars of leaves and an egg to keep them away. I needed to regain my strength before moving forward, and I was going to have to call Grandma.

It took four rings before Grandma picked up, out of breath from running to the phone.

"Is everything okay?" she said without a hello.

"Hi, Grandma. How did you know it was me?"

"I had a dream about you last night. You should come home."

"I will soon. I have some things to deal with here." I paused. I didn't want her to worry, but I probably needed to tell her the truth. Instead, I lied. "I'm okay, Grandma."

"You need to come home, Rita." I could hear the shakiness in her voice. "Tonight."

I thought about Mr. Bitsilly's words all those years ago. I couldn't risk bringing this brood of spirits into the last safe place I had in the world.

"Grandma." I felt the ache in my stomach. "I can't."

"Send me your clothes, then," she said. "Take off what you're wearing right now and send it to me. I'll go over to Mr. Bitsilly's house right when I get them."

I knew that nothing would happen if I sent the clothes. There was nothing that Mr. Bitsilly could do to get me out of what was happening now. I pulled my clothes off anyway and folded them in a stack on my couch.

"I'm sending my clothes to you, Grandma." I looked at the blood stains on my shirt. "Don't worry, though. I'm fine."

Grandma was silent.

"Grandma? Are you there?" I stared at my phone.

"Send them to me. I'll take care of it." I could hear in her voice that she was worried.

"I'll tell you more later, Grandma. Don't worry."

I was scared. It was going to take a lot more than Mrs. Santillanes or Grandma or Mr. Bitsilly to deal with Erma. Her ghost was giving me a reprieve for the moment, but I could feel her rage building when she wanted to make herself present to me. In life, I could only imagine Erma being a force that couldn't be reckoned with.

I retrieved a box from my closet and packed my clothes inside. I was going to have to overnight it. When my clothes arrived in the tiny post office back in Tohatchi, Grandma would take the box straight over to Mr. Bitsilly so that he could sing for me.

Mr. Bitsilly didn't necessarily approve of my profession. "Sometimes I guess people like you have a calling," he had explained. "And the fact that you're Diné doesn't change that. All we can do is say prayers for you so that the holy ones will protect you from the evil you don't know."

My phone buzzed, startling me. The two voicemails were from Dr. Cassler, one of the psychologists at the department. I listened to them as I washed my face.

"Ms. Todacheene. We are attempting to schedule an appointment on a referral from Sergeant Seivers from the Field Investigators Office. Can you please give us a call today? Thank you."

The phone rang again.

"Rita here," I grumbled.

"Ms. Todacheene? This is Robert Declan with Internal Affairs. I spoke to you last week."

"Oh, yes." I remembered the suit, and I was thankful it wasn't the shrink. "How can I help you?"

"Well. I was wondering if you wouldn't mind meeting with me. I am working on a case that you might have some information on."

"Well, today is my first day off that I've had in a really long time." I looked at myself in the mirror across from my kitchen. I looked terrible. "I was hoping to not go anywhere."

"If you could just meet with me briefly. I'll take you to lunch while we talk," he offered. "It won't take too long."

I stared at the nearly empty refrigerator humming in my kitchen and thought of the mustard sandwich that awaited me.

"Okay," I agreed. "Where shall we meet?"

THE CAFÉ ON Gold Street had been there for years, but I rarely stepped inside. It was somewhat high dollar and filled with lawyer-types on perpetual lunch break. Small round tables and black iron chairs ringed the exterior, their attempt at Parisian décor. I stuck out in there, the only brown face aside from the workers. I felt the stares, especially from the lawyers. They always looked me up and down. I hated them almost as much as the police.

Today, the café was nearly empty. Declan sat staring at his phone in the corner, a coffee mug at his side. He set his phone down when he saw me.

"Lieutenant Declan." I extended my hand.

"Thank you for meeting with me on your day off. I know that you keep very odd hours."

"Oh, yeah? How do you know that?" I didn't trust him already.

"I was a cop once too, you know." Declan stirred his coffee. "I guess I still am."

"I'm not a cop," I said. "I'm a photographer. A civilian in the Crime Scene Specialists Office."

"I understand," he said. "But you do work for the police. How long have you been with the department?"

"I guess about five years, almost six," I said.

The waitress interrupted. "Can I get you two lovebirds anything?" Declan's face lit up and turned tomato red. The embarrassment looked good on him.

"What? No birdseed?" I joked as I glanced at the menu. I hadn't eaten in three days. "I'll take the burger, some of this soup, and a salad. And a cup of coffee and an iced tea. What about you?"

Declan smiled. "I'll have the pasta salad, please." The waitress grinned and gave us a wink. Lovebirds, I thought. What a bad read on *this* situation.

"So, what did you bring me down here for anyway?" My stomach growled like a junkyard dog.

"Do you know Detective Martin Garcia?" Declan began to pull a file from his bag. "He was on scene with you the other day, right?"

"Yes. I know Garcia. I have to . . . the honor of working with him." I noticed that Declan had perfectly trimmed fingernails. He was also wearing cufflinks. He had pale brown eyes clear enough to direct light through. Not like my dark brown ones that swallowed up the sun.

"We're investigating Detective Garcia on a few cases that he handled a couple of years back." He wrestled with the huge file and took out his notebook. "Has he done anything that you've seen that can be construed as . . ."

"Crooked?" I offered.

"Well. Have you noticed anything suspicious or out of the ordinary?"

"He's a jerk. But, aside from lifting money off a few hoods and stealing newspapers from the café in the courthouse, no, I haven't seen anything." There was something nagging at the edge of my blurred recollection of the hours before I woke up in the hospital—Judge Winters's little boy's ghost pointing at a crowded doorway.

"Are you on a lot of the same calls as Garcia?" Declan frowned.

"Yes. Unfortunately." My salad had arrived. I worked hard not to send bits sailing across the table as I attacked it.

Declan took out a couple of photographs and laid them on the table. The two men in the picture were gruff and haggard. Their style made me think of the drug dealer types we'd see coming up from cartels in Mexico, with their fancy sweat suits or embroidered jeans. One was gigantic, with curly, dark hair and hands that looked like the ends of wings. He sported a huge scar that crossed his neck from ear to ear. I was pretty sure I had seen him before, or at least his silhouette—suspending the desperately struggling Erma over the highway. The other man had eyes the color of the ocean, which looked strange when coupled with his deep brown skin and black hair.

"Have you ever seen Garcia with either of these men?" Declan stared at me. "Look at the pictures closely."

The cartels were the source of a lot of drug- and property-related crime in Albuquerque. Whatever these guys were involved in, I was sure Garcia had the capacity to be involved. The pieces were coming together in my mind, but telling Declan about my dreamy night with Erma wasn't going to help. I had to think quickly.

"I think I would remember the big guy," I said. "That is an incredible scar he has on his neck. It's surprising that he survived a cut that big." I scooped up the last crouton on my plate. "You know, Garcia was on that murder case I was on the other day. A real mess."

"What case was this?" Declan was finally perking up.

"Erma Singleton. The fatality that was pushed off the bridge the other night. Or jumped," I corrected myself. "We aren't sure yet." I hoped that Erma didn't hear that.

Declan was quiet. His forehead buckled under the pressure of his next question.

"Are you going to tell me what's going on?" I asked. "What is Garcia involved in?"

"We don't really know yet. Our witnesses have been dropping like flies. If you know something, my hope is that you would tell us."

"Well, the other day, when I first met you at the drive-by scene—you know, at the hotel . . ." I wondered if I should even say anything. "He was acting a little strange. He watched me like a hawk and looked pretty pissed when I noticed some coke spilled on the rug."

Declan was scribbling in his pad. "And?"

"And? Well, that's it."

The rest of our food arrived, and I dove right in. My body forced me to.

"Is there anything else you can tell me?" He seemed disappointed, and I'm sure he was disgusted by the way I downed my burger.

"Who are the two guys in the mugshots?" My mouth was full.

"They were two former higher-ups in a huge drug and gun cartel that has been shipping all their product through Albuquerque for the past two or three years." He pulled one of the photographs out again—the guy with the huge cut on his neck. "Ignacio Marcos has a network here in town. They get called on to move the product on to other states and up to other networks in Farmington, Las Cruces, and some reservations." Declan pulled out another photo. "This is the man they are working with."

I knew who "El Mayo" Zambada was. He was a major player in the Sinaloa Cartel in Juárez, México—a lieutenant in El Chapo's army. This guy was no joke. At the southwest command center, the department always brought up the Sinaloa Cartel and its

easily negotiable border through our state. We knew that the
Nogales and Tijuana portal used to be the major hubs, but the cartel
was beginning to push even more cocaine, meth, and heroin
through our isolated border into El Paso.

Declan was looking through his files. He laid another photograph on the table.

"This is Cedric Romero. The cartel has between five and
seven cells here in Albuquerque, and he is one of the leaders. His
family runs an upholstery shop and has a *taqueria* up on Fourth
Street." Declan finished his coffee before continuing. "He relates
to Garcia in some way. We haven't figured out how—haven't
made the connection. But money is passing between them."

"I've never seen him." I handed back the photo.

"Neither have we, really. He keeps a low profile." Declan put
the photo back. "APD is busting some of these meth traffickers,
but a lot of them are still getting away with murder."

"And you think Garcia is the eyes and ears of the cartel inside
the department."

"Yes. We do. And we think he'll do anything to keep that a
secret."

I picked up the photographs and looked again, staring at the
cut on the guy's neck. It was brutal. I needed to figure out who
he was.

"I don't know." I gave Declan back the mugshot. "I'm sorry."

"Well, if you see him or see anything that doesn't look right,
can you please contact me at Internal Affairs?" He handed me
his card.

"I have your number already." I pushed a few crumbs off my
shirt and drank my cup of coffee in one full gulp. "Thank you for
the lunch, by the way. I was starving."

"I can see that." He smiled, projecting the shadow of a dimple on the right side of his cheek. He stood and pulled my chair out for me. "Thank you for coming down here, again."

"No problem. I'll let you know if I hear or see anything. Or if I get really hungry." I returned the smile.

"Please do," he replied.

CHAPTER EIGHTEEN

Kodak Instamatic 77X

MY FIRST YEAR in the city with my mother, as summer moved into fall, the air was cool, especially at night when you could expect a gentle rain or a downpour with equal anticipation. I missed Grandma and Tohatchi, but I had become accustomed to the convenience of the city. I was anonymous.

I attended Our Lady of Guadalupe Elementary, since my mom and grandma agreed that a good Catholic upbringing might have some sort of effect on my "visions," as Grandma called them. I thought the school was spooky. Gigantic crucifixes stood ominous and stiff in the front doorways. The shiny linoleum floor was a checkerboard of red and an aged-guacamole green.

"Students, we have a new classmate." My teacher seemed as uncomfortable as I did. I looked at the floor. "Do you want to get up and introduce yourself?"

I stood in front of all of them in inescapable silence, my throat dry, my tongue a pink log of steel. "My name is Rita."

"Rita is from the Navajo reservation. Right, Rita?"

I nodded.

"Class. Remember when we talked about the Navajo in our

history lesson?" There was silence. "Well, you can go ahead and sit down, Rita. Thank you."

I watched the girls point, cupping their hands around their faces and cackling at me. My voice was still steeped in the language of the reservation—my heavy Navajo accent digging in deep and hanging on my words.

Celina, the blonde who headed up most of the cackling, described it best. "You talk like a caveman," she yelled during lunch. The laughter spread like an infection, with each young throat coated in hate. My new classmates glowed with the excitement of knowing I was different. The dirty Indian, now sitting among all the white and Spanish faces, all who disliked me more than any reservation schoolyard bully ever could. I knew then I would hear the echoes of their laughter for the rest of my life. So I stood at the back of the class and took their picture with my 77x Instamatic. All their little faces were surprised and bitterly white from the flash. I got those angry little bastards. Their souls were in my box. The teacher took it away, seizing my arm with her pinching fingers.

"You can have this back at the end of the day, young lady." Her white face and red lips were tight with impatience. I know she thought I was a dirty Indian too.

Then a small brown face emerged from the back of the class with a smile as big as a slice of grapefruit. Her name was Shanice, and she was an Indian too. She came from a pueblo only thirty minutes away from the city. We quickly became friends. We found that the two of us were a force that kept the creepy kids and nuns away. We might not have been from the same area, but we didn't care. We were brown, uncomfortable, and out of place, being forced to learn about Jesus and how to throw the perfect punch when we were cornered. After a while, most of the kids and nuns knew to just leave us alone—the untamable, wild, and godless heathens at the back of the class. We were inseparable.

Shanice had irresponsible parents who rarely came home, and my mother was working. We pretty much wandered the city by ourselves, me taking pictures and Shanice posing in most of them. We roamed around the plaza, getting free food from some of the street vendors when we picked up trash and brought them customers. We were a couple of cute little Indian girls and sometimes earned money by letting tourists take our pictures. I'm sure we were a novelty in our Catholic school uniforms, our cheeks shiny with dry skin and our hair in coils of wild black. We would smile and take their money—a dollar here and there. No one asked questions.

We grew into our strange, new, and awkward bodies together as we explored the people and the places in our town. We were happy. No one bothered us. I slowly surrendered to the cosmic easiness of the city, its movie screens and video games. Its quadrants of stale and empty banality became my home.

During junior high school, Shanice's mother took to coming home more often, mostly because the state told her they would take Shanice away if she didn't. It was good there was someone else at home, though, because Shanice's grandma barely spoke English and coughed all the time. I was surprised she had lived as long as she had. When Shanice's grandma died, her mom decided to move after the summer was over. I was sad for days. Shanice and I decided to spend every day of the summer together, earning as much money as we could so that we could visit each other.

About a month after Shanice's grandmother died, we sat in her room, surrounded by boxes with the radio on, looking through trashy magazines and counting our change for the weekend. On the chair by the window, Shanice's grandma sat smiling and watching us like she used to when she was alive, except she wasn't coughing. I couldn't help but stare.

"Rita, what are you looking at?" Shanice stacked quarters at her desk. When I didn't answer, Shanice's grandma turned her attention to me too.

"Can you see me, Rita?" Her grandma's ghost smiled right at me. I must have nodded.

"Earth to Rita." Shanice waved her hand inches from my face.

Shanice's grandma walked over to the shelf and pointed at a book. I could hear her infectious laugh as her spirit dispersed into the sun at the open window.

"Are you on drugs?" Shanice was right in front of me, her nose touching mine. I stood up and looked at the shelf where her grandma's ghost had been pointing. A Bible. I pulled it from the shelf and handed it to Shanice.

"Why are you giving me the Bible, Rita?"

When she opened it, a crisp twenty-dollar bill floated to the floor. She picked it up and glared at me, half curious and half scared.

"Shanice. What if I told you that I can see things that other people can't see?" I was afraid of her reaction.

"What do you mean?" She stood with the bill in her hand. "Like money in books on shelves?"

"Like people who are dead."

"Ghosts?" Shanice sounded excited. "Did a ghost tell you to hand me my Bible?"

I didn't want to tell her that I saw her grandma. "I've been able to see them for a long time." I wondered if this was the last time Shanice would ever consider me her friend.

"How come you never told me?" Shanice looked disappointed, but not for long. "I have a million questions! Do you talk to dead people? Do they answer? Have you seen any famous dead people? Like, you know, Elvis or anyone like that?"

"No, I haven't seen Elvis. No, I try not to talk to them. I've learned to turn them off, just like a switch. But some sneak in."

Shanice circled me, examining me like a lab scientist. "I can't believe this is the first time you are telling me about all this!" She grabbed my face. "I thought I was your friend."

"What do you want me to say? It sounds like a bad movie."

"Well, our Halloweens certainly could have been a little more interesting." She was bubbling with excitement. "We should go to that haunted house out by the church or over to the graveyard and see what happens."

"No," I said.

BY THE TIME the sun was setting, we were at the haunted house where the widow Mrs. Gutierrez used to live. The house, on the hill behind the elementary school, was boarded up and desolate now, the adobe wall crumbling at the gate. At Halloween, all the kids would go to the house to play with Ouija boards to scare the hell out of each other and prank the gullible. The story was that Mrs. Gutierrez had killed her husband and child after she found out that Mr. Gutierrez had another lady friend in town. She had meant to kill her husband, yes, with a poison pie that she had baked, but her poor daughter decided to share a piece and died too. They said you can hear her crying up a storm every night.

I didn't believe it, but I felt an uneasiness. I remembered Mr. Bitsilly talking to me about playing with these forces.

"You never know what path a spirit has taken until they are in your head. Don't let them know that there is a door. Don't let them know that you are the key."

We pulled our bikes along the tree line and leaned them

against the withering gate. Shanice and I walked all around the house, shining a flashlight into windows and dying cottonwoods. The sun had gone down, and the full spread of darkness had moved into the Gutierrez house.

"Well? Do you see anything?" Shanice shivered in the dark.

"No," I said. "I'm starting to get cold. Let's go."

We rode off that night without seeing Mrs. Gutierrez or her family. I was glad. I didn't know what kind of person that Gutierrez woman was. For all I know, she could've haunted me forever. Shanice never mentioned it again, and we never went back. Maybe she got spooked.

The next morning, we rode into the parking lot of one of our main summer hangouts—the pool—only to see that the park adjacent had been closed for the day. Yellow tape lined the grassy border as cherry and silver lights turned in the summer sun. Police were scattered throughout the park, talking among themselves and taking photographs of whatever was behind the sheet they were holding.

We rushed through our swim lesson and hurried to the locker room, overcome by the morbid curiosity of whatever was being concealed beyond the yellow tape. We threw our clothes on over our wet swimsuits and ran for the soccer field, where we could get a better view. One man was still taking photographs, and I whipped out my 77x and took a few pictures myself. I had never seen a scene like this. The sheet was now gone. A young man's body lay there in the heat beneath two giant cottonwood trees, one shoe missing, his arms outstretched. We watched in silence as the men moved the body into a body bag, then into a waiting car. The men left one by one, taking with them the streams of yellow tape, leaving behind only their footprints.

When the last of them were gone, Shanice and I walked across the street toward the trees. The blood had dried in the summer heat and pooled into the dark, thirsty soil. I saw white flecks of tissue in the deep cracks of the cottonwood bark. We stared for a long time. As we turned to walk home, I found myself looking off into that tree line, hoping that the man who left the earth was at peace. It made me sick.

"Well, that was scary," Shanice said. "Don't you think, Rita?"

I stopped. I almost couldn't breathe when he walked in front of me and stared into my eyes, a confused look on his face.

"Rita? Are you okay?" Shanice said.

I couldn't break his stare, no matter how many times I tried. It was as if he willed me to hold his gaze.

"He's right there. Right there," the man spat. "Rodrigo. He stood right there and watched them take me away. Do you see him?" I hadn't felt a force so full of hate before. His finger pointed at a thin man in a black and orange shirt. When he saw me looking, the so-called Rodrigo began walking away fast, his hair wet with sweat.

"Let's keep walking, Shanice. Keep walking." We pushed our bikes faster.

"You're seeing something right now, aren't you?" Shanice sounded scared.

"Just keep walking." I kept us moving so fast that cramps rose in my shins.

"Just go over there and tell him you know." The ghost trailed us. "Tell him that you're gonna tell the cops. Tell him!" His voice was a scream now. "Go tell him, you ugly little bitch. *Tell him!*"

We kept walking. His presence made my stomach ache, and each step made it worse. Shanice struggled to keep up. "Are you okay, Rita? Look at your face. Your nose is really bleeding. Hold it like this and sit down."

As she wrapped my hand around my nose, I turned around to see nothing. The screaming man had disappeared as quickly as he had materialized. I pinched my nose tighter, but the blood kept coming, puddling on the sidewalk.

Shanice walked into the corner store and bought us some water, putting one of the bottles on the back of my neck.

"What did you see back there, Rita?"

"I'm afraid to say. I don't know if he'll come back."

We drank our water in silence. The bleeding eventually stopped, but I couldn't help looking back at that tree line, knowing that a man took another man's life back there.

"He told me who killed him, Shanice; he showed me."

Shanice's face filled with fear. "What are you going to do?"

"I don't know. What would I say? 'I know how that guy at the park died because his ghost described it to me?' I don't think they would believe me."

"Are you just going to keep it a secret?" I could hear the pressure in her voice. "You should tell the cops. You don't have to tell them how you know, but you should tell them something. Like the guy was looking suspicious or something like that."

Shanice was right. How bad could it be?

We arrived at the police station about twenty minutes later. The inside was sterile, four sets of four chairs attached to each other in rows. We waited for the woman at the reception desk to get off the phone. She wore heavy eye shadow and chewed gum like it was supplying oxygen to her brain.

"Can I help you?" the woman barked. Her fingernails were bright orange with black dots, like ladybugs.

"We had some information on the body they found in the park by the north pool," Shanice said, suddenly sounding like an adult.

"Hold on. Have a seat and someone will be up here to talk to you."

We sat there for thirty minutes, watching people come in and go out. There were people in handcuffs, some spitting and carrying on. There were crying women and babies. It was quite the spectacle. I wanted to leave before any angry dead people decided to make an entrance.

"Can I help you two?" The detective was in a foul mood and reeked of coffee and cigarettes.

"We had some information on the body over at the park today."

"Come to my office."

His office was a desk in the middle of a loud room full of sweaty men on the telephone, typing away at their computers. He cleaned some crumbs off his desk and pulled a file from underneath a crinkled sandwich wrapper.

"Well, I'm Detective Walsh. I'm working on the case. Where are your parents?"

"My mom is at work," I said.

"Mine too." Shanice elbowed me in the side.

"Well, I'm sure that we'll need to let your parents know that you're here. But for now, tell me what you know."

"It's my friend Rita," Shanice said. "She's the one who knows who did it."

"Well, kind of," I said. "I saw a suspicious guy over by the park when we were watching you guys take pictures and stuff. He had an orange and black shirt and a funny mustache. He was really skinny."

"And how do you know it was him?" The detective seemed skeptical.

Shanice and I looked at each other.

"I just have a feeling."

"What if I were to tell you that another witness reported that there was a girl there right before this guy died wearing a black shirt and cutoff jeans? Just like the ones you're wearing right now."

This was not working out as planned. "We were at our swimming lessons this afternoon," I said. "You can check with our teacher, Ms. Leslie."

"She's telling the truth, Officer. Why would we come and tell you if we killed the guy?"

He eyed me up and down. "I think you two might know a little more than you're telling." He pointed at Shanice. "You come with me. We're calling both of your parents." The officer pulled Shanice out of the room by her arm.

I knew they had to be calling my mom. I was a minor, after all. But I didn't want that screaming ghost coming back to me. Not in a million years.

When the creepy detective returned, he sat uncomfortably close. "When are you going to tell me the truth? How do you know who killed our victim? Do you know him? Are you one of his dealers?"

I didn't know what to say. I certainly couldn't tell the truth.

His craggy face leaned into mine as he put his hands on my knees and separated my legs. "You can tell me. I'm here to help you."

I snapped backward in my chair, forcing my legs shut. The cop mimicked my move and cocked a smile. I just wanted out.

"His name is Rodrigo. He was wearing a black and orange shirt."

The detective was silent. Then he stood and led me to a holding cell next to Shanice, who was already in tears.

"I believe you, Rita," she said. "But my mom is going to kill me."

"We should have never come," I said.

When Shanice's mom showed up, she was mad as hell. "Don't you think I am letting you spend one more day with Rita this summer. We're moving out to Mesita this weekend."

We both knew right then this meant goodbye.

An hour later, my mom came into the station with a look of panic. When she saw me behind bars, she started to cry.

"What did you do, Rita?" Her mascara was running. Her business suit looked wrinkled.

"Nothing. I was just trying to help." I couldn't look at her. I stared at the bench across from me, focusing on a heart with the name "Donnie" carved in it. I began planning my own prison carvings in my head. I was sure I was never getting out of here.

While my mom spoke to the police, I laid my head against the bars and closed my eyes. Shouts erupted from the stairwell. The next thing I knew, the bars on the adjacent cage closed on a new occupant. He had changed his shirt, but it was him. He was sweaty, breathing heavy and labored into his chest. It was Rodrigo.

After that day, I learned to keep my mouth shut.

CHAPTER NINETEEN

Pelco EH16-2MTS CCTV

Dr. Gwenn Cassler's office was on the third floor of the
City Building, a bland, crypt-like block of cement two streets
from the center of downtown Albuquerque. The whole building
was painted a cigarette-stain brown. Long, empty hallways were
divided by thick glass walls. Cassler's office didn't make any effort
to stray from the pseudo-'70s motif. Her tables were Formica, her
chairs pleather. All she had for reading material was *Highlights for
Children* and the *Albuquerque Journal*. Up in the corner above her
door was an old mid-'80s CCTV camera. I watched its eye focus.
I shifted in my chair.

"Miss Toda," her secretary stammered, looking confused.

"Todacheene. Yes. I have an appointment."

"Go ahead and go in," she said.

I poked my head in the office cautiously. There was a giant
pink brain model on the doctor's desk that really centered
the room. Another CCTV camera panned to my chair and
stopped.

Dr. Cassler was wiping her hands with a paper towel. "Can I
call you Rita?" She extended her hand, then proceeded to dust

crumbs from her blouse. "I apologize. I had to have lunch on the run this afternoon."

"I understand how that is," I said. My chair squeaked. "I'm surprised that you had me in here so soon."

"Well, I understand you have been under a lot of duress lately." She opened a file on her desk. "Sergeant Seivers described you as hallucinating two days ago. Is that true?"

"I don't think I would describe them as hallucinations." Why had I told Angie? What had I been thinking? "I think what was going on the other night was best described as fatigue."

Dr. Cassler sat quietly, staring at me. I was uncomfortable. The camera in the corner buzzed.

"It's my job to make sure that our officers are prepared for the job they are undertaking. You've been with the Crime Scene Unit for about five years. Is that correct?"

"About."

"And where are you from?"

"I grew up on the reservation. On the Navajo reservation on the western side of the state." I knew she had this information in front of her. Why was she asking me?

"I used to work out there, after my residency. At the IHS in Fort Defiance." Dr. Cassler seemed pleased to have made a connection with me, flashing a smile. "So, what brought you into this kind of work? Aren't Navajos scared of death?"

"Aren't we all?" I answered.

She wrote something on her notepad. "Why did you take this job?"

"Because I needed a job after college. I couldn't find a job anywhere else doing photography."

"And why have you stayed?"

"What do you mean?" I asked. It seemed like an odd question.

"I'm just curious. I imagine it's not easy, the work you do." She looked up from her notepad. "As a Navajo. The work you do must be distressing to you."

"I don't believe in all of that," I answered. "It's superstition."

"Do you believe in God?" she asked.

"No," I said. "That is also superstition." She wanted the truth. She was going to get it.

"Sergeant Seivers mentioned that these hallucinations that you're having have to do with ghosts. Do you want to talk to me about these ghosts or spirits that you're seeing?"

I sat in silence for a few seconds, my chair squeaking again as my foot drummed out an uneven beat.

"I was tired. I worked almost fifty hours that week. Work has been busy."

"So, you didn't tell Sergeant Seivers you see ghosts?"

"I can't remember what I said to her." I watched her pen. "I was delirious."

"Is working fifty-plus hours a week the normal thing in your unit?"

"Not every week, hopefully. But Albuquerque is getting bigger, and the crime hasn't showed any sign of stopping."

She paused and poured herself water from a plastic bottle. "Is most of the work you do homicide?"

"Not always. Suspicious deaths, suicides, car accidents." I wondered what she was getting at.

"But those all seem to involve a dead body. Am I right to assume that?"

"Yes."

"Would you be interested in transferring out of this unit?" Her pen was already pressing into the paper. "Maybe do something else in the Crime Unit, ballistics or . . . ?"

"Are you asking me this because I'm Navajo?"

"Well, no." She straightened in her seat. "I'm just a little surprised to see a Navajo so long on this kind of unit—that's all."

It had become quiet in her office, with just the hiss of the heater vents.

"What if I told you that I've been like this for years—seeing ghosts, I mean? What would you do?"

"You've been having hallucinations for years?" She scribbled furiously. "When did they start?"

"You didn't answer my question." I was angry at that point. "I'm not hallucinating. But I have a feeling that you think I'm going crazy."

"I don't know what I would do, Rita. What do you think I should recommend? How do you feel about this whole situation?"

Behind Dr. Cassler, Erma sat on a stool, shaking her head, her feet resting on the doctor's file cabinet.

"I'm ready to work, doctor. I don't know what else to tell you. And I'm in the middle of something right now that needs to be finished." I got up to leave.

"You need to speak with me if you intend on going back to work," she said. "I would hope that in the interest of keeping your job, you would answer a few questions about your current state of mind."

I sat. "Aside from being tired and a little hungry, there is nothing wrong with me."

Erma eased up to her ear. "You need to let her go, doctor. She has work to do."

"Your coworkers are . . . concerned about your behavior over the last few weeks." She put her notepad down. "Are you taking any medications that we should know about?"

"I'm not taking any drugs, Dr. Cassler." My face churned with heat. "I'm under some pressure right now, that's all." Erma threw herself back onto the stool, frustrated.

The chair creaked. Dr. Cassler turned to look.

"Why don't you just tell her that I'm sitting here?" Erma offered. "I bet that would convince her."

"Do you want to talk to me about that, Rita? What is it that you need to take care of?"

"I need to wrap up this case. They're waiting for some photos. I really didn't think this was going to be a full-on shrink session. But I need to leave."

Erma and Dr. Cassler stared at me in silence until Erma's ghost rose from the stool and moved toward the door. Dr. Cassler turned to see what I was looking at.

"Maybe I'm just easily distracted." I followed Erma's ghost out the door.

"Maybe it's finally time that you helped me find out how I ended up dead," Erma said.

CHAPTER TWENTY

Mom's Cameras

I was a senior when Mom got sick. Her kidneys were failing, and no one could figure out why. Mom wanted to pretend it wasn't happening, but I could see that she was in pain. She ate less and less and had to go to dialysis more and more. I just wanted to stay with her, to make sure that she was okay.

We started playing hooky all the time. She would call into work and would call in for me at school. Mom had it down.

"She's been throwing up since last night," Mom would report. "We can come pick up her homework."

We would pay to see one movie at the first morning showing at the multiplex, then sneak from one show to another until we couldn't take it anymore. Then we would go out and buy horrible food and rent bad movies and go home. There was no mention of homework or schedules. It was just me and my mom, all day, every day, for a couple of weeks.

I was always eager to drive, so my mom and I went all over. We drove for miles, to ruins, to the tops of mountain ranges, to churches and ashrams up in northern New Mexico. We talked about movies and books as we drove home in the orange of sunset, like we were enduring friends. I learned a lot about her during those three weeks.

"You're going to go to college, aren't you?" Mom asked on one of those days. She sat in the dirt and sketched a small drawing of the canyon below.

"That was the idea. Isn't that what you wanted?"

"What do you want?" She stopped her sketch.

"I want stability. And I want to fix Grandma's garage."

Mom laughed. She turned away from me and dug into her knapsack, a green bag full of holes. She brought out a square of fabric wrapped around the body of a slightly used Hasselblad 500 C/M. She held it with both hands and looked out into the breezy canyon. I waited to hear the snap of the exposure. Instead, I heard nothing. Just the building of the wind beneath our perch.

"You know, I took a picture of your father with a camera just like this. Well, older, of course, and heavier."

"My father?" I was surprised. "I thought I just hatched." There was an uneasy silence for a few seconds. "I never heard you talk about him before. Not since I was a baby."

"You can't remember being a baby," Mom said. "That's impossible."

"I can do a lot of things that I've never told you about." This was the first time I had ever challenged my mother. I didn't like it. "I can remember. And I'm sorry. I'm sorry I ruined your plans." I rose and shook the dust from my jeans. "I'm sorry."

She handed the camera to me.

"This is yours, now. You'll have my cameras. All of them."

I was stunned. "When did you buy this, Mom? It looks brand-new."

"A while back." She stared at the camera in my hands. "I thought about getting back into portraits. You know, just mess around with a nice camera again. I took it out to Grandma's last week—I have a nice print of her in front of the house. I'll show you later."

"Mom, you need to keep this." I pushed the camera back onto her lap. "You can take a picture of me. Right now. Do my portrait out here!" I was excited as I turned around and around, searching for the best backdrop. My mom stepped a few feet to the right.

"Right there. Stop." Her hair rippled in the wind.

She put the camera on top of a flat rock and pressed. I could hear the shutter open and close even through the relentless wind at my back.

After that, my mom showed me how the camera worked, and I was able to frame a great shot of her with nothing but the heavens behind her, a sea of blue and white. She was so beautiful.

WHEN THEY STARTED calling and threatening my graduation date, I finally went back to school. It felt weird to leave my mom at home alone, to leave her sick like she was.

"I'll be fine, Rita," Mom said. "Just go to school."

The first day that I returned from my "sickness," I was summoned to the guidance counselor's office. I was only a month out from graduation, and it probably hadn't been the best timing for a two-week absence.

Mr. Kepthart wore skinny ties and silk shirts and combed his hair into a two-inch black helmet. He loved to eat peppermints and always kept a huge jar of those soft ones on his desk.

"Want some candy?" He pointed at the jar.

I shook my head.

"You're about graduate. Aren't you even the tiniest bit excited?"

"I guess I am. I haven't really thought about it." I noticed hummingbirds outside his window.

"Rita? Everything okay at home? Plans still the same?" Mr. Kephart rummaged through my files. "You still going to that photo school in . . ." He couldn't remember.

"In San Francisco. No. I've decided to stay home."

"When did this happen?" he said.

"Last month." I closed my backpack and began to eye the door. "My mom's just having a hard time. She's sick."

"Oh." He shifted in his seat. "Is she okay?" He looked concerned.

"She was okay when I left her this morning," I said.

"Let me know if you need anything." He wrote a number on the back of his card. "That's my home phone if you need to call me outside of school."

I HEARD THE scratch of a record on the turntable when I came home. It just crackled and whirred, then popped. Over and over. I knew something was wrong. I ran through the door to find my mom on the floor. I tried to shake her awake, but her eyes stayed shut. I called the ambulance.

On the ride to the hospital, my mom's eyes opened to small crescents, and she smiled and took my hand. She was entering late-stage renal failure. Her liver was also not working, and her creatinine levels were through the roof. It was all just happening so fast. I called Grandma that night and she was at the house by dawn.

I was thankful that Mom's doctor was in a new hospital wing. The older hospitals were the worst as far as seeing ghosts goes. We made the trip to the hospital early every morning, and while the dialysis machine performed its magic, I would go to school. Mom and Grandma would sit there and watch soap operas and do crossword puzzles. But my mom wasn't getting any better. The doctors had no idea how her kidneys had become so weak—one was barely functioning, and the other had stopped functioning altogether. My mom was in her late thirties, so her diagnosis left the doctors with no explanation. They tried to question her about exposure to chemicals, gave her a million tests, but it was a mystery. They started talking about finding a donor.

"She can have mine," I said as I watched the dialysis machine work.

"Hey, kid, you can't give me your kidney. What if something happens to you? Who's gonna take care of me?" She smiled and nudged my elbow.

"I'm old enough to decide for myself." I couldn't look at her.

"Happy birthday," she said. "What a horrible way to spend it. Why don't you and Grandma go out and get something to eat? And when is graduation? In about three days, right?"

"Yes. But don't worry about it. I didn't think you would be up to going." I could feel myself starting to cry.

"I'm going. There's nothing you can do about that." She laughed.

I put my head in her lap. Grandma woke me up an hour later. The machine still whirred.

We left the hospital knowing that Mom's days were numbered. At home, I stared at her constantly, waiting for her to become faint or weak, but she only smiled at me and endured. I convinced Mom to let me give her my kidney. We were scheduled for the test to make sure that I was a viable donor.

"Stop worrying," she said, smoothing the frown lines on my forehead. "Pretty soon, I'll have a sexy new kidney."

But two days after graduation, Mom didn't wake up. I walked into her bedroom, and even though she looked like she was sleeping peacefully, I knew she was gone.

I sat and stared at her in her bed for fifteen minutes and waited for her ghost to come to me. She never came. The one person I wanted to see, and she wasn't coming.

Grandma walked into the bedroom and immediately knew. She just stood in silence with tears coming down her face.

"I can't see her, Grandma." I was crying. "I can't see her. Why can't I see her?"

Grandma and I sat there for almost an hour before we called the ambulance. When we heard the knock at the door, Grandma stood and hugged me so hard my sides ached.

"I think your mom had made her peace with her body. She was in pain. Now the pain is gone."

Grandma was right. It was me who wanted her here. I wanted to cut myself open and put my kidney inside her, to bring her back with the electricity of my own flesh. But she was gone. There was nothing I could do.

It took Grandma and me a month to clean out the house. We still owed a lot on the mortgage, so I decided to go back home with Grandma. When all was said and done, my life had been reduced to a few boxes and two suitcases of clothes. Mom's car was paid off, but we left it in the city, storing it in a friend's driveway until I came back for school in the fall. I had all my cameras with me, and they rode up front in Grandma's pickup on the way back home. I took a picture of Grandma in front of our house before we drove away. I used Mom's Hasselblad and noticed that only three shots remained. I knew I had to save them.

The house looked so lonely when we pulled away. The windows were wet with the condensation of early morning, but they were empty, the glass reflecting the image of whoever was staring in. Houses are just like bodies. When there is no spark, no life force to fill them with warmth, they're just vessels.

CHAPTER TWENTY-ONE

iPhone

THE DAY AFTER my session with Dr. Cassler, I spent my morning sorting through the work of the last week. I cataloged the photos, filled out forms, and tried to find a way to work my clues into a narrative. It wasn't easy, but most of the time, the photos could tell the story.

I would be turning in my reports on the rollover and the drive-by soon. I would be turning in Judge Winters's case and Erma's file too. But something was still tugging at me; something was still incomplete. It was Erma herself.

Erma's ghost picked at her fingernails. "I've been cheated. I don't know what happened to me. One minute I'm leaving work, the next minute I can't breathe because I'm falling."

"I don't know what happened to you either, Erma. I only see what you can show me." I was exhausted. "Now, give me a minute to go save what is left of my job." I gathered my files and headed for the crime lab.

Dr. Cassler had sent her report over to Samuels almost immediately. By the afternoon, they had me scheduled for a sit-down with Samuels and Angie. I had a feeling that all of it wasn't going to go over well. As I walked down the hallway to Samuels's office, I could feel eyes on me. There was probably a pool on how long I had left.

"I heard that you were less than cooperative with Dr. Cassler yesterday," Samuels boomed.

"I thought I was very cooperative."

Angie Seivers was standing in Samuels's office with her hands on her hips. "Apparently you are refuting my statement about your behavior at the scene and at the hospital. I saw what was going on with my own eyes. Now you're calling me a liar. As far as I'm concerned, you're not fit for duty."

"We're suspending you, Rita." Samuels laid a page in front of me. "You will be reevaluated in three months."

My heart raced with the panic of losing my job. "Reevaluated for what? What am I supposed to do for three months?"

"You should have thought of that before you put every case that you've ever worked on in jeopardy." Samuels grabbed his pipe and chewed the tip. "All this talk of ghosts and visions only clouds our path of evidence. People will think we're having séances to get through case files. And here you are, one of my best investigators, turning into some kind of damn psychic detective."

"I've never done anything that would jeopardize my cases. Never. Angie, you know this." I turned to her, but she was just as angry as Samuels.

In the corner of my eye, I could see that Erma had followed me in. She stood against the wall, listening.

"Right now, all of this is unknown outside of this office. I want to keep it that way." Samuels pointed at the paperwork. "You need to sign this. It guarantees that you will continue to be evaluated by Dr. Cassler once a month until your suspension is over."

The paper was freshly printed and already signed by Samuels.

"What about the cases I'm working on? Judge Winters and Erma Singleton on the overpass?"

"Miss Singleton's case was ruled a suicide," Angie said.

"A suicide? Already there's a ruling on that case?"

From the corner of the office, a gravelly scream came from Erma's outstretched mouth, so loud that I winced, trying my best to keep my eyes on Angie.

"We will need all of your storage devices, photos, diagrams," she said. "Anything related to the cases you're working on."

"A suicide?" Erma continued screaming. "Suicide!"

I handed Angie my files, my stomach churning.

"This is all for the best, Rita." Angie placed her hand on my shoulder. "Take this time to rest."

"There'll be no rest for you, Rita!" Erma unleashed another scream. "I didn't kill myself!"

FIVE YEARS OF work was slipping away from me, and there was nothing I could do about it. Maybe I could find a better job. Something nine to five—taking pictures of school kids, or birds, or anything.

Erma Singleton was turning into the biggest wrecking ball I'd ever encountered. She sat with me in silence, riding in the backseat of my car. Her rage had drained us both.

Once I got home, all I could do was lie on the couch and close my eyes. I didn't care who was in there with me. I just needed to rest.

I should've known that wouldn't last long. The knock at the door was not going to go away, no matter how hard I shut my eyes.

"Let us in, Rita!" It was Shanice.

"Come on, sister! Open the door." And Philip.

My only two friends. Philip lived in my building, always smelled of expensive cologne, dressed impeccably, and was a great person to talk to. He also had no interest in girls. It was a shame. Shanice was my sister. After years of separation because of our junior high school jailhouse experience, we had managed to find each other again. The two of them had become quick friends and bar buddies.

"I'm not here. Go away," I yelled.

I tugged my blankets over my head but could hear my locks opening anyway. Shanice knew where my extra key was. She crashed with me all the time when she was between places. Just like any other Native relative, she was known to show up whenever the hell she felt like it, stay a few days, then leave without notice.

I threw my balled-up sock at Philip's head as he yanked off my blanket. Shanice was already looking through the photos on my table, mixing up the stacks and piles, grimacing at a few. "Where are those pictures that you took of me last week? I called you, like, three times and you never answered."

Shanice was taller than Philip and I, especially in her four-inch heels. She was now a part-time actress, catching odd roles in small films and plays that rolled through town. She had pure, impeccable olive skin, well-shaped eyebrows, and supremely sculptured hair, which made her a simple, beautiful everygirl.

I pulled a red folder from the drawer, then threw it on the table. "Red, for the devil!"

Shanice and Philip were on it within seconds, like ravenous animals.

"Look at you, Shanice!" Philip gushed.

I lay back down and covered my head with a pillow.

"These are wonderful, Rita. Thank you," Shanice said.

Philip tore the pillow off my head. "These photographs are perfect, Rita. Have you ever thought about being a photographer?"

"You think?" My head pounded, but I smiled anyway.

"Let's go celebrate!" Shanice squeezed me, feeling my ribcage. "When was the last time you ate?"

"Shanice, I'm fine." I squirmed.

Philip was already looking in the refrigerator. "Mustard and beer." He shook his head.

"Please, you two. I just got home from getting suspended from work."

"What?!" Shanice shrieked, not making my headache any better.

"Yes. I've been suspended for three months, and I have to go see a shrink if I want my job back."

"Holy shit! What did you do?"

"Got worked too hard. That's what. I had a little episode on a scene and now I'm crazy."

"Now what?" Shanice said. "Are you just going to stay here for three months and sleep?"

Before I knew it, they were dragging me into my room, forcing off my crinkled work khakis and dusty black shirt. Shanice pushed me into the shower, then they dressed me in a few clothes I didn't know I owned and rushed me out the door. After going a few floors down, I glanced back up and saw Mrs. Santillanes watching me from the ledge of the top floor.

We walked up to the new hipster bar at the corner of Second and Gold and sat just inside the front windows. The city in the dark was sometimes more appetizing than it was during the harsh desert light of day. In the dark, the city was cavernous and strange and full of the souls of my ancestors. I felt them every day, but especially at night. They didn't talk to me. It wasn't that way with them. I just knew they were there.

The bar was loud and crowded. The small dance floor pulsed at the back of the long, thin room.

"Do you want one drink or two?" Philip asked. I couldn't even answer. "Right. Two drinks." He walked into the darkness of vibrating bodies and conversations.

Drinks in hand, Philip vented about his grumpy clients, and Shanice expounded upon the new guy she met at her last job— some actor who was following her around like a lost puppy. That was not out of the ordinary.

"Ugh. But he's from Utah, so I might need to make some trips up there. But whatever it takes." She tugged at her earlobe, stroking and pulling, something she did when she was serious. "Oh, and by the way, I'll need to stay with one of you guys for a few days." She sat back and lit a cigarette.

"You know we have lives, right?" Philip said.

"Rita doesn't." They stared at me.

"Yeah. Whatever. I'm never home anyway," I said.

"Can I buy you a drink?" a voice called out across our table over the roar of music. No one replied.

"Rita?" Shanice directed her eyes toward the man standing by our table. "Can this gentleman buy you a drink?" I guess I just assumed the drink was for Shanice, or Philip for that matter. They were just as shocked as I was.

"Me?"

"Yes. If that's okay."

"Sure." Why not. He seemed nice enough and wasn't dressed like a lawyer. "Do you want to join us?" I presented the empty chair at the end of the table, which he took and sat down.

"My name is Chris." He extended his hand out to each of us. "I just moved here about five weeks ago. For work and school."

"And what is it that you do, Chris?" Philip smiled broadly when Shanice jabbed him in the rib.

"I'm a land surveyor. But I'm going to school right now for engineering. I've been working so much that this is the first time I've been able to get out and talk to someone."

Chris was tall and had broad shoulders and semi-long hair that hung into his eyes. I kept catching him staring at me, then looking away when I looked back. It was kind of . . . interesting.

"Well, you're in luck, Chris." Philip stood and pulled Shanice's hand. "Our friend Rita here needs some company because we're gonna go for a dance, then go home. Right? Shanice?"

"We'll see you later, Rita." Shanice was already dancing as Philip dragged her out in the crowd. She pointed to Chris's head and opened her mouth wide.

"So, what do you do?" Chris smiled at me.

"I'm a photographer." I remembered my afternoon. "Well, I was."

"You're not a photographer anymore?" He sat down across the table.

"No. I'm still a photographer. I just found out I'm starting a three-month unplanned hiatus from my job this afternoon."

"Did you want another drink?" He raised his hand for the waiter.

"Maybe one more."

We sat at the table for two more hours until the lights blinked off and on. Philip and Shanice had long since giggled themselves out the door. Chris was smart and, for some reason, wanted to hear all about me. I kept it simple. He liked to read and go to the movies, two things I also loved to do but rarely found the time for anymore.

When we left the bar, we staggered out into the winter air, tugging at our scarves and laughing into the cold. He refused to let me walk home alone. We had about seven blocks to go before we came to my apartment building. The streets were glistening from the icy rain and snow that had fallen during our hours at the bar. Except for a few passing taxis, we were alone in downtown Albuquerque. A faint hint of police sirens cried out from miles away, and one lonely, wet dog skittered by, turning to look at us, then walking into the empty street.

Chris moved into the echo of my building with me and shuffled the five stories to my apartment. By the time we got to the door, we were both out of breath.

"Thank you for bringing me home." I smiled.

"Anytime." He raised his coat collar. "I have to leave for a little over a week for work tomorrow. Maybe we can see a movie when I come back?"

"I would like that." I felt so awkward and small. I didn't know what to say. As he moved in closer to me and pulled me to him, I could only feel a flood of heat as I kissed his lips. I think it surprised both of us. But once that had happened, I couldn't help but bring him through the door with me.

We didn't separate from each other for hours and didn't say a word. I felt the shame in knowing that I had only met this man about five hours ago and had only his words to trust. For all I knew, he was a killer or a sociopath or a narcissist. But right now, I didn't care. There was something about him that reminded me of home, of warmth and deep embraces. He kissed me, nuzzling his hot breath into my neck. He knew just where to touch me, and there was nothing I could do to fight it, so I didn't. He flooded over me like a warm light. I hadn't been this close to anyone in years, but I welcomed all of it, then wound myself around him and slept a deep and unwavering sleep to the sound of his breath. Shortly after, I began to dream.

In the dream, I sat on the swings in Nahkai Park, a sparse collection of aging playground equipment. Next to me was Erma. Our feet carved parallel tracks into the ground. Snow began to fall just as Erma disappeared into the abyss, leaving me rocking in the swing.

The front of Grandma's house appeared before me just as easily as the swing had suspended itself from the nothingness of the sky. Snow and frost covered every leaf and rock as I ran into the garage door. Grandma stood in the open doorway of her kitchen, the hot liquid of her coffee sending clouds of steam out of the backdoor screen. She looked out into the vast white and cried. Her face did not turn to me.

I pushed her front door open and walked into the winter nothing, where the sky and ground were indistinguishable. There was no horizon for me to find my way. I panicked and turned to follow the path I had made, but my own tracks had vanished, covered by the blowing snow at my back. It was then that I noticed the light in the distance. It moved quickly. I had to shield my eyes against its yellow glare. As it came closer, I realized it was *the* red truck; it was moving again, the evil ghost of a horrible memory. It slowed and the window rolled down.

"Get in," Gloria barked.

"I'm not waiting for you, you know," her boyfriend offered.

I looked through the window, trying to see his face, but he was only a shadow in the darkness, a voice coming from nowhere. No matter how hard I tried, I could never remember what that man looked like. The dream did not want to help me remember either. I used the door to pull myself into the truck.

"Where are we, Gloria?" I asked. It was dark outside, but I could see the lights of traffic passing by. We were moving.

"Shhhhh." Gloria put her finger over her mouth.

"Rita. Rita. Take my picture." Erma put her hand over Gloria's mouth and laughed.

The voices echoed between dream and reality. My eyes opened, sticky and tortured. There Gloria sat, her head wound fresh as the day she died, her gaze strong and intense. I could smell her, like sweet corn and the exhaust of the road. Gloria, here in my bedroom with Erma's ghost. Gloria seemed unable to speak.

"Rita? Take my picture!" Erma's anger boiled.

This time her voice was deep and sinister. The force of it shook me awake. I looked over at Chris, who was still in a deep sleep. I couldn't stay in that bed, no matter how much I wanted to.

"Rita!" Erma yelled, then pushed Gloria out of her way.

She lunged at me, trying to reach for my hand, but I turned and ran into my bathroom, slamming the door behind me. I pushed my face against the linoleum of the bathroom floor and peered beneath the door. Nothing. Maybe it was the booze. Or the lack of sleep. I was seeing things. Then, Erma knocked. Hard.

"*Rita!*"

The knocking was constant until its beat matched the pulsing of my heart. I feared that the wood in the door might splinter. I watched four spots of blood from my nose appear on the bathroom floor as the walls of my vision closed in. I lay down in a panic and went to sleep.

CHAPTER TWENTY-TWO

Plaubel Makina I—Folding
Bellows Plate Film Camera

GRANDMA SAT BESIDE me in the truck, her head moving back and forth with the shifting traffic. As Grandma's truck jetted toward Gallup, I felt the weightlessness of home and smiled at the landmarks that still stood. Nothing had changed.

As I drove us toward the sun, Grandma's chin touched her chest, her snores moving in and out. I couldn't believe that I had spent so much time away from home. That haunting connection I had to this land had become weak in my time away. Phone calls replaced visits.

"I don't want you coming to see me out here," Grandma would say. "There is nothing for you." This was her mantra.

Grandma enjoyed some of the comforts of the city. She never denied that. She loved to go to the grocery store most of all because there were so many more good vegetables in the markets, beautiful bunches of lettuce and brightly colored fruit. But when I offered to bring them out to her, she always claimed she had plenty and insisted on coming to visit me instead, sometimes bringing Mr. Bitsilly along for the ride.

"It's too hot out there," Grandma explained. Or, "It's too cold and the roads are bad." I knew she was just keeping me away.

There was only one Christmas that we spent at Grandma's house—the Christmas when I was twelve years old. Grandma knew it was going to snow for Christmas, knew how much I loved the snow, and made sure that I was there. On Christmas Eve, the snow began to fall at about six o'clock in the evening and didn't let up. When I woke on Christmas morning, the snow came up to my hips and was packed all the way to the screen door. I made a path for Grandma out to her truck with the ash shovel from the fireplace and brought in six or seven armfuls of wood from the garage. We were stuck in the house for two days, stoking the fire until the sun came out and made the land as bright as eternity.

"The devil is whipping his wife," Grandma said, and looked into the sky. I ran out to play in the snow and saw the ghost of my cousin Gloria in the haze of white. I called out to her. I saw her head turn to look, then she disappeared into nothing. Maybe it was just me wishing that I saw her. Unfortunately, Grandma heard me. I still remember what she said.

"You talking to ghosts is going to come back and bite you like a snake. Do you hear me? Like a snake." She turned and went back inside. I felt the sting of sun and snow on my cheeks and followed Grandma into the house. All these years later, I realized she was right.

When I pulled into the driveway, Grandma was still fast asleep, head against the window, her purse in her lap with her hands perfectly folded over the leather. Grandma's grizzled dog Zoe greeted us with a faint bark, her fur matted with reservation dust. When I got out of the car, she jumped and barked at my feet until I paid attention.

I couldn't believe I was home. I pulled Mom's camera out of

my backpack in the bed of Grandma's truck and carried it with me. The dirt under my feet welcomed me, yielding as my weight pushed into the clay. I walked up to Grandma's gate and took it all in, breathing the deepest breath I could, absorbing the comforts beneath the mountains. I snapped a picture of Grandma's house: the front walkway, the white mailbox with GALLUP INDEPENDENT written on its side, and Zoe, her bottom teeth protruding from her mouth.

I went back to the truck and woke Grandma from her deep sleep. I strapped her purse on one shoulder and held her hand all the way to the entrance to steady her gait. The door opened easily.

"Grandma, I've told you to make sure to lock the door before you leave. What if somebody tried to break in while you were gone?" I was nervous, looking around every corner of the house for whatever squatter had taken up residence.

"That is the city in you talking, dear." Grandma let out a big sigh. "Around here, people know better than to steal from an old lady. Especially me." She walked into the kitchen, filled a pot with water and Navajo tea, and lit the stove pilot. "Get me that big pot down and take that mutton from the icebox. I'm making you a welcome home feast."

The broth boiled and hissed, steam coiling up from the corn and meat. Grandma and I sat at the kitchen table drinking our hot tea. It reminded me of how wonderful it was to be a child again, to be here with Grandma, without the weight of the city upon my shoulders. I wanted to stay forever in these walls, at the bottom of the mountain, for as long as I lived.

"You really have grown. Look at you." Grandma held onto my forearm.

"Grandma, you see me all the time," I said.

"But not here. In this house, I only remember you as a little girl. And seeing you here, sitting at the table with me, just makes me realize how many years have slipped by. What are your plans? When does school start?"

"I don't think I'm going to go to school right now." I was afraid to look at her. "I think I'll stay here with you for a semester before I go back. I just need a break."

There was an awkward silence.

"You're not staying here, Rita." Grandma took a sip of her tea. "You're going to school just like you planned. Aren't you going to California? Aren't you going to study your picture-taking? That's what I always thought you wanted."

"I didn't accept the scholarship, Grandma. Not the one in California." I'd thought Mom would still be alive. Now that she was gone, I honestly didn't know what I was going to do. "I'm supposed to start in Albuquerque in the fall."

"When was all this decided?" Grandma looked disappointed.

"When Mom was getting real sick. I didn't want to be too far from her in case something happened. I wouldn't be able to afford to come back from California. But I guess that doesn't matter now. It's done. And I'll be closer to you, too, Grandma. I'll be closer to home."

The only things that could be heard were the sizzle of the liquid on the stove and the ticking of Grandma's scarecrow clock, his arm hitched up on an aging yellow stalk of corn. I could feel that scarecrow looking down on me from the wall, as if barely able to recognize my face after ten years away. I looked at the table, at Grandma's beautiful hands, the soft skin now draped and dotted with age. Her jawline remained straight and refined; her hair was still perfect, coiled into pin curls. She sat with her hands folded, her eyes closed as if in prayer. I reached for the Hasselblad on the chair at my side and sat it on the table, pulling out wide. My finger pressed the shutter, capturing the moment, the memory forever fused onto film. The click opened her eyes.

"You and that camera." She laughed. "Do me a favor and go into my closet and pull out the trunk. I think it's time."

"Time for what?"

"Time to show you."

Grandma's closet was just as I remembered it: handmade dresses on quilted hangers and boxes of sewing patterns. Even my hiding spot was intact, with Grandma's brown leather train case serving as my seat in the corner. As I pulled down worn boxes and scuffed shoes, I came to a green trunk with brass corners and a thick leather handle. I had to use all the leverage I had to get it out of the closet. Whatever was inside was hefty. Memories, maybe.

Grandma sat on the bed opposite me. Her fragile hands opened the trunk, releasing a million bright speckles of dust into the light of her window. Inside, there were boxes, notebooks and photo albums, pictures randomly escaping from book covers. On top, there was a picture of Grandpa smiling, his eyes squinting at the camera, the single dimple on his cheek that I remembered from his light. He was handsome in his army uniform, pressed and crisp, every hair in place. He stood by a giant shelf of shiny bottles and containers. Grandma took the photo out and stared at it for almost a whole minute before she laid it on her nightstand.

There must have been a thousand photographs in that trunk. There were some early photos of relatives that were gone long before I ever came into this world. They wore woven dresses and handmade shirts and pants. Their hair was groomed into tight buns and wrapped with sturdy woolen ties.

"That is your great-great-grandfather and great-great-grandmother," Grandma explained. "That was my grandma and grandpa. Oh, look at them. They were always so happy together. They would spend hours out on the mesas with their herd of sheep and goats. They had a beautiful garden in Lukachukai, with lots of corn and beans and pumpkins. They were never apart from each other. When your great-great-grandpa died after a sickness, an infection in his lungs, your great-great-grandma went with him three days later. I remember she explained to me in Navajo that she hoped he had taken her lungs with him too because she no longer wanted to breathe in this world. She cried after him."

Grandma kept pulling things from it and gazing at them longingly, reliving her childhood and her past in front of me. A piece of me wanted to look away. Another part of me knew that this could be my one opportunity to understand the mystery of my past and to learn about the ancestors that came before me.

"Give me that red leather book." Grandma pointed to the corner of the trunk. "This was the beginning of all of it. Right here." The outside said PHOENIX INDIAN BOARDING SCHOOL, 1931 in faded gold letters. When Grandma opened it, the pages creaked with anticipation—the years in storage stifling its remembrances, forgetting the feeling of human contact.

"This is me. This is your grandma, a long time ago." She pointed to a large picture of herself as a young girl—maybe eight or nine years old, her hair cut into a bob right above her shoulders. Grandma wore a boxy dress and sagging white socks pushed into black-and-white saddle shoes. She stood next to an antique camera, the kind with a huge leather bellows and the sort of flash that could catch fire to anything or anyone standing too close to it. A throwback from the early days of portraits, with their dangerous chemicals and blasts of light. On the other side of the camera was a haggard man, his deformed fingers sticking out of his vest pockets.

"That was Mr. Wilson." Grandma paused. "He taught me how to take pictures." There was a huge space of silence in the room. "I was about seven. It wasn't even a year after your great-grandma passed. I had just come in from helping your great-grandpa with the shearing. It was hot, right before the summer's end, right before we were going to do the last of the harvesting in the peach orchard. It was a still day, no wind, not a cloud in the sky. We could hear the approaching roar of an engine way out there on the dirt road that led up to our home site. He and I watched as the black car came closer and closer, a huge plume of dust and smoke in its wake, finally coming to a stop near our hogan door. Your great-grandpa came out, waving his hand at the dust and smoke that settled around us. We watched as two white men with powder-white shirts and black ties came up to our home. They held papers and leather satchels. One of them stopped and smiled at me, but I ran away up into the hills. I knew they were there for me. They had come and taken my friend Esther two months before, sent her off to school. She never came home. Not even in the summer. I haven't seen her since."

Grandma shifted in her seat. The bed had no back support, so I moved out of the way and helped her onto her rocking chair. She sat quietly, remembering things. I could see her mind at work, her two thumbs twiddling in her lap. In the kitchen the sizzling continued, the walls and windows filling with condensation. I brought her another cup of tea. Grandma sighed and started her story again, her feet up on a footstool.

"My dad walked to the hilltop and sat with me as we watched the two men sit under our cottonwood tree. I always wondered what they were saying down there. But Dad was there to tell me that I was going. 'I don't want you to be stuck in this place all your life,' he said. 'I want you to go and learn about the world.' I didn't care about the world. I remember being happy there in the homestead; the water was so pure up by the springs, and we had lots of sheep and land. I did not want to leave. But we walked down the hill together anyway and packed a small flour bag full of my things—some clothes and a tintype of my mother. I was so sad. My father cried, and I cried too. I got into the black car with the two men in ties. My feet hung just over the seat, my toes touching the back of the passenger side where this white man with teeth the color of butter kept turning around to smile at me—nodding up and down." Grandma set her tea on the floor and slowly started to rock her chair.

"An hour up the road and we were in Gallup, where the big train would head toward the ocean. The train was gigantic and made of silver. I made my way up to the train with the two men on each side of me. I guess they thought I would run away. I thought about it, I'll admit. But when I got on the train with my little flour sack, it was shocking to see fifty or more kids just like me sitting in every aisle. The younger ones, who sat up at the front of the train car, cried—the kind of cry that makes your whole body shake. They didn't look like they could breathe in between. They were saying 'I want to go home' in Navajo, over and over. It was heartbreaking. Before I knew it, I had tears of my own stinging on my burned cheeks. I sat down in the back row with two brothers who just sat there looking out the window. The cries would only stop when the little ones fell asleep, then they would wake up and see where they were and start crying all over again. It was a relief to get to school, to not hear them cry anymore."

I really wanted to ask Grandma a million questions, but I

knew the story was not over. I wanted to hear about this one picture of Grandma that rested inside the box. The quality was perfect, even though the photo had been taken years ago. I could see the determination in Grandma's eyes.

"When we got to Phoenix, they took our pictures first. They would bring us all up one by one and that man, Mr. Wilson, would hold a bulb over our heads and take our picture with a flash that would cut through our eyes. I was mesmerized by that flash and by the big camera. I knew about pictures—that in the cities, there were cameras that could capture people just as they looked. I think Mr. Wilson could see I was interested. I remember his hands were all curled up at the fingers and he could barely use them." Grandma looked down at her own hands and rubbed them. She stopped rocking.

"Next, they cut our hair real short. The scissors would slide right beneath our tsiiyéeł—right under our thick hair and cut through, just like that." She snapped her fingers together like rusty scissors. "The rest of our hair would let go and fall around our faces. The boys had theirs cut even shorter, right up to their ear. The girls went through school with their hair short right above their shoulders, just as the scissors had left us. Then we went back to the room with Mr. Wilson and his camera, and they stood us all against the wall and took our pictures again. They did it so that they could make sure all the Navajo had been cut and shaved from all of us. They wanted all of it to be gone."

Grandma stopped her story and looked toward the chest. "Pull those two boxes out, the ones right there." I moved to the corner of the chest and grabbed two heavy boxes. Right below was an ancient Plaubel Makina in almost brand-new condition, with a leather bellows and flawless glass, lens, and surface. It was like it had been pulled from the 1930s. I took the camera out carefully.

The viewfinder was a little bent, but I used it anyway to frame Grandma there on her rocking chair. She smiled.

"That is my camera." She laughed. "I guess we all have the bug, don't we?"

"How come I am just learning about this now, Grandma?" I held the bulky camera in my lap. It must have weighed at least twenty pounds. I tried to imagine my grandma, her arms young and strong, keeping this camera steady, holding her breath.

"Mr. Wilson could see that I was absorbed in what he was doing. I watched everything he did: loading the camera, focusing with his crooked fingers, and the painful pressing of the button. He called me over and pulled out a stool so that I could look through the viewfinder. I could see the two little boys who had traveled here with me in the frame. The image was backward, but showed their hair still long and tied, their skin still burned by the sun. Mr. Wilson would have to pull the lever down from the front of the camera to take a picture. It was hard on him. You could see the pain in his face every time he snapped the frame. When he saw me watching, he showed me how to work the lever. It was easy for my little fingers. From then on, I became his assistant.

"They took me from whichever class I was in every time a new trainload of Indians came to the school. After a while, I did all the work—loading the film, changing the lenses, moving the camera around campus. Even though I was a little girl, I knew my way around that big camera. Mr. Wilson died when I was twelve. I took all the pictures after that. But it became a chore." Grandma handed me two framed photographs of a beautiful Navajo girl—her skin brown, her hair pulled back. She wore a nice rug dress and moccasins. In the second picture, her long hair was cut to her shoulders, her beautiful dress replaced with a symmetrical black-and-white dress—the same one they all wore.

"I got so tired of watching all the Indian being taken out of these kids, one after another, year after year. I felt like I was trapping their souls in a box. As they aged, they had no Indian in them left. Just like me. When I finally went home twelve years later, the land had become overgrown, the herd scattered in all different directions. My father had become a shell of the man I left behind. I think when my mom died, he died too, but he stayed here on earth to watch me because he knew I would one day return and would take care of what I needed to take care of."

"Is that why you don't take pictures anymore?"

"I took pictures for a long time after that, until your grandpa died. He liked to take pictures too. But when he passed, I didn't want to do it anymore. I put that camera away along with all those memories and kept them locked up so that I wouldn't cry after him. It made me sad to think of what could have been, of what should have been. The pictures always made me cry for him, and I knew that I had to let him go."

I started to put all the boxes, books, and photographs away—back into that vault of pain that Grandma kept in her closet. I didn't think I ever wanted to open it again. As I scooted the chest closer to the closet, Grandma stopped me.

"You missed a box. Up there on the bed." There was one orange box by Grandma's pillow. When I opened it, I saw her—my cousin Gloria. Gloria with her long, shiny hair and her infectious smile. I remembered that day. She was so happy. We sat on the roof until it was dark and the neighbor's dogs began to howl. We took that picture with her friend's Polaroid right before the sun set. It was two weeks before she died. This trunk was full of ghosts, full of reminiscences—brimming with the pain of loss. I stuffed Gloria's picture into my pocket and closed the box. Grandpa's picture stayed on the nightstand. It was a memory that she could probably enjoy, I thought. Grandpa could look after her.

After digging through the trunk, Grandma grew tired. I helped her to bed, brushing her long white hair and massaging her hands with her "magic rub," as she called it. It was a Bengay rip-off that smelled terrible, but Grandma didn't mind if it kept the pain in her hands away. She called the pain "Arthur Yazzie," the Navajo personification of arthritis, and cursed him every night as she rubbed heat into her skin. "Damn him," she'd say.

After I turned off her light, she was asleep within ten minutes. I sat outside on the porch beside her western door, the one that flooded with rainwater all the time, and watched the sun go down beneath the mountains.

Shame enveloped me. Seeing Grandma living alone in her outdated house made me feel sick and lonely. I wanted to bring her with me, but where? Albuquerque wouldn't be safe for her.

I needed a drive, to clear my head, to do something besides sit in the house and watch TV. Grandma's keys hung on a nail in her kitchen. I grabbed them and my camera bag and walked to the truck.

One blank frame remained on the roll of film inside my mother's Hasselblad, and I hoped I would find that final photo somewhere tonight, wishing that it might close a chapter. I needed to let go of this weight, to find something that could give me hope for my future and the wisdom to cope with my ghosts.

The engine sputtered as I turned the key, finally turning over after a couple of chokes. I drove down the road from the house, dodging a few packs of stray dogs and the occasional pothole. The houses had become unkempt and dilapidated, many of the tribal government homes replaced with trailers and model homes with fake adobe and white frames. The trading post was closed and so was the park where Gloria and I would swing. The town was becoming a memory too, with all of Grandma's friends leaving the world one by one, replaced with kids and grandkids that didn't want to be there. I could see why Grandma wanted me to leave, to put behind me the history of this place.

I drove through town slowly until my eyes called out for sleep, but I didn't want to go home. Instead, I thought of Gloria. I thought of that white house on the mesa where I last saw her alive. I wondered if it still stood, if the things that happened there were cemented in its walls. I was compelled to drive up Choosgai Hill to see if it still mocked me with that one childhood photograph that I could not burn.

I saw it in the distance, standing defiantly. The outside was covered in graffiti, color over color. I drove right up to it, directing the headlights at the front door, and got out. I fished a pack of cigarettes out of my backpack and my mom's Zippo lighter that she kept with her camera bag. I had no flashlight, so this had to be my torch.

I walked to the front door and kicked it open, flooding the walls with the silver light of the headlamps. The elements had taken their toll. The wind whistled through the bare walls and occasional pink wisps of insulation. On the back of the door were the marks I had left all those years ago, when I raged, trying to set myself free. You could still see where I had banged on the wood until it began to splinter. That is when I saw her.

"Rita, what are you doing here?" She was smiling. "It's too late for you to be up here." Her hair was long and straight, her skin a perfect olive hue. I started to walk toward her, inching toward the warmth of her voice. Then, just as suddenly as I saw her, she disappeared through the rays of the headlights.

I came out of that house and cried. I had received my answer. That night still haunted me.

I reached into the back of Grandma's truck and pulled out her nearly empty gas can. I sprayed the walls, the insulation, the sink, what counters remained. I sprayed more on the trash-covered floors and on the doors and hallways in the back. But mostly, I sprayed the front door—the door that had kept me locked in, that still held evidence of my fear.

I stepped outside. When I scraped the Zippo's wheel, the light shone on my face and on the cigarette in my mouth. I took a deep drag, feeling the smoke down my throat, finding its way to my lungs. I walked to the door and threw the cigarette in. The light flickered and grew. Within fifteen minutes, the entire house was engulfed, sending the splintered wood and blood stains into the sky.

I pulled Mom's Hasselblad out of the truck and rested it on the cab as the fingers of the fire swayed, the smoke trapped under the eaves. The house was choking and dying in front of me, and all I could think of was that picture. I wanted to remember the death of this house for the rest of my life. I wanted to see its evil soul lifted into the permanency of eternity. If this curse had to stay with me, I prayed that this purge could bring me some peace.

The fire had become perfectly balanced, the flames and smoke turning the white paint into the dead shade of gray. I looked at the house in the viewfinder and pressed the shutter release. The photograph. The last memory—finally dead.

CHAPTER TWENTY-THREE

Pictures of Dreams

THE KNOCKING ON the bathroom door woke me. I sat up, still in Chris's T-shirt, my head throbbing from the booze, my heart aching for Gloria. It had been years since I had seen her, and last night was bittersweet. I could feel her presence still, as well as the fear that Erma was pressing into her. Now Erma was coming for *my* ghosts, and I was letting her.

"Are you okay in there?" Chris spoke through the door.

I looked myself in the mirror, stained with the remnants of my nosebleed, and splashed some water on my face. "Yes. I'm fine." I opened the door to the sight of him wrapped up in my sheets.

"Do you know where I left my pants?" We laughed. It saved me from bursting out in tears and confessing everything.

We walked out into the kitchen to search for the rest of his clothes. "I just want you to know that I've never done anything like this before." I was embarrassed, both that I jumped on him last night and that I woke up on my bathroom floor.

"I haven't either. For the record." He smiled and picked his pants off my kitchen counter.

"And this is yours too. I'm sorry." I began to remove his shirt but realized that I had nothing underneath. He pulled it off for me and began to kiss me again, right up until there was a knock on my door.

"Just a second." I let go of Chris and ran to look out through the viewer. My grandma and Mr. Bitsilly stood right outside.

"Jesus. It's my grandma." I hurried back into my room to put some clothes on.

"Your grandma?" Chris put his clothes on faster.

"Yes. And the medicine man." I fixed my hair into a tight bun and opened the door.

"Is this a bad time?" Grandma asked, staring at Chris as he buttoned his pants. I threw my arms around her.

"Grandma. It's never a bad time. What are you doing here?" I looked around my kitchen to make sure there were no articles of clothing lying around. "Mr. Bitsilly. I'm really surprised to see you here. All the way to Albuquerque?" He, too, stared at Chris.

"Who is this?" Grandma pointed at Chris, who was now in his coat with his backpack in hand.

"My name is Chris." He extended his hand, which Grandma weakly accepted.

"Chris. This is my grandmother. And Mr. Bitsilly. They both came from the reservation out by Gallup."

"I'm working out there in the next week or so doing some survey work for the highway. Beautiful place." He looked at me.

"Come in, Grandma. You guys sit down. I'll make you some coffee."

"It was great to meet you all," Chris said, and I pushed him toward the exit.

"I'm so sorry about that. I wasn't expecting them."

"Don't be sorry. Next week. Promise." He handed me his phone. "Can I have your number?"

I smiled as I entered the digits, still feeling the heat of embarrassment. He bent down to kiss me, then walked down my stairway.

"Who was that?" Grandma was now standing in my doorway, livid.

"Just a guy, Grandma." I moved quickly inside and tried to make coffee. Anything to keep me from having to look them in the face.

"Oh my *God!*" The front door swung open. "Did I just see that guy from last night make the walk of shame down the stairs? Rita, you animal . . ." Shanice rounded the corner and saw Grandma and Mr. Bitsilly waiting for coffee. "Oh. Hi, Grandma." She lunged to the couch and gave Grandma a hug.

"I see the two of you were out and about last night." Grandma started to straighten out the magazines on my coffee table. "You both smell like a bar."

"I'm sorry, Grandma." Shanice smiled. "It's never Rita's idea."

"Listen to her, Grandma. It's never me." The coffee steamed from its spout. I was feeling sick to my stomach. I could sense their eyes on me, waiting to make contact with mine.

"What is everyone staring at?" I was turning red with embarrassment.

Mr. Bitsilly stood. "We came to see you because we know that something is going on. Something more than you're telling."

"All I had to do was walk into his house with your clothes in a bag for him to turn as white as snow." Grandma glanced over to Mr. Bitsilly. "He knew right away that something was wrong, that you had gotten yourself into something you couldn't get out of."

"Wow." Shanice gulped her coffee. "You knew all of that because of laundry?"

"We have been more than patient with this profession that you've chosen, but I think it has gone way too far." Grandma scolded me like a spoiled child. "And then we come here and find you with a strange man, smelling of booze. No wonder."

"Rita, I think I'm going to shower over at Philip's. I'll catch you later, right?"

I nodded.

Shanice mouthed "sorry" as she snuck out of the door.

I knew right then I had to come clean.

"I have this spirit that won't leave." I put my head down. "She will not leave me alone until I help her solve her case. That's what's going on. And there is no amount of praying that you can do to make her leave. Nothing will make her leave until I do what she wants."

"I'll never understand why you think you need to help these strangers. These people are stuck in this world and you're only pro-longing the agony. You need to stop what you are doing now. Stop before one of these things finally kills you." Mr. Bitsilly was angry.

"She has opened a portal," I explained. "There are people coming in and out all the time, and I can't control it anymore. She is too strong. Last night she even pulled Gloria through."

Grandma gasped.

"I can't close it. I've tried. She's just too powerful."

"You need to quit this job of yours." Grandma was shaking. "You need to quit it for all of us."

"Grandma. It doesn't matter if I quit. She will just keep fol-lowing me. It's what she does." I glanced over at Erma, who turned to me and shrugged. "Either way, yesterday I was put on suspen-sion. Now I have three months before I can go to work again."

"Good." Grandma sat up from the couch. "Now you can come home. Leave all of this here."

Mr. Bitsilly took a bundle from his coat and began to sing and bless my apartment. My grandma hugged me as tightly as she could. He came over to me with his whistle in his mouth and pushed his prayers into my body, singing louder than I'd ever heard him before, until his voice became raspy and weary.

Once done, he wanted to leave. "I can still feel that thing here," he said. Grandma agreed.

"I'm not letting the two of you drive home alone." I began to pack a small bag. "I'm driving you back to Tohatchi. I'll catch the train back here tomorrow."

"We drove the three hours here; we can certainly drive the three hours back home," Mr. Bitsilly said. "These ghosts that you see, they are obsessed with this world. Did you know that? These things are still so attached to their memories, their possessions, that they have no desire to move on. It is evil. This . . . thing. It's evil." There was a long silence. I didn't know what to say. "These . . . people that you help. They are strangers. Why would you risk giving up your life to help someone whose life is already over? What would your grandma do if you left this world? Who would look after her?"

"I guess I would," I answered.

Mr. Bitsilly sighed. He was still angry with me. I could feel it. Grandma hugged me one last time with all her strength, then walked into the hallway. Mr. Bitsilly followed. I felt terrible.

The weight of Erma returned, constant and immediate. She was ready for me to get back to work. I turned on the heat and pulled some Navajo tea from my bag. Erma sat on my couch.

"We missed you, Rita," Erma said.

"We?" I stared at the boiling water on my stove, the tea bundle moving around the rim.

"Erma said that I could come along." A little boy's voice arose from the couch. I turned to see Judge Winters's son jumping on the cushions next to Erma as she smiled. He made my pulse rise.

"I thought you could use a little incentive." Erma watched as the boy ran around my apartment.

"Erma. That's not fair." I watched him, his wound still visible over his bruised face and happy smile. "It's too hard on the little ones."

"Hey, he wanted to come. You want me to bring his father instead?"

"Why are you doing this to me?" I was angry now. "You know I can't just snap my fingers. That is not how this works, Erma. I don't even have my job right now. What am I supposed to do?"

"You're supposed to make sure that the man who did this to us dies a horrible and deserved death." Erma spoke like she was reading a bedtime story.

"Erma, we still don't know what happened to you. *You* don't even know."

"Isn't it your job to find out? I don't care what that police report says. I didn't commit suicide."

"I understand that," I said. "But I don't understand why it matters anymore. You're dead."

Erma sat the boy on her lap.

"When I died, I left everything I had in the world. My little daughter is probably still waiting for me to come home from work." Erma began to radiate heat and put the boy down. "They took me away from her, and if they tell people that I killed myself, there will be nothing left for her."

"What do you mean?"

"I was working a good job, making good money, and had insurance. All of it was going to my baby. If they say I killed myself, she will get nothing. And the visit. After Matty went to jail, they came and asked me where he hid it. I didn't know what they were talking about. Those men will keep coming back until they find whatever they were looking for." Erma's voice was pained. "They could be looking through my house right now."

"I promise to help you, Erma." I poured myself a cup of hot tea. "But you have to close the door. What you're doing isn't helping."

Erma darkened. "You're gonna figure out who did this to me, or I will make your life a living hell forever."

The little boy stopped jumping. I hurled my cup of hot tea right through Erma's head and heard it shatter into a million pieces on the wall behind her. Erma and the boy were gone.

CHAPTER TWENTY-FOUR

Hasselblad

THAT WHITE HOUSE was still with me when I woke in the morning. The final death of that building was like a ray of sunlight, an exorcism of the memory that had haunted me for so long. It felt good.

When I came into the kitchen, Grandma was already sitting there, her newspaper opened, her legs covered with a blanket. The coffee boiled on the stove, the brown liquid percolating up through the glass opening on top of the coffee pot.

"Good morning, Grandma." I shuffled toward the stove.

"Good morning, she'awéé'. Did you sleep?"

"I did. I slept better than I have in a long time. It's good to be home." I poured some coffee. "Do you need some more?" I held up the coffee pot.

"No. The doctors up at the clinic made me stop drinking so much coffee. It's not good for my stomach."

I sat at the table with her, and she passed me the cartoon section, just like she used to. I don't think Grandma really wanted to admit that I had grown up. I guess I didn't either. We stayed in silence as we read our sections. I didn't even recognize some of the new cartoons on the page. I guess it really had been a while since I had been there. But everything else was just as I remembered: the turquoise-and-copper containers for flour, sugar, and coffee; the matching bread box with my handwriting still all over it; the percolating coffee pot; the same dusty clocks. The only things in that room that changed were me and Grandma—my body taller and both our bodies weaker.

"Grandma. Is Mr. Mullarky still alive?"

"No, dear. Mr. Mullarky died years ago. I think they said he had a heart attack. Something like that. Poor man."

"What about the photo shop? Is that gone too?"

"No, the photo shop is still there. There is an art supply store in there now too. But the place is run by someone else. Someone from another country. I can't remember which one." Grandma strained to remember, her eyes turned up to the ceiling.

"I want to go in and see if I can get these photos developed." I had pulled the 120 cartridges from the Hasselblad. I wondered about the mystery of the other photographs on the roll since I had only taken the last four or five of them. It was exciting to think about just how many pictures Mom had taken before she died. What had caught her eye? What would be revealed about her that I never knew?

"Grandma, let's go to town. I'll buy you some lunch over at Earl's."

"Earl's has gotten expensive. Where did you get money?"

"I save my money, Grandma. Every cent from every job I've done over the years." I stopped when the memory came. "Mom also used to give me ten dollars every time I got an A in school."

Grandma smiled. "Well, you must have lots of money then."

WE HEADED OUT into the early sun, me at the wheel of Grandma's truck. The green and vibrant land that I remembered was now waterless and brittle. Little trailer houses and hogans dotted the landscape from the road to the hillsides. Every now and then I would see wandering groups of sheep move along the road, their pastures reduced to the occasional bush and sprig of sagebrush. This place had changed, and not for the better.

When we pulled into Gallup, I noticed so many new places. There were twice as many buildings, people, and restaurants. There was Chinese food and an Italian restaurant. There were rows of payday loan places and car dealerships. Hundreds of Navajos I didn't know were walking and driving on the potholed streets. Dozens of withered Indians held out dollar bills on the roadsides for anyone who would pull over and drive them home.

It was the first of the month, so everyone was in town, spending their grandma's social security checks. I knew that Grandma got money too, but I didn't want her to spend a dime of it. I wanted to take care of her. I wanted to stay with her for the rest of my days and make sure she never had to suffer any of the indignities I saw in town. As I stopped at a red light, I looked over at her, sleeping against the window. Her face was soft and flawless, her breath steady. Her hands, as always, were folded in her lap. I pulled up to the Mullarky building and turned off the engine. Grandma woke. She pressed at her hair and looked out the window.

"Are we here?" She was already opening the door.

I walked around to help her as she slowly moved her feet to the ground. I reached out to steady her.

"I'm fine." She pushed my arm when I offered it to her. Always the independent one.

THE BUILDING WAS just as I remembered it, except that the new owners had an entire section set aside to make way for paper, pencils, paint, and canvases. The wall of film rolls had been reduced, but the display cases were still full of shiny, new cameras that I probably couldn't afford. All the pictures of Navajos on the walls remained.

"Can I help you?" A young East Indian man came out from a curtain behind the counter. He was slight, with narrow shoulders and large, deep-set eyes. He carried a sandwich wrapped haphazardly in paper towels and foil.

"Yes. I was hoping that you might be able to develop this roll of film for me." I handed him the roll wrapped in a handkerchief.

"Wow! A roll of 120. I haven't seen one of these since I lived in Los Angeles. Do you live around here?"

"Yes. I live on the reservation with my grandmother." I looked her way and saw her staring at the photographs on the wall. She adjusted her glasses, straining to see.

"And you have a Hasselblad? Can I see it?"

"I left it at home." I wouldn't have shown him anyway.

"Well, this roll might take me an hour or so." He bit into his sandwich.

"Okay. But please be careful with it. It's important to me—I really can't have anything happen to it."

"No problem." He pointed to a sign above the register that read, WE CARE ABOUT YOUR MEMORIES.

"Good," I said. "I hope that's true."

GRANDMA AND I went to Earl's and sat at her favorite corner booth so that she could people-watch. The place hadn't changed much, although it had expanded its western wall. Navajos still visited the tables, selling their jewelry and pottery to all the customers. Grandma always wanted to buy everything. This day was no different. An older woman came up to us first, holding a velvet board with dangling silver and turquoise earrings on its surface. She had a beautiful smile and knotted, overworked hands.

"I want to buy that first pair." Grandma pointed to oval-shaped turquoise stones in silver bezels.

"Fifteen dollars," the woman said.

Grandma handed her a twenty and told her to keep the change. The woman smiled deeply and shook Grandma's hand. When the woman stepped away, Grandma shook her head. "Fifteen dollars wasn't enough. She probably worked on that a long time. Now, put these on." I pushed the silver through the empty holes in my ears and felt the jewelry swing on my neck. "So pretty," Grandma said.

Grandma and I both ordered hot roast beef sandwiches with mashed potatoes and gravy and cups of coffee.

"You're turning into an old lady." Her shoulders shook with laughter.

"We just have good taste, Grandma," I said as the waitress brought our steaming cups to the table. I added four small containers of cream and two heaping spoons of sugar.

"You haven't changed. You've just gotten taller." With that, we both laughed. It made me so happy to see her chuckling, to see the perfect white ridges of her smile.

THE ANTICIPATION OF the developed roll was almost too much. After lunch, Grandma stayed in the truck and read her *Reader's Digest*. I walked into Mullarky's and straight to the counter.

"Oh, hello," the man bellowed from the back room. "I just finished the roll. I'll be right out."

I walked to the corner display case and looked at a dusty

Polaroid just like the one Gloria had brought home, with the same silver knobs and shutter button, the rainbow Polaroid sticker on its front. Gloria was weighing heavy on me; I couldn't shake her. I even smelled the faint hint of smoke in my hair and jacket. She was still with me.

"Here they are. There were twenty-four on the roll. Beautiful stuff. Did you take all of these pictures?" He was smiling.

"No. My mother took most of them. I only took the last four or five. I can't remember."

"Well, that last one is a doozy. Loved it. Here you go."

He handed me the packet of photos in a black plastic container. Their weight was awkward; I had to take it in two hands. I could feel a lump in my throat rise and fall. My hands were damp with sweat, my mouth dry and cramping.

"Are you okay?" He stooped to look into my eyes.

"Yes. I'm fine. Just a little anxious." I must have looked pale. I could feel my blood rushing down to my feet. "How much do I owe you?"

"That comes to forty dollars. Sorry I had to add a little extra, you know, for the rush and the special care. One of the spindles on the film cracked, but other than that, all the photos were there."

"That's fine," I said, and handed him the money.

"Well, are you going to open it?" He smiled. "If it were me, I would be tearing them open. But, hey, I've already seen them. What do I know?"

"I'm waiting to open them with my grandma. She's in the car."

"Well, if you're ever in town with your Hasselblad, come and visit." He shrugged. "Sorry, I've never actually seen one in the flesh, you know, in my hands."

"Okay."

When I opened the truck's door, Grandma already had a smile on her face. "Well? Open them up."

I jumped into the cab and pulled up the folded plastic. My fingers stuck to the back of the stack. The first photograph was of Mom. It must have been her first photograph with the camera—a self-portrait. I could see her hand clenched around the shutter cord; her finger pressed down. She wasn't smiling, but she had a look of wonder on her face, like she was trying to imagine the photograph burning into the emulsion. It was as if she were watching us opening the envelope. There were three generations of memories all there together on the pages.

I could feel tears burning on my cheek. She was so beautiful. I noticed Grandma was crying too. We looked at each other and smiled.

"Grandma, maybe we should save the rest until we get home."

"I think you may be right," she said.

I pushed the stack back into the envelope.

THE ROAD HOME was long and hot—the winter sun was surprisingly warm. In the cab, Grandma had dozed off again, holding the black envelope in her lap.

With nothing to distract me, I couldn't stop thinking about the rest of the photographs. Although I knew Mom was gone, that first picture had really forced me to realize that her presence was no longer here. I felt slighted that I could not see her. I was willing to give up my self-exorcism from seeing the ghosts if it meant I could see my mom again.

Once home, I helped Grandma into the bathroom, leaving the photos on the kitchen table. I put on some tea, staring at the envelope. I could hear laughter coming from it like a whisper. I picked up the envelope and held it to my chest, then laid the photos out on the kitchen table one by one.

The first was the one that Grandma and I had pulled from the envelope this morning. Images two, three, and four were of my mom accidentally pressing in the cable release.

Photos five and six were of Tohatchi from high above the town. I knew right where she was sitting when she took this picture—on the west side of Chuska mesa, looking down at Grandma's house. The second was very wide, capturing Tohatchi and the still snow-covered peaks of the Chuska Mountains. On the top of the print, the clouds spread out over the peaks like melted marshmallows, effervescent and seamless.

The next five photographs were of Grandma. They were beautiful portraits as I had never seen her before, her Navajo blood shining deeply through her eyes. Photos ten and eleven were of Grandma and Mom together. Mom was dressed in a black T-shirt and a gray vest with khaki pants and boots. Number ten must have just been a random shot—my mom pointing to the lens and Grandma looking into it. But eleven was great. Grandma had her arm around Mom's neck, both of them laughing hysterically. Just seeing them made me smile.

Photo number twelve was of a Navajo lady with her hair pulled under a blue handkerchief. When I looked closer, I realized it was Mrs. Bitsie, Grandma's neighbor. She was standing at her garden gate, holding her shovel. Her dog, George Bush, sat by her side. Photo thirteen was of George Bush, his mouth open in a smile, his bushy tail wagging behind.

Photo fourteen was of Jasper, the Laguna Pueblo man who sold bread halfway between Tohatchi and Gallup on Saturday afternoons. It had been years since I had seen him.

Photo fifteen was the WELCOME TO GALLUP sign with an elder

holding a wrinkled dollar bill in his left hand and a cane in his right, trying to hitchhike somewhere. Sixteen was of the man getting out of my mom's car. In the background you could see the yellow and blue squares of the Indian Hospital on the top of the hill.

The next photo was of me sleeping at the desk in my room, my face pressed against some homework, hands flat. I had no idea how she'd taken it without waking me, but she hovered above me, catching the perfect symmetry of light circles coming from the lamp bulb and the serpentine coils of hair that spread out from the top of my head.

A huge lump in my throat rose when I saw image eighteen. It was the one she took up on the canyon that day we played hooky. The next picture was the one I'd taken of her, the back-drop nothing but the blue of sky and white of clouds. The next photo was one we took together, the frame skewed, the background asymmetrical, but the smiles balanced it. I could finally see myself in her—the smile, and the face in the same identical shape.

Image twenty-one was of Grandma and me standing out in front of the house Mom died in. You could see the exhaustion on our faces. The bare space called out my mother's name; you could see my own extended arm with the cable release in hand. Image twenty-two was of Grandma's house the second I came home, her perfect fence, her newspaper mailbox.

Twenty-three was the picture I took of Grandma sitting at her table, capturing the curtains floating, her coffee mug steaming, her smile, her pin curls, and the scarecrow clock ticking.

I pulled twenty-four out and stared at it for a long time. It was the white house that had terrorized my dreams for years, consumed in flames. Trails of flame bled deep into the stars, the eyes and mouth of the house billowing with fire. The smoke coiled at the corners.

The bathroom door closed behind me as Grandma came up and touched the small of my back. She gasped when she saw all the photos spread out on the kitchen table, all in order by the image number. She kept her small handkerchief over her mouth and cried and laughed at the photographs that my mother and I had taken. When she came to the last one, she hugged me until I couldn't breathe. We went to bed that night in silence, leaving the pictures on the table.

CHAPTER TWENTY-FIVE

OMAX 40X – 1600X Lab Binocular
Biological Compound Microscope

I HAD A few months of "vacation" coming up, but Erma was never going to let me rest.

I had no idea how I was going to change her report, especially now that I had no access. No one cared about what had happened to her, and that was the tragedy. Garcia wasn't going to help me. He had called that case before we had even finished picking Erma off the freeway. I was going to have to find out how he was connected to her on my own.

I thought of Dr. Blaser, the medical examiner who had been at Erma's scene. He was a forensic pathologist and had worked for the Albuquerque Police Department as a field deputy medical investigator for years before coming to the ME's office. He was in his sixties and liked to wear Grateful Dead shirts under his lab coat. He always narrated his autopsies like crime novels and tried to make you smile if you had to be a part of it. When I had the chance to work with him in the field or in the lab, I always learned something new, and he was eager to teach me. I knew if anyone would be straight with me, it would be him.

I tried to call him, but it went straight to voicemail. I would have to go to his office. I'd had to visit the Office of the Medical Investigator on a regular basis since I started. I hated it.

I managed to get my car to whine and rattle to a start and sat in the garage listening to my police scanner, letting the beast warm up.

"I'm thirsty." The voice of the ghost child spoke in the passenger seat.

"Jesus!" My heart raced in my chest. They always managed to sneak up on me.

"I'm thirsty," the little boy said again.

"Get used to it, kid. You're dead." Erma's voice was different today, weaker—like it was two spots off from a radio frequency.

"Erma." I looked at her in the rearview mirror. "I'm working on it."

"Not good enough." Erma moved toward me, draping her arm over my shoulder. "I need you to work harder. I need to know that nothing is going to happen to her."

I put the car into gear and pulled out into the light, where pools of melting snow stood on every corner. The boy peered out the window.

"You had a job, Erma. What was it?"

"I was the manager of the Apothecary on Central, that new bar right off the freeway. I was about to take over as a part-owner with Matias. Everything was about to change."

"Who is Matias?"

"He was my husband—well, common law. You know. Living in sin. Well, sometimes."

"So, off and on?"

"I don't think that has anything to do with this." Erma sounded annoyed, as usual.

"Well. Do you want help or not? It doesn't hurt you to share what you know. You're dead. What are you afraid of? Your boy-friend?"

"Matias is dead." Erma's voice scratched.

I was pulling up to OMI, a four-story battleship in blue, silver, and orange right off the freeway. The new building's glass was blinding in the morning light. Luckily, security buzzed me right in since I had been there before. I was glad that news of my suspension hadn't spread further than the crime lab.

Dr. Blaser was in the laboratory, examining something through an impressive microscope on the counter. He was surrounded by jars upon jars of specimens—fingertips, ears, organs, all preserved and labeled like fall canning season.

"Well, are you gonna stand there in the doorway being creepy, or are you going to ask me a question?" Dr. Blaser looked up from his work. "Rita! It's been a while. I thought you didn't like it out here in the lab."

"A forensic worker who hates OMI." I smiled. "I like irony."

"Me too." He moved to his microscope. "We just got a camera added to our OMAX 40X and I cannot get it to take a picture. Everything is plugged in, but I press this button and nothing."

"That's a reset button." I looked at the screen next to the microscope and reached behind to the unit power switch.

"It's always the simplest thing," he said. "So, what brings you up here?" Dr. Blaser took a sandwich out of his lab coat.

"The last time I saw you, we were out on the overpass that night—the Singleton case."

"Oh, yes." He took a bite of his sandwich. "The overpass."

"Do you know what the ruling on that was?" I tried to concentrate on something besides the sandwich. "I was told it was suicide."

"That was hard to determine. There was no evidence to prove

otherwise." He moved over to the corner and pulled a few files from the cabinet, turning pages. "Manner of death, undetermined. That is what I put in my report. There was so little to go on since the body was so badly mutilated. No ligature marks or signs of a struggle. Her family insisted she would have never committed suicide, that she was on her way to a meeting and never came home."

"Do you know why the report would say she committed suicide?"

"Maybe because the detective on scene said it was." He handed me the report. I saw Garcia's name scribbled on the last page, but it wasn't followed by the stamp from the coroner's office. The final determination was never made until the coroner signed off on the death certificate, and for now, that signature line was blank.

"We *were* able to determine that she was pregnant." Dr. Blaser moved into an adjacent closet and began to put on his scrubs, booties, and face protector as two ambulance drivers brought a gurney into the room next to us. "We found a six- or seven-week-old fetus in what was left of her."

"I think there is much more going on here than any of us even know." I closed his report. "This woman deserves the benefit of the doubt. I wonder if she knew about the baby."

"That's hard to say," Dr. Blaser said. "Some women claim they know from day one."

"I know she didn't jump, Dr. Blaser. Garcia is a lazy investigator."

"Follow your guts, Rita. Your guts are right most of the time." He smiled. "And you're right. Garcia is a lazy investigator."

"Thanks, Doc."

"I'll be honest with you, Rita. We processed Judge Winters a couple of days ago, and our field investigator agreed with us on this, it wasn't a murder-suicide."

"You mean someone really did murder the whole family?" I hadn't let myself think about that scene since it sent me to the hospital.

"The trajectory of his injuries made it almost impossible. The starlight tearing you see with a self-inflicted wound wasn't there, nor the muzzle imprint. I thought it was intermediate range at best, with some soot around the wound." Dr. Blaser walked toward the autopsy room and began to wash his hands. "The bullet exit was through his cheek, so someone stood next to him and shot. That simple."

"Do you think there is something bigger going on here?" I wanted to know where he stood.

"I know that Judge Winters didn't pull that trigger on himself. Garcia was the lead detective on scene and concluded it was a murder-suicide—just like that."

"Do you think Garcia is involved?"

The doctor shifted his weight. "I don't know, Rita. Maybe you should ask Armenta. If anyone knows, it's that man. Garcia and Armenta spent over twenty years as partners. They saw each other more than their wives did." He gave me another one of his kind smiles. "Let me know if there is anything I can do to help." He turned, eager to get to the autopsy.

I stopped him. "What happened to Armenta? Is he still in Albuquerque?"

"No one knows what happened to Armenta," he said. "We had a retirement party for him, and he never showed up. Good guy, though." He opened the autopsy room with his hip. "You take care, Rita."

CHAPTER TWENTY-SIX

Nikon F5

THE MORNING AFTER Grandma and I developed Mom's Hasselblad, I woke up and found the house empty. Grandma was already awake, praying to the morning sun. The coffee perco- lated and hissed on the stove. As I turned the fire off, I could see Grandma returning to the house, holding onto the bent fence line for balance. Zoe trotted slowly beside her through rows of knee-high corn and squash plants. I walked out to join her.

Two cars, a burned-out Chevy that looked like a recycled police car and Mrs. Bitsie's blue truck, were pulling into the long stretch of the driveway. They came to a stop, waiting for us. Grandma squinted, wiping the sweat from her brow, then put her glasses back on.

"Oh, no."

A young man got out of the truck. "We lost Grandma," he said.

"What happened?" Grandma was tearing up. Mrs. Bitsie was her dear friend. They used to talk, drink coffee, and share their garden vegetables with each other. I felt a lump rising in my throat.

"They said it was a stroke." The young man wiped away tears. "We're going into town to meet with the people from the funeral home right now. Her services will be up here at Saint Mary's. We had to let you know. You were one of her only friends."

"Thank you, dear," Grandma said.

I helped Grandma into the house. Sadness filled the room, expanding out and up, enveloping the two of us in an uneasy silence. I poured a cup of Grandma's thick coffee.

"Grandma, are you hungry?" I wasn't, but I knew she should eat. Sadness had a way of starving our bodies.

"No," she said. But her stomach growled loudly right on cue. We looked at each other and laughed.

"I'll make us some sandwiches," I said.

Grandma sat at the table and watched as I chopped up onions and pickles and boiled eggs. Tuna fish salad was always her favorite, on wheat bread. Out the window, I could see Mrs. Bitsie's dog, George Bush, standing at the gate of her garden, still guarding her treasures from the roaming packs of strays.

Grandma was staring at the Bitsie house when I placed her sandwich on the table. Cars were beginning to gather—some rusty trucks and tattered ten-year-old cars. George Bush barked and barked but never left his post at the front of the gate. No one was getting into that garden.

"Grandma, did you want to go over there?"

"No. That would just make me miss her more." Grandma shifted in her seat. "I guess all of us old people are just going to start dropping one by one."

"Don't talk like that. You're healthy and you're not going any-where." There was panic in my voice.

"Even if I died, I could probably still come and talk to you every day. You still do that? Talk to dead people?" Grandma looked at me sideways.

"No, Grandma, I haven't done that in a long time," I lied.

"Not even your mom? You've really never seen her again?"

"No, I haven't," I said.

Grandma kept watching everything across the street, pushing away the plate I just set in front of her. I couldn't eat either. The thought of Grandma leaving this earth had haunted me forever. She was all that I had left—my whole family. And here she was, refusing to eat, her heart reaching and shuddering from all the death and tragedy that was befalling us. I ached to protect her heart from the pain, to fix this battered house. But there was little I could do except keep her company.

When Grandma fell asleep that evening, I walked out to the eastern side of the house and watched the clouds curling and swelling, the flashes of lightning in the distance over Albuquerque. By the time the sun was getting ready to settle down for the day, the storm was practically on top of me, my lungs and nose filling with the smells of wet sagebrush and heavy-soaked earth.

"Can I ask you about something?" The voice came from nothing, just a faint white flicker in the darkness. It didn't matter. I recognized her immediately.

"Yes, Mrs. Bitsie. You can ask me anything." I tried to make out her features or a silhouette—anything. She was only a glimmer now.

"All those kids at the house are fighting." Mrs. Bitsie was angry. "They never cared about me when I was alive—never came to visit me. Now that I'm dead, they're sure over there dividing up all of my things and moving in."

I didn't know what to say. I wasn't even supposed to be talking to the spirits, especially here at Grandma's house.

"I need you to go over there. I never had the chance to tell anyone about my will. I have everything arranged, just like I wanted. It's all in the blue lockbox up in the crawlspace in my closet. Let my grandsons know that it all goes to them. Their mother left them here years ago and never bothered to come back for them. They were all I had."

"Do you want me to go over there right now?" I asked. But she was gone. There was no voice and no light. Just me again. Alone. In the dark.

Back in the house, I checked on Grandma, still asleep, her radio on low, KTNN's canned voices coming out in Navajo. I sat in front of the living room television. I wanted to ask Grandma what to do, but I had the feeling she wouldn't want me to go through with Mrs. Bitsie's request. She didn't want people to know about my curse. She'd protected me from it my whole life. But I didn't feel like letting Mrs. Bitsie down.

My shoes sunk into the still-soft mud in our driveway as I walked to Mrs. Bitsie's house, which was surrounded by cars I didn't recognize. George Bush left his post to come over and greet me, wagging his tail, and I wondered if he could see Mrs. Bitsie's ghost too. I could already hear voices arguing inside the house. Five or six kids played outside with sticks and a weathered kite that couldn't catch a breeze. Even if it did, the kite would have been lost to the dark or to the abandoned power lines on the side of the rugged mesas.

The wooden steps outside the entrance creaked and moaned as I went to the door and knocked. At first, no one heard me. I knocked again, harder, until my knuckles stung. This time, an angry woman opened the door. I tried to smile, but the heaviness in the room pulled my grin to a slim, flat line. I shook hands with everyone: the two grandsons, a girlfriend of one of the grandsons, two older Navajo men with cowboy hats, thick necks, and bulging bellies under tight western shirts. Both had those long stringy mustaches that Navajo men try to wear, just ten to twenty hairs that grow from the edges of their mouths. I knew they had to be Mrs. Bitsie's sons. Then there was a woman with lots of jewelry and makeup who had the most damaging glare I had ever seen. I knew her as Rosie, Mrs. Bitsie's daughter, a Mormon who reformed after twenty years living out of the bottle. They all were mad as hell—Mrs. Bitsie's ghost included.

I offered condolences. "My grandma was a good friend of hers. She's going to miss her." Everyone was looking at me, wondering when I was going to leave so they could carry on with the arguing. "I know there is a service at the chapter house, and I just wanted to tell you that we are willing to help with anything you might need." I looked over at the grandsons and smiled. They smiled and nodded in return.

Rosie was already opening the door for me to leave. "Thank you for coming over," she barked. I followed her, wondering how I would ever deliver Mrs. Bitsie's message.

I resorted to lying. "Can I ask one of you to help me out at my grandma's house? I have a box in the back of the truck and wanted to get it out of the rain."

One of the grandsons stood right away. "I'll help." We walked out together. Once we were past the parked cars and away from the house, I extended my hand.

"What is your name again? I'm sorry. I have a bad memory."

He shook my hand. "My name is Arvis. I'm the older one. That's my little girl in there."

"Your grandma was really close to you two, huh?"

"Yeah. Real close. She was more my mom than Rosie was." He looked to the ground.

I stopped him before we got to Grandma's driveway. "Listen, don't ask me how I know, but you need to go up to your grandma's closet and look up in the crawlspace in the ceiling. There is a blue lockbox in there that has all your grandma's paperwork. She left what little she had to you and your brother."

He looked at me like he had seen a ghost. The irony.

"Did you see her spirit?"

"What makes you say that?" I already knew, but I wanted to hear it from him.

"Everyone says that you used to see spirits and stuff when you were a little girl. I thought maybe you were still seeing them." He stood with his hands in his pockets, half scared and half curious.

"People sure like to talk, don't they?"

"Yeah. I guess they do." He shrugged.

"Let us know if there is anything you need. Okay?" I began to walk back to Grandma's house. Arvis stood there watching me until I was almost to the door, then turned on his heel and walked toward Mrs. Bitsie's house. George Bush howled in the distance.

When I came in the door, Grandma was sitting in the kitchen with the lights off. I could smell reheated coffee and hear the television in the living room.

"Where did you run off to?" Grandma asked. I knew she had probably been watching me the entire time.

"I just went over to Mrs. Bitsie's house to let them know we were here if they needed help with anything."

"That doesn't sound like you." Grandma was onto me.

"Mrs. Bitsie asked me to."

"I knew it. What did I tell you about that?" Grandma was on her feet. I could see her rage even in the dark.

"I know, Grandma. Did you want me to tell her no? Did you want me to let her down?"

Grandma was silent. I heard the ache of her chair as she sat back down.

"What did she want?"

"She needed me to tell them where all her paperwork was. She had a will and some money and things and wanted me to tell her grandsons where it was."

"I just don't understand why she would do that. She knew how I felt about the things you see. She knew I didn't want anyone to know." Grandma leaned over and turned on the lamp on the table. "Someone is going to say something. I just know it."

MRS. BITSIE'S SERVICES were well attended by most of Tohatchi. It was shocking to see all of Grandma's friends completely gray, their skin softly wrinkled and peppered with spots from the sun. The group stood together, talking in Navajo and often shaking their heads, pointing at the parts of their bodies that ached and pained, sharing stories about their terrible kids or grandkids. It was sad to see Grandma's generation slowly slipping away, taking with them all their knowledge. The new generation lived without the ingrained commitment to look out for one another, to be a part of the community. But I couldn't complain. I was getting ready to leave this world behind too. School was only a month away.

Rosie and her brothers had been watching me during the services, and I knew it wouldn't be long before somebody shared a few choice words with me. It was Rosie who marched over to me the moment she spotted me at the reception. "So, you're the one that can see the spirits." She stood inches from my face. "You're a witch. That's what you are."

By then, the entire chapter house was staring at me—the

elders embarrassed for me, for my grandma, and for the soul of poor Mrs. Bitsie.

"I'm not a witch," I whispered. "It's not my fault that she didn't trust you." I walked out and went home. Grandma was right. No one would ever understand this thing that haunted me.

But Mrs. Bitsie deserved to be at peace. The sky began to open again, bringing the rain and the sunshine all at once. Maybe it was Mrs. Bitsie's way of saying thank you. The raindrops were wide and heavy on my skin.

AFTER MRS. BITSIE'S funeral, I spent the summer on Grandma's porch watching people drive by, slowing to get a glimpse of me, sure that I would witch their families or levitate them off the road. It was beginning to get old. I sat there anyway as a kind of defiance.

Grandma and I planted lots of corn and squash, some radishes and onions and baby carrots. I had stocked Grandma's little pantry with canned peaches and pears—the ones in water she liked—and the usual cans of corned beef, tuna, and deviled ham. The thought of leaving Grandma alone terrified me. She was slower and more fragile than I remembered. She walked to the gas station and sometimes to the chapter house to keep her legs strong and her heart pumping, but she couldn't really get anywhere else. I let her drive her pickup to the post office every day, but I found myself digging my nails into the seat cushions when she would turn into parking spaces and come up hot on cars before she would finally step on the brakes.

"Why don't you come with me to Albuquerque?" I'd say.

"And stay where? In the dorms with you? In some old folks' home? No, thank you."

"What are you going to do if you need help, Grandma? Who is going to take care of you?"

"I am going to take care of me. That's who. And you're going to live your life and have adventures and not come back to this place. Promise me."

"I promise, Grandma," I said. "But as soon as I have money, I'm fixing your house. Promise that you will let me, then I'll promise."

"Okay, I promise."

"Then we'll both have a place to come home to. I need a place to come home to."

"This will always be home. But there is a whole world out there that you should see. I've only seen it in books. I don't want you to say that. I want you to see it. I want you to smell it. I want you to be able to tell me all about it as you're showing me the pictures."

I really wasn't going that far away, two and a half hours by car, but the distance felt like a gigantic divide. I knew I would feel alone there, even if I was going to be beyond busy. I had registered for eighteen credit hours for my first semester, anxious to move beyond school and into the real world of photography. I was ready to tell Grandma the stories and show her the pictures.

The day before I had to leave for school, Grandma took me over to Mr. Bitsilly's house. It was important for the both of us to have a prayer said. I didn't know if I believed in Mr. Bitsilly's medicine, but I still wanted to see the man and hear his voice, to hear him talk about dreams and the Arizona Cardinals.

When he opened the door, he smiled wide and shook my grandma's hand, leading her into the house and straight to a chair. A couple of great-grandkids sat on the couch watching cartoons, the youngest one drinking a can of Shasta like it was his last bottle. Grandma and Mr. Bitsilly spoke in Navajo as he shuffled to pour her a cup of hot Navajo tea. She was worried about me being in the city by myself and wanted Mr. Bitsilly to give her some semblance of security. I'd be happy if he could, but I knew if something was going to happen to me out there in the world, it was going to happen, no matter what prayers Mr. Bitsilly offered.

"So, Rita," Mr. Bitsilly asked me. "Still seeing your friends?"

"Just here and there, I guess," I admitted. It did no good to lie to Mr. Bitsilly.

Mr. Bitsilly rubbed his freshly shorn hair and shook his head. "Your grandma told me that you had finally learned to put that away. She said that it had been years. Is that true?"

"Yes. It's true. It had been years—they'd forgotten about me."

Mr. Bitsilly handed me a Shasta. "And now? Did you invite them back in?"

"No. Mrs. Bitsie. That's all," I said. "She needed my help, and I didn't want to let her down."

The kitchen was quiet except for the screeches of the cartoons coming from the other room. Grandma sipped her tea as Mr. Bitsilly got up from the table and headed toward the attached hogan that jutted out from the house, its door facing the east, covered by the same worn blue Pendleton blanket I remembered from my childhood. Mr. Bitsilly was worn too, his back hunched as he grasped chair backs for balance.

I helped Grandma into his hogan and sat with her on some of Mr. Bitsilly's creaky wooden chairs. Smoke began to snake up toward the ceiling. The smells of burning cedar and sage coiled inside of me. Grandma and I breathed it in as deeply as we could, our eyes closed, our chests rising and falling. As Mr. Bitsilly continued to sprinkle dry plants on the gray coals, I opened my eyes and watched him carefully circle the fire. He was deliberate with his movements, his hands, and his heart. He caught my gaze and smiled at me as he began to sing. This time I let it happen. I allowed myself to be part of the moment, to join them both in the prayer. I was scared and I needed to admit it.

I prayed that Grandma would be okay, that Mr. Bitsilly would continue to live a good life and keep his blood pressure and diabetes at bay. I asked the spirits to watch over the two of them, to make sure that nothing evil would come to them. All I could do was hope that those same spirits and entities that thought it was reasonable to talk to me would find it in their hearts to do what I asked: to keep the two people that meant everything to me safe from the world that I already knew was out there—one that I never wanted them to see. The world that I was resigning myself to had already broken my heart.

THE NEXT DAY, Grandma and I drove into town together so that I could catch the train into Albuquerque. I couldn't help but cry as I packed my bags. Grandma would have been upset with me. It was bad to cry after someone. I knew that. But all I could imagine was Grandma helpless on the floor, or sick and unable to call. The unrealized tragedies of life consumed me.

I put my duffle bag in the truck, hoping to hide my tears from Grandma. I could see Arvis, Mrs. Bitsie's grandson, coming down our driveway with his hands in his pockets.

"So, I hear you're leaving us." Arvis offered a huge smile. "Moving to the big city."

"It's not that big. But, yeah, I'm going to school. How are things going over at your house?"

"My mom has stopped fighting us and finally just left us alone.

I'm glad, too, because my little girl doesn't know any place else as home. Just here."

"I don't either. This is home." I tried to hide a tear that had escaped. "Can you please check in on my grandma for me?" I pulled out a piece of paper from my pocket and wrote my phone number on it. "If anything happens to her or she needs anything, can you call me?"

"Yeah. I can do that. That's no problem." He stared at me for a moment. "We owe you and your grandma a lot. She's like my grandma too. We'll take care of her."

The slam of the screen door turned my head. Grandma was on the porch in her coat, her purse clasped to her arm, her hair in place. She looked so together, suddenly twenty years younger in my eyes, standing in front of the house that she built. Just seeing her like that, so full of power, made me feel better. It made me remember all the things that my grandma had already endured in her life. She was so much stronger than I was giving her credit for. That, and I now knew that Arvis would watch out for her. He just seemed like someone I could trust, someone who had the same heart as his own grandmother. He smiled and waved goodbye as he walked back toward his house, wedging his hands back into his pockets.

Grandma pulled the truck into gear and drove out onto the highway with several feisty reservation dogs following us to the cattle guard, barking and nipping at the rubber. I watched Grandma's house until it disappeared under the first hill, the roof sinking beneath the rows of sagebrush.

The Gallup train station had been newly renovated, with art on its walls and benches. It had a clean bathroom with shiny mirrors and electronic hand dryers. Inside the station, two elder Navajo ladies were selling their jewelry on a red-velvet table spread, their laughter filling the room to the high ceilings. I walked to the platform window. The silver Amtrak was sleek, modern, and looked like it went on for miles. This was my first train ride, and I was excited to watch the world go past, to see the small, significant details I missed when I traveled the highway. When Grandma stepped up there with me, she stared straight ahead. It made me think of her time on this same track, a path that led her away from home for thirteen years. I could see the memory in her eyes.

Grandma pulled a box—wrapped in lavender paper with tiny honeysuckle clusters traced in white—out of her purse. I was surprised I hadn't seen it earlier. She smiled and handed it to me. When I opened the corner, I could see a glossy black box with a brand-new Nikon F5. This was the first camera I had ever seen with a green digital display.

"Grandma, you can't afford this. Where did you get it?" I caressed the camera box, pressing it into my chest.

"I wanted you to have a good camera for school. Your own. Not a hand-me-down, but something that can finally really be yours." I grabbed and hugged my grandma so fast that it startled her. I held on to her as I watched everyone getting on the train, didn't let her go until the attendant began her last calls. I fought hard to keep my tears back, the lump in my throat a throbbing ache. Neither of us said goodbye.

CHAPTER TWENTY-SEVEN

Sony Cyber-shot S-600

I KNEW I was going to have to find the former Detective Armenta if I wanted to get any information on Garcia. I had gone to a party at his house once after one of those policemen vs. firemen softball games—some of us from forensics were invited. Armenta lived in the north valley in a modest but nice house with an acre or two attached to the back. It was surrounded by a tall adobe wall, and the yard was full of rose bushes that his wife grew.

I drove to the valley, weaving through hibernating lavender fields on the Los Poblanos Farms. I remembered how their fragrance had permeated the party. I followed the long driveway past the old adobe wall to the house. It was empty, a FOR SALE sign attached to the outside gate. I got out of my car and peered in. All the rose bushes were brown.

"Can I help you, miss?" A frail man came to the wall from next door, leaning on a muddy shovel. Behind him, I saw a second man still digging.

"I was looking for a Detective Armenta. I thought that he lived here."

"Armenta has been gone for a while now." He looked into the sky as if trying to retrieve a memory. "His wife has Alzheimer's. He had moved her up by her family."

"Do you remember where?"

"Hey, Miguel!" he shouted to the other man. "Where did they move? Armenta!"

"Taos. *A la vuelta de la esquina.*" They both laughed.

"That's right. Now I remember." The man took off his hat and scratched his white hair. "His wife is at a facility up there in Taos."

"Thank you. I didn't mean to interrupt your work." The two men waved and went back to digging.

I stopped for coffee and gas on my way north to Taos, which was about two hours away, with an approaching storm at my back. By the time I arrived in Taos, it was starting to snow. I followed the highway to the one nursing home in town and headed inside. When I asked to see Mrs. Armenta, the woman at the front desk glared at me.

"Are you family? I've never seen you over here before."

"No, ma'am. I was actually trying to reach Mr. Armenta and I knew his wife was here."

"Mr. Armenta lives down by Mora, not here."

"I'm with the Albuquerque Police Department. I have an urgent message for him," I lied. "If you could let me know where I could find him, it would really save the department some time."

"You would think that the police would know where one of their own was." The woman looked suspicious, her arms crossed.

"You're right, ma'am. Detective Armenta left without giving us his permanent address." I showed her my ID. "I'm from the forensics unit."

"He's in Ledoux, past Mora," she said. "He lives in the old

bottle house down by the lake." The phone began to ring, and she answered. I walked out into the billowing snow. I shuffled through my glove compartment and found my little Sony camera wrapped inside my folded map. It was strange to be alone, but the quiet was inviting. I figured if I just kept working, it would stay that way. I raised my camera and turned it on, taking a photo of the nursing home sign covered in snow. I was surprised it still worked.

By the time I made it up the twists and turns of the forest road by Ledoux, the snow had turned the landscape a rich and vast white. I took the lake road until a local in a rattling pickup rolled down their window and waved down my vehicle.

"I don't think you're going to make it much further up this road. Not with that." The man pointed at my car.

"You're probably right." I smiled. "I'm looking for a Detective Armenta. I heard he lives in the old bottle house. Do you know where that is?"

"Yeah." He signaled up the road. "You're almost there, maybe a half a mile more." He began to roll up his window then stopped. "I didn't know old Mr. Armenta was a detective. He never told us that."

I wondered if I should have divulged it.

"Thank you for the directions." The snow was already stacking on my door.

"Be careful out there."

I pulled up to the bottle house. A steady stream of gray smoke billowed into the sky from the stacked stone fireplace. I could tell why they called it the bottle house, as I could see the different colors of bottles built into the walls, giving them eyes even through the thickly falling snow. I walked toward the gate in absolute quiet, except for the wind shaking a chime on the porch.

Then: the click of a gun being cocked.

"Stop right there."

I stopped and raised my hands above my head. The gun poked into my shoulder.

"Who are you? They called me from the nursing home and told me you were coming."

"My name is Rita Todacheene." I tried to turn around, but the gun poked me again. "I work at forensics at APD."

"And what the hell do you want with me?" I felt him lower his gun. He stepped in front of me and stared like I was familiar, but he couldn't quite place me.

"I'm working on a case and thought you might be able to help me." I kept my arms raised. "I'm just a photographer in the Crime Scene Unit."

"I remember you. What do you want to know about?"

"Garcia."

"I have nothing to say about Garcia."

"Please, sir. I know there is something going on—we just need your help to figure it out."

"I came out here to get away from what was going on in the department, and here you are getting me involved in it again."

"I think he may be involved in something much bigger."

"And you're a photographer? What is that to you?" He turned and headed toward his house.

"Please, sir."

He paused and looked at me, shaking his head. "Well, you might as well come in. You're not getting out of here tonight in that little car."

I followed him inside and looked around his cabin as he made coffee. The drinking glasses stacked on the shelf made prisms around the room.

"I moved here for my wife. So she could be near her family."

"I heard what happened. I'm sorry." I looked at his photographs on the wall. There were two of him and his wife standing by the lake, holding their catch.

"Life," he said. "The department isn't for everyone."

"How is your health since the heart attack?"

"I didn't have a heart attack." The coffee maker hissed, then dripped into the glass. "I had to get out, and it had to be quick. I was tired of getting sucked into things I wanted no part of."

"What were you getting pulled into?" I watched the man stare out of the window. "Can you tell me?"

"Why are you investigating anything if you work in the crime lab? If you want to know about Garcia, wouldn't you be with the IAB?"

"He's already being investigated." I tried to think fast. He was right. Why would I be the one asking? "He is putting a couple of my cases in jeopardy. I don't want to be pulled into it either. I think he would kill me if he knew what I already know."

Armenta sighed deeply. I could see that he was trying not to tear up.

"When you get to be my age, you really began questioning your decisions in life. I wished I had brought my wife up here a long time ago. Instead, I worked. It took its toll on both of us." Armenta took a mug from the cupboard. "Now my wife doesn't even know who I am and my doc says my diabetes has done a number on my body. It's only a matter of time. With both of us."

"Are you in as deep as Garcia?" I was as straightforward as possible.

"Garcia has been in deep for as long as he could walk." Armenta took another mug down from the cabinet. "I knew

Marty since he was a kid. Both of our dads were cops. We knew the life."

I shrugged off my coat, feeling the heat from the woodstove. "He has put in quite a few years of service, just like yourself."

Armenta sat across from me at his kitchen table. "His father, Jose, was the kind of cop you would see on the television shows—helping everyone who crossed his path, saving cats trapped in trees, the whole nine yards. He received merits and outstanding service awards from the mayor. It wouldn't have mattered how many years Marty's dad worked for the department, though, he would never make detective. He studied for the test, always waiting for that promotion that never came. That's how it was back then." He poured two cups of coffee. "In the seventies, Marty's dad joined a group of Chicano police officers who decided to sue the department and the department head, Chief Shaver, since their surnames and the color of their skin seemed to be making hiring and promotional decisions for all the higher-ups. The case was eventually settled after years and years of back-and-forth. During the eight years it took to get up to the Supreme Court, Officer Garcia was never promoted to detective, even after he had passed the test."

"Did he leave the department?"

"Jose left and took his family south to Belen. He joined their three-man force for twenty years until, at sixty-five years old, he finally became the police chief." Armenta took a huge gulp of the hot coffee. I wondered how he could stand the heat without even blinking. "Marty had told me the story a million times, especially after a few drinks. That badge wasn't enough for him, not like it was for his dad. He worked around the clock and had a wife that he never saw. He had a mortgage on a house way too expensive for a detective's salary. Every now and then he might pick a few bucks off some drug dealer, that kind of thing. Four years ago, that all changed."

"What happened four years ago?"

There was a long pause. A small dog stirred to life in the corner, then came to sit next to Armenta.

"It was the beginning of the Marcos cartel's move into meth trafficking. With safehouses all over, Albuquerque had become a central hub. It was the perfect town, midway between hubs in California, Mexico, and Texas, with interstate systems that moved north and south, east and west, right through the center of the city. We were about to end it." He picked up the little dog and rested it on his lap.

"I remember that bust," I said. "You guys stopped a lot of product. Wasn't that a good thing?"

"It was. Garcia and I had tracked a major shipment coming up through Mexico into Albuquerque to be processed and distributed by the army of soldiers that the Marcos cartel had assembled around the city. When Garcia ordered the apprehension of two appliance trucks, we thought we had stopped about two million dollars in product." Armenta looked out the window as branches from his iced-over trees scratched on the glass. "On the I-40 shoulder, with the winds blowing over forty miles per hour, Ignacio Marcos sat handcuffed beside our squad car while we searched through the back of his truck." There was another long silence. Even Armenta's dog looked up to his owner, waiting for his story to unfold. "'I can make you a rich man,' he kept saying. Garcia kept telling him to shut up, but Marcos kept talking. 'I'll give you one hundred grand. Right now. It's in my duffel bag on the front seat,' Marcos said. 'I'm not that stupid,' Marty said." Armenta shook his head. "I could see his hesitation. I knew he was thinking about it."

"Did he take it?"

"Ignacio told us that the truck had nothing in it, and when we went to check, he wasn't lying. There was nothing there. Our big bust was going to go nowhere. We searched that empty trailer, knowing the real shipment had to be miles away." Armenta got up and fetched himself another coffee, the hot steam rising as he gulped again. I hadn't even touched my mug.

"Did you have to let him go?" I was almost afraid to ask.

"We didn't have to, but we did." Armenta peered out the window again. "We sat with Marcos on the side of the highway, the wind blowing through to our bones. Garcia walked to the front of the truck and opened the door. He walked away from the truck with that blue duffle bag and was never the same."

"How much is he into the cartel for?" I began to think about the repercussions.

"Now? Who knows. Marty spent that money in a few weeks, paying off his mortgage and student loans. It didn't take long for him to need more. Before long, he was turning a blind eye on certain Marcos deals and helping some of the small-time dealers stay out of jail. He obsessed about the money, saving it all over the place, even burying some in his backyard. I'm ashamed to admit it, but he gave me money to get this cabin."

"Every person I have talked to says you just kind of vanished off the face of the earth." I finally took a drink of my warm coffee.

"It was getting to be too much—the constant lies, covering our tracks, all of it. I took some money and I left. The Marcos family knows that I am part of this. I was Marty's partner. I knew I had to stop being on the take and get out before I lost my pension. Now I have my pension and no more time."

"I had a couple of cases in Albuquerque that were marked by your old partner." I thought about how to phrase the question without scaring Armenta into kicking me out. "Judge Winters and his entire family were killed just this past week. Garcia has reported it as a murder-suicide, despite inconclusive evidence. And another young woman—"

"Judge Winters is dead?" Armenta seemed shocked.

"Yes. Someone shot him and his whole family." I lowered my head. "He was just getting ready to start trial for the incident that had him thrown off the bench."

"I tried my best to convince him to come back to the land of the living—back to putting these kinds of people in jail. But there was a huge batch of heroin and oxycodone coming, three million dollars' worth." Armenta picked at his cuticles, his fingernails bit down to blood. "It was coming up from Sinaloa through the rough territory out by the Antelope Wells Port of Entry, where there's only one border agent stationed, right across from El Berrendo in Chihuahua. They were doing the same run at least four times a month. And Marty was set up to get thirty percent of the take."

"Did you help him with this deal?" I watched Armenta's eyes.

"I was working with him," he answered.

"What did you have to do?"

"It was supposed to run the way it usually did. Matias Romero, Ignacio Marcos's right-hand man, waited on the US side of the border for the drop, then drove up Interstate 25 to Albuquerque and brought the drugs to Pino's Upholstery. It was our job to keep a distance and keep Matias from being busted."

"Something went wrong?" Night had fallen—the snowdrifts outside the window were reflecting purple from the shadows. Armenta walked to the woodstove and threw two logs on the fire.

"The DEA didn't care about Marty's agreement with Marcos.

About an hour from Albuquerque, Matias Romero's SUV was swarmed by three dark trucks with hidden flashers between their front grills. We drove by the scene like we knew nothing about it. Ten DEA agents had Matias on the ground. They charged Matias with drug trafficking, and there was really nothing that Marty could do to change it."

"How was Judge Winters involved?" I couldn't figure out how a buttoned-up guy like Winters could have been so deep into a thing like this.

"Judge Winters was the one who gave Matias twenty years. Marty tried to derail the investigation—threatened Winters to get him to drop the charges." Armenta looked at the floor. "When Winters wouldn't budge, Marty set up his bust."

Armenta described how Marty Garcia had paid for the prostitute and planted the drugs in the car; he then took Winters out for a beer and dropped in a Rohypnol. When Judge Winters woke up in the downtown lockup, he knew nothing except that his career was over.

"He was fighting the charges when he died," I said.

"Marty thought arranging his downfall would be enough for the Marcos family. But it sounds like they wanted their own revenge on Judge Winters."

"And I guess they got it," I said. "They even killed the kids and the dog."

Armenta avoided my eyes. "Were you on scene?"

"I took the photos. It was horrible." I got out of the chair and peered out the window at the piling snow. I had no idea how I was going to get out of here. At this rate the roads would not be passable in the morning. "Did Detective Garcia know an Erma Singleton?"

"That's Matias Romero's girlfriend. She ran front of house at the Apothecary while Matias ran deals out of the back room. He was cutting the drugs with her and making a fortune." Armenta took down a bottle from the top of his fridge. He poured pills in his hand and swallowed more coffee. "Erma Singleton was trouble and Marty knew it."

"A loose end." Why hadn't Erma told me what she was involved in? What had she dragged me into?

Armenta came over and stood by the window with me. "Erma couldn't stop talking and spending Matias's money. I knew something bad would happen to her." Armenta paused. "I'm sorry I didn't do more. All I could do was get away from it. Faking a heart attack was as simple as paperwork. I haven't spoken with Marty since I left."

"Thank you for telling me what you know, Detective Armenta." I began to gather my things.

"I'll make up the spare room, Rita. You're not going anywhere tonight."

I hesitated, wondering about Armenta's intentions.

He smiled and handed me a few blankets. "Don't worry. I'm not going to hurt you."

CHAPTER TWENTY-EIGHT

Hasselblad Portraits

THE UNIVERSITY WAS a lonely place, though I was never physically alone. There were long lines of students everywhere—for financial aid and housing, for food, for registration and schedule changes. I navigated through the process, finally finding my way to my dorm room. I could hear Bauhaus thumping from speakers. The door was open.

The girl sitting on the bed—Megan Ulibarri, according to my paperwork—had long, shiny black hair and black eyes accentuated with black eyeliner and mascara. She wore a black leather choker with silver spikes, matching bracelets, and tall, calf-length black leather boots.

"Hey," Megan said.

"Hi. Megan, right?" I offered my hand. "I'm Rita. I'm studying photography."

"Hey," Megan said again.

"So, what are you studying?" I tried again while I unpacked my bags.

"Medicine," Megan said and lit a cigarette, then sprayed a blast of air freshener to cover up the smell. "No. I paint. This one is mine." She pointed to a giant black-and-white portrait of Robert Smith from the Cure. The portrait was well done.

I sat on the bed and took out the new Nikon box. I opened it slowly, watching it unfold, and pulled the new camera out. The plastic was smooth and perfect. I took some film from my bag and loaded it into the back. I could hear the mechanisms moving and turning inside. I was so used to turning and spinning that tiny wheel to load the camera that the automation of the Nikon F5 had me marveling.

Megan stubbed out her cigarette on the small coffee table that separated our beds, yanking me out of my admiring reverie. The room was small and uncomfortable, and now it was filled with smoke and cinnamon apple spray. But this was my new space. It felt wonderful and terrible all at once to be in this tiny room with this girl and her dark, depressing psyche.

"Can I take your picture?"

"Why?" Megan fished around for what I assumed was another cigarette.

"Because you're interesting," I answered.

"That's the first time I've ever heard that. Shoot." Megan stared blankly into my lens as I took her picture. Then she asked, "Want a cigarette?"

How could I say no?

I SPENT ALL my spare time in the chemical smell and dark red of the photography studio. I loved to watch the images reveal themselves in the developing tanks. The film racks, tongs, squeegees, and dryers became my life.

Over the first two semesters, I maintained above-average grades in my required classes, but only really devoted myself to my film and photography classes. Megan had managed to get me completely addicted to nicotine. She took me to strange experimental film events around town and introduced me to her unsavory love castoffs. I never did take the bait, but I was able to get some great photos of Megan and her punk rock love monkeys she paraded around town. There were a lot of Native and Mexican punk rockers in Albuquerque. I began to develop a collection of portraits of them, especially taken at the run-down Sunshine Theater, where many of them ended up every weekend. The club was dark and had a cheap miniature bar with three lonely red stools and ten plastic chairs. The plumbing was terrible, so the whole place smelled like a urinal cake, but the drinks were cheap and some of the best punk bands would come through the club. Sunshine's black-painted walls and chain-link fence motif ended up being the backdrop for a lot of my work.

Photography classes lasted six hours every Tuesday and Thursday. I learned a lot about both the process and the art.

"I like this one," my journalism professor said when I presented the portrait I took of my grandma sitting in her kitchen with the scarecrow clock. The class all stared at it for a while. "If you can capture her spirit, then you can capture anyone's spirit. You just haven't done that in the work you've been doing here."

I had to agree. My work had become sloppy and uninteresting. I was shooting the photos, but I wasn't getting to the humanity inside of them. Between my photojournalism class and my portrait class, I still had a lot to learn.

With only a few days left in the workshop, I wandered the city looking for "the shot," to no avail. I sat and had coffee, and as the café filled, I began to shoot the movement of the city, the commuters, the cars and taxis, the bicycles, the baby strollers. I stayed in that café until it was dark, walking past the cemetery on the way back to the dorms.

The cemetery was one of the oldest in the city and had survived the fate of having a freeway or an apartment building built over it. During the day, I cut through the graves to get to the 7-11 on the other side of campus. The gravestones were dated from the early 1800s, when Albuquerque was still part of the Wild West. It had been a hard life, I was sure.

This was the first time I'd walked through the cemetery at night. The moon was bright, illuminating all the gravestones in the older part of the cemetery. I pulled out my Nikon and framed what looked to be fireflies hovering over cracked gravestones. I had never seen anything like it. They danced for me and my camera in the moonlight.

When I went back to the photography studio the next day and developed my work, I was shocked to find the hovering flashes of light in the photographs. Some of the lights streamed, some just floated, but they were beautiful. The spirits had come to visit, and I was lucky that none of them wished me harm.

My professor took one look at my last images and told me they were "tragic, but in a good way," and wondered how I got that light to work in the cemetery. When I told him I did nothing to alter the light, he didn't believe me. He just laughed and gave me an A. I went home two days later with a box full of photographs to show Grandma, but the more I thought about it, the more I realized that my favorite photographs and stories would not be shared with her. She would be horrified if she knew where I had been.

MY GRADUATION WAS only a few months away when I realized that finding a job wasn't going to be easy. I'd known all along that it would be a miracle if I could find a way to make a living taking photographs. I applied everywhere: newspapers, local magazines. No jobs came my way. At graduation, all I could think about was how I was going to take care of Grandma and how we were ever going to fix up that house. Not that it mattered either way—Grandma didn't even want me back out on the reservation. I was going to have to figure out a way to maintain my life here and save money for Grandma.

FORENSIC PHOTOGRAPHER WANTED. That's how the ad started. They offered a salary, benefits, and quick certification. Forensics. It made me giggle. That has got to be the worst job for a Navajo, I thought, but a salary and benefits sounded like something I could get used to. I called the number, spoke to a gruff man who told me to come by the next morning about 9:00 A.M., then hung up abruptly. I drove out to Tohatchi to tell Grandma the good news.

Mr. Bitsilly and Grandma were sitting in her kitchen around some sweet rolls and steaming cups of coffee when I arrived. I brought my box of pictures, some fancy coffee, and a large sausage pizza from Godfathers Pizza—Grandma's favorite, all the way from Albuquerque. Mr. Bitsilly laughed and grabbed a huge slice to have with his coffee.

Grandma was furious about the job interview. "Why are you still obsessed with dead people?"

"And your ghosts? Have they been bothering you?" Mr. Bitsilly munched on his pizza. "Something like this could make it worse."

"It's not always going to be dead people. It's evidence, car crashes, investigations. Things like that. I'll be with the police, so I'll be safe."

"I don't know about that." Grandma looked out the window.

"Just be careful out there," Mr. Bitsilly spoke up. "And if you feel like something evil has you, send me your clothes and I will pray over them." He took another bite. "You can't bring those evil spirits back here to your grandma's house."

CHAPTER TWENTY-NINE

Nikon AF-S DX Zoom-Nikkor 55–
200mm f/3.5-5.6G IF-ED

Erma had no intention of letting me sleep. In my dream, I sat inside the Apothecary, like a quiet drunk at the end of the bar. The place was buzzing and classy, the sun just setting and pulling the deep light from the table candles into the outdoor patio.

I watched Erma take inventory from a supply room as a man with a blue duffel bag hanging over his shoulder came around the corner, startling her. She dropped a bottle of scotch on the floor, shattering the glass. He laughed and grabbed her around the waist.

"Come on, Matty." Erma squirmed out of his arms and moved to pick up the glass. "We're slammed tonight." She threw her bar towel at Matias and he kneeled down to scoop the glass and scotch into the trash.

"I'm sorry. When are you off?"

"I don't know," Erma said. "I told Mom I wouldn't be home too late."

"I'm leaving my bag here, babe." Matias shoved the duffle behind the racks of booze and margarita salts, then came out and kissed Erma on the forehead. "Don't work too hard."

Erma smiled and walked back to the bar. I watched her shelve more bottles and count money. The stool screeched as I propped myself up again, drawing Erma's gaze. She came over and looked me straight in the eye.

"Wake up!" she screamed. The air became cold around her breath.

I jolted up on Armenta's couch, my boots still on. It was freezing. The dream had felt too realistic, as if I had spent the night drinking at the Apothecary, headache included.

I could hear the roar of a tractor out in the front of the cabin. I folded Armenta's quilts on the couch, watching him maneuver his tractor on the snowy path. The sun had already begun to cast its rays through the valley, melting the fresh snow.

I stepped outside and trotted toward the comfort of my own car.

As the tractor rolled up to the last bit of driveway, it pulled hard to the left, and the gravelly hum of the engine stopped. Armenta jumped out of the warm cab, looked my way, and waved as I backed out of his driveway. I rolled my window down.

"I'm sorry. I didn't mean to wake you," he said. "I had to clear the way so I can go see my wife for breakfast."

"No need to apologize." I smiled. "Thank you so much for letting me stay. You're very generous."

"Be careful, Rita." He unfolded the collar of his coat up around his neck. "This whole thing with Garcia . . . it's better to not even get involved."

"Thank you, sir." I reached out my hand and he shook it. "I'll be careful."

ONCE I WAS home in my apartment, I yearned for sleep, but there was just so much to process. My mind whirled around everything Armenta had told me, all the things Garcia had done over the years. I never thought he would go so far as to be caught up in cartels and backdoor judicial extortion.

"You're not going to go to sleep, are you?" Erma perched next to me like a raven, stiff with urgency. "The more you find out, the more I can remember. You can't stop. Do you hear me, Rita? You can't stop."

My living room had gone cold. I had not even been here an hour, and Erma was already working on me.

"You were part of the whole thing, Erma." Her lies were making my headache worse. "Don't act like you didn't know what was going on."

"I wanted to make life better for my baby; is that so wrong? I can only hope that she is safe with my mom. They wouldn't really go after her, would they?"

"They went after you, didn't they?" Erma's rage was pulling on me. "They killed you and the baby you had inside you. They will kill whoever they want until you give them what they want."

Erma's fury and sadness hit like a brick. Her scream rang so loud and cold that I thought even Mrs. Santillanes would hear it—and every other tenant, for that matter. I curled myself into a ball on the sofa to escape it.

"Rita! Are you in there? Please tell me you're in there. It's me. Philip. Rita? Rita!"

I sat up, startled from the dream. I turned to look at my clock: 4:30. From the glimmer of light I saw coming into my window, I could only assume that meant 4:30 P.M.

The knocks on my door continued.

"What do you want, Philip?" I yelled.

"Rita, please open up." When I opened the door, Philip had his hands pressed together in supplication. "I'm really in a bind right now." As I turned, I could smell his cologne—thick and heavy as the taste it left in my mouth. He followed me in like a hungry puppy.

"Are you going to tell me what this is all about, or do I have to guess?" My patience was short. I took the one beer from my fridge and finished it in two gulps, then set the empty bottle on the counter. "I'm still recuperating, I guess."

"I have this huge client party tonight—lots of rich people, friends of the lady who bought that huge McMansion up on the mountain. She's very artsy. Anyway, the photographer I hired fell through. The hostess was insistent we have a photographer—the mayor is coming." He picked up the beer bottle to take a swig, then saw it was empty. "Are you working?"

"Not at the moment. I'm kind of on mandatory vacation."

"Oh, right." He stared dejectedly at the beer bottle.

"So, what? You need me to take pictures of your rich friends?"

"They're not really my friends. My clients. And I'll pay you. Fifteen hundred dollars. You can ride with me down there now. The party starts at six thirty."

"Fifteen hundred dollars?" I could use the money. "How many hours?"

"Six thirty to eleven o'clock," he said. "After that, everyone will be too drunk and sloppy to get their picture taken."

"Okay. Let me get ready." I steered him by the shoulders toward the door. "And can you get me something to eat . . . and something to drink? And get me one of your valiums, too."

He turned to me, surprised. I closed the door in his face.

It had been at least four years since I had taken pictures of people who were still alive. I had to remind myself about the rules of the living. I walked to my closet and pulled my ghost clothes from the hangers. Everyone who works behind the scenes anywhere has a set of ghost clothes—a pressed set of nice black pants, black shirt, black shoes, and black socks. When you wear this attire, no one notices you as you lurk in the shadows, taking pictures. They're not supposed to. You are not there. You are the flash of light that pulses from the darkness, the action of a finger on the button. That is how you get the best stuff, people smiling or having a quiet moment (hopefully somewhere with nice lighting or architecture in the background). I never liked staging people and giving them the option to know how to stand, how to look. They become self-conscious. The trick is to take the picture seconds before that moment, before they think about their teeth or their hair, while they are still spontaneous.

My camera bag was full—maybe I'd done a little too much planning. I brought four lenses, all my filters, two cameras. A quick, well-paying gig didn't come every day. I saw my huge 200 to 400 lens sitting by my computer and figured, why not?

As I put the lens in a second bag, a huge crash echoed from behind my bedroom door. I almost didn't want to see what it was, but curiosity got the best of me. One of Mrs. Santillanes's bottles of herbs had been shattered, random pieces of green settling into dresser tops, the gold lid still spinning on the wood floor. Erma wasn't there, but I knew it was her. I grabbed my two bags and headed out the door.

Mrs. Santillanes was in the hallway. "Are you okay? I heard a big crash coming from your place."

"I'm okay, Mrs. Santillanes."

"What was it?" she asked, but I think she already knew. Her little hands rubbed at her red rosary beads.

"It was one of your jars." I couldn't look at her. I just locked my door.

Mrs. Santillanes made the sign of the cross and pulled me

into a strong embrace. Thankfully, I heard Philip coming up the steps. It was time to go.

"I'll pray for you, *mija*." She looked worried. "Be careful."

"I HAVE BEEN kissing this lady's ass for the last six months," Philip told me as he steered wildly through the stacked sets of switchback turns that took us up the mountain. "I mean, I even drove her dog to the vet and bought her some Epsom salts on the way home. I'm her designer, for crying out loud. But I was good. I did what I was told, and we got this huge bid."

I never realized that they built houses that far up into the canyon, but apparently these people were so loaded they could have built on the moon. Philip explained that the Benavidez family, his biggest client to date, had spent over two million dollars decorating their house—nine bedrooms and nine baths. I needed to make sure to get Mr. and Mrs. Benavidez in pictures with every single influential person who was at that party. That was my job. To make them look glamorous, important, and connected.

"What exactly is it that Mr. and Mrs. Benavidez do for a living?" I asked.

"Something involving money and politics. But don't even ask. I'm in my boss's good graces right now, so don't mess that up, okay?"

"So, it's a politician party."

"Anyone who is anyone in this rotten little metropolis!" Philip pulled up to the front door. He pointed his manicured finger at me. "Don't make trouble."

"I know," I said. "I'm here to work."

The Benavidez mansion was gigantic, rising three stories above the sand and sagebrush, a perfect brown stucco that blended into the surrounding land. It was like a ranch house, except for the addition of a stucco skyscraper with cobalt blue windowpanes.

I sat in corners and stairwells, just inside doorways and right in front of windows. Everyone was dressed in tuxedos and evening gowns. The men had platinum cufflinks and the woman wore huge diamond rings that dug deeply into their flesh. Voices blended into a muffled drone, with the occasional whoop of fake laughter. I recognized people from the police department—the chief of police and county sheriff were there. Politicians, city and state officials, and local celebrities stood around sipping wine and picking finger food from silver platters. It was lovely. I took picture after picture of smiling faces, hands shaking, deals being made, promises being broken. After four hours, I had taken almost 1,500 photographs. A dollar a photo, I guess.

I caught sight of a spark through the window—a cigarette being lit. I let my addiction lure me out to the balcony.

"Excuse me, but can I get a cigarette from you? I'll pay you." I held out a dollar. The man just shook his head and handed me one. It was flat, as if it had been in his pocket all day. The man took a long drag off his stogie and stubbed it out in one of Mrs. Benavidez's glazed ceramic flowerpots. He smiled as he turned and went back inside, leaving me alone.

I enjoyed the night air in the silence of the canyon. I was almost done with the cigarette when a voice carried up from below me, hushed but clear as day, every word echoing in the high walls. Down by the temporary valet, away from the party, more voices began to gather.

"Who the fuck told you that it would be okay to add him?"

"Not here, man. This is not the place."

I hunched over the railing to take a peek. From what I could tell, there seemed to be three men dressed in tuxedos. Something about their body language, the way they stood together, felt dangerous. The sun was setting, so it was impossible to see their faces, but I had seen Martin Garcia's silhouette at enough crime scenes to recognize it anywhere. I'd spent four blissful hours not thinking about Erma Singleton, but now everything Armenta had told me came back to me in a rush.

"I don't care. I'm not going to be screwed on this." It was Garcia's voice. I was sure of it. "You said it was taken care of."

My heart pounding, I moved to grab my camera and telephoto lens. I peered back over the balcony, focusing on their faces. Garcia finally turned toward me, and I filled the frame with his face. I laid my finger on the shutter release, taking shot after shot of his face, then pulling out to get everyone else in there with him.

The men began to walk away, heading toward their cars. I took one last wide shot with all of them together.

It was that very moment that I saw it all happen: Garcia, at his car door, took four quick steps back toward one of the other men and shot him the back of the head. Even though he had a silencer, the hiss and thud of that man's life force filled the air. My auto shutter just kept clicking, breaking every second into its own frame of what was unfolding below. As I leaned dangerously far out on the balcony, my camera slipped from my hand, the flash hitting the railing and lighting up the entryway like a flare.

I hauled myself back up, my skin scraping against the stucco. There was no way they hadn't noticed the flash. I collected my gear in a hurry and headed toward the exit.

Philip spotted me and cut across the room. "Are we having a problem? It's not quite eleven o'clock." He tapped his watch.

"Philip, I need to leave right now." I was panicked. I started to look for a place to hide in case they came looking for me before I managed to escape the house.

"Okay. Rita. What's going on?"

"Let me borrow your car. I have to get out of here," I pleaded.

"My car?" Philip shook his head. "You know I'm not going to let you take the car."

I gave up and left him without a goodbye. I was out of breath by the time I made it to the bottom of the stairs. I slowly opened the huge oak door and stepped outside. No one was there. My head spinning, I searched the asphalt where I'd seen the cars parked just minutes before. I didn't know where they had put the body. I didn't see any blood. No cars. No Garcia.

I looked up into the dark sky to the balcony where I'd just perched and wondered what had happened. Had I imagined the whole scene? Was it one of Erma's vivid dreams?

I ducked into the shadows of the Benavidez's garage to fumble through my bags for my phone. That is when the man sat up from where he was dumped in the bushes, his face an explosion of flesh and blood.

The man turned and saw me ogling. "Did you see that? Did you see what just happened?"

I caught a better look of his wound. The gunshot had left a sizable star-shaped hole right at the bottom of his eye socket. The flesh was popped open like a blossom, the center filled with the white cloudy fluid of his now-deflated eyeball. The empty eye sack rested on top of his cheekbone like heavy, wrinkled skin. I stared in stunned silence, finally finding my phone at the bottom of my camera bag.

I dialed 911.

"Bernalillo County 911."

I gave the address. "We need to get some units over. There's been a shooting." I hung up the phone.

The ghost started to approach me. "You can see me?"

I tried not to react—tried to pretend I was looking past him. I recognized him, even with his eye blooming from his skull. It was Ignacio Marcos—the much-feared second-in-command of the Zambada drug cartel.

"Did you see what happened to me?" He wiped blood from his face with the back of his hand. "It was Garcia, wasn't it? Who else would do this to me?"

I needed out of this place as quickly as possible. I called Shanice's cell.

"Listen to me, you bitch," he screamed as I held the phone to my ear. "That fat fucker Garcia isn't getting it all. That wasn't the deal. They will kill us all."

His form lunged out, but his ghost fingers passed through my skin. Shanice's phone rang and rang, eventually rolling over to voice mail. I hung up and dialed again.

The ghost kept at it, limbs swinging through my body. "I know you see me. I can feel it. I can tell you are listening to every word!"

Finally on my third call she picked up.

"Hey! Philip said you're up there with the greaseballs!" She sounded so happy.

"Shanice, come and get me now," I begged. I could hear the approaching sirens.

"Rita, I'm not going anywhere tonight. Oh, and by the way, I'm at your apartment right now. I need to stay for a couple of days."

"If you don't come and get me right now, I will break your neck when I get home. Now, Shanice!"

"Okay, okay," she said. "What's the address?"

CHAPTER THIRTY

f/32

As I WAITED for Shanice, I hid from the awful ghost in the shadow of the stone wall that surrounded the mansion. While out of view, I watched a man with a blunt, straight jaw and giant shoulders come out of the oak door and walk straight to a limousine. As he popped the trunk, I recognized his face: Garcia's new partner, Detective Vargas. Another man in a tux stepped out of the limo and walked toward the bushes. The two men lumbered over and picked Ignacio Marcos's body up from behind the bushes. They clasped his arms and legs and easily threw him into their trunk with a thud. Both paused to look around for witnesses—for me. I crouched against the wall, ducking from shadow to shadow as quickly as I dared, trying desperately to put distance between myself and the scene of the murder.

By the time Shanice rounded the corner, I had run almost halfway down the hill. Her aging Mercedes wheezed to a stop.

"Hey, I thought we were going to the party." Shanice's red lips pressed together in disappointment. Her dress was the color of panic buttons.

I threw my cameras and bags into her backseat and slammed

the rattling doors. "Just get us out of here. Don't go up to the house."

"What's going on, Rita?" Shanice turned her car into a bus stop and drove us back down the hill, tagging the curb with her tire. "What did you do?"

"I just need to get somewhere with a computer." I looked back at the gate again, wondering if the ghost might still be trying to follow. I could only hope that the two men hadn't seen me either. I was in trouble.

Shanice pointed to her backseat. "My laptop is back here. Will that work?"

"Perfect. Let's get somewhere with Wi-Fi." I dug my phone from my pocket, hoping I'd saved Declan's number. The phone was dead.

There was a Satellite Coffee up on the north side of town, right as we came down from the foothills. The café was basically an adobe box with a giant neon coffee cup and a UFO on its sign, but they had free, semi-fast Wi-Fi and decent coffee and stayed open all night. I snatched Shanice's laptop out of the backseat and turned it on the moment we parked. I needed to put these images somewhere besides the original cards as soon as possible. It would be too easy to destroy this evidence if I carried the only copy.

"I need caffeine," Shanice said, reaching for her purse. "Come on, let's go inside."

"Can you get me something to go? I've got to sit here and pirate some Wi-Fi."

"Suit yourself."

Once the Wi-Fi was connected, I took the card out of my camera and clipped it into the laptop dock, bringing up 1527 images. I bypassed the handshaking and backslapping of the

Benavidez event and opened the last twenty-seven, which were so clear I had to look twice to make sure that my eyes were telling the truth.

They were.

The first was Garcia coming out of the party in a group of seven men, including Ignacio Marcos, the soon-to-be ghost. He was walking right behind Garcia, his arms and mouth in motion. Shot 1,527, the last shot, was a perfect photo of Garcia looking straight up at the camera and the blinding flash, right into the lens. That was the one that was either going to save me or kill me. I looked around, wondering if Garcia could be watching me right now. He couldn't be. Otherwise, I would be dead too.

I highlighted all the photos of the incident and pulled them to my Flickr account, then attached them to emails I'd send to three different accounts I maintained for alternate backups. The upload bar ticked slowly. Too slowly. I dug in my photo bag for Declan's card and composed an email to him with the relevant photos attached. I needed to get the photos to Angie and to Samuels—I needed to stop Garcia from taking this any further, and I needed to prove I wasn't insane. But would that be enough? These people were dangerous, and the police offered no protection. The emails finally went through. I popped the card out, put it back into its sleeve, and stared at it.

Shanice eased her way into her car and handed me my coffee. "I know you don't like all that fancy stuff, but I put some milk and sugar in it for you."

"Thank you." The computer whirred as I burned my tongue on the first sip. "Just right."

"So, can we go?" Shanice started her engine.

"Take me home," I said, wondering if that really would be a good idea.

"Oh, no you don't." Shanice touched up her red lipstick in the mirror. "You are going with me to the club tonight. I'm not wasting an entire outfit on some cruise to the coffee shop."

"Shanice. There was a shooting up at the Benavidez mansion."

"You shot somebody?" Shanice barked. "What are you getting me involved in?"

"I didn't shoot anyone, Shanice. But I took pictures of the whole thing. So I might not be the best person to be hanging out with right now." Sometimes Albuquerque was way too small a town. I knew these guys were going to be looking for me for a while.

"Are we, like, in fucking danger here? Don't you work for the police? Can't you just call them up and tell them?"

"I've seen a lot of things, Shanice. Things that I can't possibly describe to police without getting my throat cut."

Shanice sat in stunned silence. "Well, it wouldn't be the first time," she said at last. The two of us hadn't talked about our last debacle with the police in a while. "Please tell me you're not seeing ghosts again."

"Just get us out of here." I kept eyes on the road. "Get us somewhere they would never expect me to go."

Shanice was in front of the Lotus, her favorite club, within fifteen minutes. The music was pouring from the front doors, which were guarded by a menacing-looking pair of muscle-bound white guys in tight black T-shirts. There was a line already snaking around the building. I knew I looked completely out of place in my all-black getup, like Shanice's weirdo goth girlfriend. Great. Shanice dragged me right by the line of waiting hipsters, who sighed and complained as we passed. Shanice was like that, and the two giants at the front door knew better than to stop her.

Shanice trekked straight to the bar. "Two cosmos, please. Okay, maybe three. I get an extra since I might be on the verge of death."

"I don't want any of your foo-foo candy drinks, Shanice," I said. Then I told the annoyed-looking bartender, "Change mine to a scotch, please. And no one is going to die."

The Lotus was filled with the usual glitter and fishnets and giant Amazon women in stiletto heels. The bartenders, DJ, and waitresses were dressed in white angel wings and red vests with bowties. It was a very '80s club scene—the air was filled with the smell of smoke machines.

"Let's dance." Shanice writhed her red body in the darkness. "Oh, look!" She pointed to Philip, who was coming toward us.

"You left early so you could come here?" Philip laughed and poked me in the shoulder.

"No. I left to go home. But this one had to come here."

"Relax, Rita. Have some fun for once." Philip tried to make me dance. It didn't work.

The bartender set our drinks on the bar. I seized my glass and drank it down.

"Make sure she doesn't leave," Shanice said to Philip with a glare in my direction. I was famous for leaving early and without notice.

"I won't."

"Hey, you know there was a guy that came looking for you after you left. He was super built, you know, in great shape. A new love interest maybe?"

I felt the heat rise in my face, and not for the reason Philip imagined.

"He wanted me to tell him where our event photographer was. I told him you left. Then he wanted to know your name."

"And what did you tell him?"

"Nothing. Just that you're a friend. Then I was called away by the hostess."

"Can I have another, please?" The bartender glared at me but poured me a new glass. I was pissed and paranoid. I now knew for certain that Garcia and his men were looking for me. Maybe I had to worry about Philip too. "Did the police ever show up?"

"Police? You mean besides the chief of police?" Philip was already drunk.

"Yeah. Units. With the lights and everything. You know. The police," I said.

"Not while I was there. I left about fifteen minutes after you did. Why? What did you do?"

"Me?" I knocked down my second shot and turned to the bartender, who picked up the scotch bottle to pour me another.

"You sure do put that away."

The voice came from behind me. When I turned around there was no one there except a petite blonde waitress with her tray full of drinks.

"I never really liked scotch myself." Erma circled to stand in front of me. "You're wasting time, Rita. You have to fix this."

I pulled on my drink again and ignored her, closing my eyes.

"Don't try to pretend you don't hear me. I can bring everyone with me."

I opened my eyes and scanned the pulsing crowd, watched the ghosts lingering, unmoving, among the dancers. Two or three became five or six, then nine or ten. I recognized some of them: the young woman from the hotel room with her nightgown full of holes, Judge Winters's wife and kids. I turned my eyes to the ground as I felt the chill of their unhappiness leach into my bones. They would bleed me dry.

Philip's strong grip on my arm brought me back. "Come with us, Rita. Stop moping around." Philip retrieved a brown vial from his pocket. "Take a blast."

"A blast of what?"

"X." He opened the lid and shook the powder into the sniffer casing, then placed it under my nose. "Just relax, Rita. You need some sunshine."

I breathed in as deeply as I could and found the heat and burn of the powder on my tongue. I poured the last of my drink into my mouth and swished it out and down, closing my eyes until the sensation made me sway. When I opened them, they were gone: no ghosts, no voices, nothing except the warmth and happiness coursing through my body. Before long, I was part of the moving mass, absorbing the heat of all the other bodies around me, Shanice and Philip spinning me through the music, the alcohol and X cascading into my body, jockeying for position. I shut my eyes and let it happen, hoping to never come out of the haze. Garcia would never be able to come in here, I thought.

BY THE TIME we left the club in the early hours of morning, the warmth was fading. The X leaving my body felt like frost creeping over my insides.

"I'm so glad we got you out and about, Rita." Philip smiled.

"Yes, that's like twice in a week!" Shanice shivered with her arm through mine. I imagined the sensation was wearing off on her too.

"I'm starved!" Philip said. "How about the Frontier?"

The Frontier was one of the mainstays of the city. The steam, heat, and coffee smell always hit you in the face, especially in the winter. The walls and booths were designed in a '70s Old West style: lots of wagon wheels and orange pleather, scattered paintings of adobes, and a couple of giant John Wayne portraits. Its bathrooms were famously disgusting, full of broken mirrors, a lingering smell of ammonia, and years of smeared phone numbers.

Frontier was famous for its gigantic breakfast burritos that you could smother in their super spicy green chili salsa, and hot, heavily buttered cinnamon rolls that were bigger than your face. It was where every local wanted to go on Sunday morning. It was also located across the street from the university, which made it the place to go after a night of debauchery. It used to stay open all night long until some of the unruly bar crawlers ruined it for us, fighting, pulling guns, and acting like fools. Now it closed in the evening and opened again for breakfast at five, when the bar hoppers were passed out cold.

Philip stood in line at the counter while Shanice and I found ourselves a booth by the window. Blue shadows of buildings stretched from east to west on the sidewalks. City buses hissed and roared, dropping off just as many people as they were picking up. Shanice was looking tired, her red lipstick gone, and her dress wrinkled and sweaty as she rested her head in her hands. It was a usual morning for her.

Someone banged on the window.

"You have to help me, goddammit, Rita." Erma. "You must help my daughter, my mother. Who knows who they will come after next, Rita! You have to help us. Right now. All of us. Do you understand what I'm saying to you?"

"Rita. Are you okay? Rita?" Shanice was shaking my arm. "Rita. What are you looking at?" Shanice turned in her seat and stared right at Erma. "I haven't seen you like this since we were kids."

I refocused on Shanice. "I guess I'm still rolling a bit." I was hoping the stuff that Philip gave me had gotten rid of the ghosts, but now they were here, closing in around me.

Judge Winters, his wife, and son stood beside Erma Singleton, staring at me. The wife held the baby in her arms. Their wounds were visible to me: the boy with his head pulled open, his mother with the bullet hole in her face, and the baby with the exit wound right below her eye.

"Her name is Rita," Erma spat. "She's the one that takes pictures of us when we're dead. Hey, Rita, remember me? Remember how you haven't even tried to help me out? Do you remember that?" I tasted Erma's hate and smelled the death coming from her gray skin.

"Now what?" Shanice turned around, trying to see what I was looking at, as the ghosts moved through the window and surrounded the booth.

"Listen to us." Judge Winters bent to meet my eye. "We will stay here until all you smell is the rotting of our flesh."

"Wow, girl. You must be tripping." Shanice waved her hand in front of my face. "Rita? Come back to us, Rita."

Philip stood at the table with our food and stared at me. He moved into the spot next to Shanice and passed around our orders. "Is she still lit?" He shook my arm lightly. "Are you okay, Rita? Take too much? Oh, God. Maybe we gave her too much."

A thin bead of blood tickled my lip. I knew there were more to come. I couldn't handle the anticipation, so I scanned the room. The booth behind me was full of ghosts, faces lost and eyes piercing. On the far left was a patchwork of body parts, held together with portions of torn clothing. Erma, as only I would recognize her.

"Listen to the man, Rita," her corpse gurgled. "I'm done playing nice for you."

Then there was the Indian man—the frozen bench-sleeper I'd photographed a few days before my suspension. He sat in the booth too, silent and blue, just like he had been that night.

"I'm surprised that you are seeing us," the man said. "Are you Navajo?"

"Yes." I realized I had said that out loud.

"Yes, what?" Shanice grabbed my shoulder. "Come on, Rita. You need to eat. Try and bring yourself down. Come on, take a bite." She dipped a napkin in her ice water and rubbed the blood beneath my nose.

Philip shook his head. "Remind me not to ever give you a blast again. I don't think it agrees with you."

I turned to the booth once more, but the ghosts had been replaced by a living family who stared at me in return, the youngest one clenching her mom's arm like a snake wrestler.

"See, now you're scaring children." Philip spoke with his mouth full.

"You're a Navajo that can see ghosts?" The Navajo's ghost was suddenly at the table adjacent to us.

"Shut up," Erma barked at the man. "When are you going to help us?"

I tried to concentrate on Shanice and Philip across the table, raising a fork full of tortilla and chili into my mouth. I chewed quickly and took a sip of my coffee. My head spun and I watched blood splatter in star shapes on the linoleum.

"Rita, your nose again." Shanice handed me a wad of napkins. "Oh my God."

"I definitely gave you too much. My bad." Philip scooped another mouthful.

"Rita. Help them. Help them so you can go home." I knew that voice. It was Gloria. There she was, sitting right next to me in the booth, her skin smooth and soft, and her hair shiny and long. "Rita, can you hear me?"

I felt myself smiling.

"There she is." Shanice raised her coffee mug. "Philip, I think she's coming out of it."

"Oh, thank God. I was beginning to think you were brain damaged."

A huge thud forced me to jump from my seat and step away from the table. Philip and Shanice looked up at me, terrified. I watched Judge Winters's ghost slam his fists into the table a second time, so hard that the potted flowers and macramé slings around the table rocked back and forth. "Help us!"

Philip and Shanice stared at me, stunned by their moving plates. I had to get out of there. I hightailed toward the exit.

"Rita! Where are you going?" Philip called after me. "Rita!"

I didn't look back. My body was exhausted in the worst of ways, but something pushed me on and kept one leg moving in front of the other. I ran full force through traffic, between cars and the morning rush of business owners and students, all the way home to Downtown Village.

When I reached the top floor, my door was already open. Mrs. Santillanes came rushing out of her apartment.

"*Mija*. Oh my goodness, I'm so happy to see that you're okay. So happy."

"What happened?"

"I don't know, *mija*. I just heard the police here early this morning banging on your door. It was still dark outside, so it woke me. I was dreaming about my husband. Bless his soul."

"Did they say what they wanted?"

"No. They eventually knocked the door in. They made such a ruckus. I didn't dare come out. And neither did anyone else."

We both looked toward my apartment. The lock was broken and the frame of my door was splintered. The apartment was completely torn apart. Every shelf was empty, every drawer pulled out and dumped on the floor. Three of my cameras, including the very first one I owned, sat by my workstation, shattered into a million pieces. My computer screen blinked, cracked right through the center. My digital archive was missing from my desk, and all the memory cards and backups were gone. Every photograph on my walls had been pulled down and torn apart, even my prints of home and my giant photo of Grandma. There was not one thing that had escaped untouched. I couldn't even cry.

"Oh, *mija*. I didn't know they were doing this." Mrs. Santillanes took out an egg from her apron, rubbed it on her chest, and began praying in Spanish.

"It's okay, Mrs. Santillanes," I said. "I don't want you to get involved. As a matter of fact, you better get home right now." I had to leave, and quick. I had a feeling the police would come looking again since they didn't find what they came for in the first place. Me.

"Shall I call the police?"

"No. Just get home and lock your doors."

"Be careful, *mija*." Mrs. Santillanes stood by the door. "If I hear anything crazy, I'm calling."

In my bedroom closet, behind some sweaters I never wore, was a small door that I had made. I looked inside to find my other cameras still hiding there, along with a box of negatives of Mom's pictures. Most importantly, my mom's camera was untouched, as were my four backup hard drives. I pulled the cards from the camera I'd used at the party and hid them with a box of negatives, then put the drives right back where they were. When

I came down from my perch and shut the door, I almost had a heart attack.

"Oh my God!" Shanice and Philip were standing at my bedroom door. "What in the hell happened here? Did you do this, Rita?"

"No. I didn't do this. What the hell do you think?"

"Well, you were still flying high back there. You went sprinting into fucking traffic. Jesus, Rita! What in the hell is going on?"

"I'll explain on the way while you drive me to the station," I said.

"Wait, I thought you got fired?" Shanice said as she and Philip followed me out.

It was just before 9 A.M. when we pulled out of the Downtown Village parking lot. "So, where are you staying?" Philip stared at me through the rearview mirror. "You can't stay at your place. Did you call the police?"

"No. I guess calling the people who want to kill me didn't cross my mind."

"How do you know it's them?" Shanice turned in her seat. "Don't you work for them?"

"Listen. I used to work for the police. They found out about me. That's all."

"What do you mean they found out about you?" Shanice hesitated. "You mean they know about the ghost thing?"

"The ghost thing? What the hell is that?" Philip rounded the corner.

"Kind of." I looked out of the windows nervously.

"Jesus, Rita. The nosebleeds. I didn't even think."

"What is this ghost thing? Dammit. Someone tell me what in the hell is going on!"

"Nothing," I said. "Just take me to the station. I'll let you know more once I figure this out. If I don't call you by tonight, something might have happened to me."

THE STATION WAS quiet for an early morning. I walked in the front door like I always did. Angie was at her desk, on the phone. She hung up when she saw me and rose.

"Rita. What are you doing here?" She looked angry.

"Angie. I have to talk to you."

"Garcia filed a warrant for you last night," she said. "Obstruction of justice. He says you may have ruined an investigation that he's been working for over three years."

"He hasn't been investigating anything. He's been committing crime after crime in this town just to cover himself. He's so involved in everything that I can't begin to tell you where this starts." I hoped that Angie wouldn't have me locked up at the state hospital after this.

Angie crossed her arms. "Do you have any idea what you're saying? The accusations you are making?"

"I understand," I said. "He's a murderer, a drug runner, and a liar. I've been watching him for a while. I spoke with Armenta and the ME. I'm piecing it all together. I already tried to turn some of this over to Internal Affairs."

"Wait a minute. Are you investigating this? Rita, you're not a police officer."

"Please hear me out. Erma Singleton, Judge Winters—all of it is connected."

Angie's face was lit with fury. "Does this have to do with the fucking ghosts?"

"It's all in your emails, Angie. You don't have to take my word. Look for yourself—it's all in there."

"Rita. Am I going to need to take you into custody until we clear this all up?"

"Custody?" I looked at the door. "You can't take me into custody. Garcia is going to kill me. You should see what he did to my apartment. He killed someone last night, Angie." I felt my blood drop into my shoes and could only contemplate how many hours I had left before he or someone from the cartel had me buried in the desert.

"Having you here could be the safest thing for you." Angie moved toward the door. "You stay here."

As soon as Angie was out of earshot, Erma's ghost took Angie's chair. "That has got to be the stupidest thing I've ever heard. Why are you coming to the police? Aren't they in on this?" Erma rocked in the chair.

"I'm doing this for you so you'll leave me alone once and for all. You want justice? Then he needs to be thrown in jail." I looked around, wondering if anyone heard how loud I was shouting. "I'm doing everything I can, Erma."

"I didn't say anything about throwing that bastard in jail." Erma stood. "He can go straight into the ground—it would make me just as happy."

Angie returned and sat at her desk, studying me silently for a moment, then dialed up a number and put the call on speakerphone. It rang twice.

"Detective Garcia here."

Angie put her finger over her lips. Erma and I stayed quiet.

CHAPTER THIRTY-ONE

1/22

"I NEED YOU to tell me what happened up at the Benavidez mansion last night," Angie said.

"A lovely party, Sergeant."

Erma and I looked at each other.

"You know what I'm talking about, Garcia. You're accusing one of my specialists of obstructing justice. I need to know what happened."

"You mean she's back on duty? I thought you suspended her. I don't see how she can be considered a part of this force. She's delusional."

"Whatever Specialist Todacheene needed to be put on leave for is none of your business. Now, explain to me these charges."

"She was up at the Benavidez party last night and almost blew our cover on the Pino case. I want those photos."

"She was working on non-police business last night," Angie said. "What does that have to do with your investigation?"

"Well, I don't know for sure until I see them. If she turns them over, I'll drop it. She's putting my cases in jeopardy."

"I had a visit with IA yesterday about an investigation they're starting. Do you know anything about that?"

A long silence. Then: "I have no idea."

"I think we're going to have to close the Pino investigation. Your case is—"

"That's unnecessary," Garcia interrupted her. "We're close."

Sergeant Seivers must have been hot with rage at being interrupted. She said, "Tell me about it, Garcia. I haven't heard you give a coherent report in months."

"We've staked out Pino's and we're about to shut it down."

"How is Judge Winters's case connected to this? How about that vic on the freeway, Singleton? Tell me what is going on."

"We've been on the Pino case for a while, and all of this is linked to them." Garcia raised his voice. "Why? You think since I'm a Mexican, I must be dirty? I'm the one who can't be trusted? Even after the Marcos bust?"

"Something is going on and I don't like it. The department needs your reports on these investigations. If we don't receive them, we'll take your badge and turn you over to IA."

"We'll close the case tonight if we have to." He hung up.

I knew that whatever Garcia was going to do to close his case wasn't going to be good for me.

Angie looked at me and put on her glasses, her hand working her mouse on the computer.

I watched the images popping up on her screen in the reflection off her lenses.

"These were last night?" She kept scrolling. "I'll call Garcia back to the precinct."

"He's never coming back to this precinct," I said. "He's either going to jail or he's going to die."

"Either way, Rita, you need to stay out of this." Angie

stood. "You stay right here." She pointed at me. "For your own safety."

Erma laughed. "Yeah, lady. Whatever you say."

Angie exited her office, heading toward the crime lab. When she was out of sight, I walked right out of the precinct and called a cab, Erma's ghost at my heels.

CHAPTER THIRTY-TWO

f/16

THE MORNING TRAFFIC in downtown Albuquerque was stifling. I directed the cab through a few alleys, dodging trash bins and the occasional residents of cardboard houses.

"I can't believe it took me this long to see the big picture." Erma sat propped up in between the front seats. "All this time it was the cop."

"You didn't know Garcia?" I doubted this, remembering what Armenta had to say about her involvement. "You were moving drugs right alongside Matias. You can't tell me you didn't know what was going on."

"Matias was helping me and my daughter make a life for ourselves."

"I don't believe that, Erma."

The driver looked at me through the rearview mirror suspiciously, wondering who I was talking to. I put my earbuds in to quell the staring.

"Matty was on his way out of the business." Erma's voice cracked. "He told me about Pino's and about what they did, but he also told me it was being shut down because there was too much attention. Some of their connections were turning on each other. He never told me their connection was a cop."

"Erma, you told me that someone came to see you. Do you remember who it was?"

Erma sat next to me now, her white eyes staring out the window. "It was Cedric from Pino's. They were so angry when Matty got popped. It was the end of their partnership."

My phone buzzed. Mrs. Santillanes. My heartbeat accelerated with fear.

"Are you okay, Mrs. Santillanes?" The cab turned up toward Central Avenue.

"*Mija*, your grandma is here with her friend. They just saw your apartment and they're scared—"

Grandma was on a phone before she could finish her sentence. "We couldn't stay away, Rita." I could hear Mr. Bitsilly singing in the background. "We just saw your apartment. What is going on, Rita?" I hadn't heard that terrified tone in my grandma's voice in years.

"I'm on my way, Grandma. Stay in Mrs. Santillanes's apartment until I get there."

When we finally rounded the corner to my apartment, I saw Grandma's old pickup sitting in the handicap space. One thing I didn't see: Garcia's unit.

"We don't have time to stop, Rita." Erma pounded on the seat. "We have to find what they're looking for. You have to help me find it."

"I have my own crisis. I have an extremely unfriendly cop looking for me, and my grandma is next door to the first place he will look."

The cab driver stared at me like I was crazy. I handed him some money, then ran up my steps as fast as I could.

"There you are." Mrs. Santillanes pulled me inside her apartment.

Grandma hugged me tight. "We thought something had happened to you."

"Look at you, Rita; you look terrible." Mr. Bitsilly walked up to me, staring straight into my eyes, then grasped my shoulders. "You just couldn't stay away from it." He shook his head and hugged me just as hard as Grandma. "We should have brought you home."

"Thank you for helping them," I said to Mrs. Santillanes.

She glanced at the three of us and pressed her finger to her lips. "Shhhh," she said as she peeked out the peephole. She moved to the side just in time for me to see two officers make their way up the stairs and look through my splintered door.

"They must have seen you." Mrs. Santillanes placed her fingers on her lips again. "Those two have been waiting for you to come back all day." She walked us into her kitchen and put the kettle on the fire. "Rita, it wasn't safe to come back here."

I watched the cops turn and retreat down the steps. "They're gone now."

"What are they looking for, Rita?" Mr. Bitsilly asked.

"Some photographs." I looked at the three of them, their eyes on me like a weight. "It's too late. I've turned them over. Now they probably just want me dead."

Grandma began to cry. I shouldn't have said it.

"I've been here praying for you." Mrs. Santillanes pointed to her altar, which lit up the entire corner of her kitchen. Burning candles and bundles of sage ringed a small photograph of me and a larger saint candle that sat closest to the wall. The saint was a woman with dark coils of hair and a smooth, peaceful face. There were also various trinkets and a small handwoven basket in which lay an egg cushioned by dried herbs. I had not seen this before.

"What is going on here?" Mr. Bitsilly pointed at the altar.

"Those are my prayer candles. It's the altar I made for Rita."

"Who is this saint?" Grandma looked at the candle.

"That's Saint Veronica, the patron saint of photographers," Mrs. Santillanes explained. "She is the woman who saw Jesus struggling with the cross and offered him her veil to wipe the blood from his face. Are you Catholic?"

"I am," Grandma admitted.

"I am not." Mr. Bitsilly reached into the pouch around his neck. He took a pinch of herbs from inside and sprinkled it on the candles. We watched the flames flicker and grow. "But I'm willing to believe anything to keep you safe."

"Wow. They really have you pegged." Erma sat on Mrs. Santillanes's kitchen counter, but I refused to look at her. "We have to go, Rita."

I went to the door and looked out. No one was waiting. I turned. "I must take care of this. I know you're scared, but I'll be okay. I'll be back, I promise." I saw Grandma's truck keys on Mrs. Santillanes's table and snatched them.

"You can't." Grandma lunged at me in a panic, but Mr. Bitsilly held her back.

"We're going to pray for you, *mija*." Mrs. Santillanes made the sign of the cross. "It's going to take all of us to bring you home."

CHAPTER THIRTY-THREE

f/11

I WASN'T SURE where I was going, but I had a feeling I'd had that dream about Erma and the Apothecary for a reason, even if Erma didn't know what the reason was. Erma took over her perch in the passenger seat of Grandma's truck. She looked like a small child. "Can we go to my house? I just want to make sure that my mom and my little girl are all right."

"That is dangerous, Erma." I stopped at the light.

"I never told anyone where my mom lives. She always comes to my house."

I didn't want to go there. We didn't know if I was being followed. But I said anyway, "Where is it?"

Erma's mom lived in the older part of town in a nice town-house with a short white picket fence around the perimeter. Erma guided me with a pointed finger, the urgency of the moment trapped in her throat. I drove by slowly, trying to take notice of who or what could be watching us. There was not a parking spot in sight. I pulled up across the street in front of a red curb marking a fire hydrant. I glanced at Erma, finally quiet, staring out the window.

We watched as people in black walked in and out of Erma's childhood home. I recognized Erma's mother from the dream. She stood by the front door, smiling slightly as guests shook her hand, offering their condolences. We had somehow managed to show up to Erma's wake. What were the odds? I wondered if Erma had known.

A little girl came out of the house with a plate full of carrots. We watched her hand a carrot to another little girl who was sitting on the porch by Erma's mother.

"There she is." Erma was raw with grief. Her weightless body began moving toward the house.

"Erma, stop." I said the words out loud, which startled me momentarily. But there was no stopping Erma, so I gave in and followed her. I felt horrible for her. It didn't matter to me anymore that she had dragged me into all of this. I saw the depth of her love for that little person sitting on that porch in a black dress, eating carrots on her grandmother's lap. In a trance, I followed Erma's ghost up the steps to her own wake.

"Mrs. Singleton?" I recognized the voice coming up from behind me and whirled around.

Garcia was staring right at me, even as he spoke to the grieving mother.

"I am so sorry for your loss, Mrs. Singleton. I'm Detective Garcia, with APD. I investigated your daughter's case, along with my partner, Detective Vargas." Vargas, silent as ever, nodded. I was frozen as Garcia gestured toward me. "This is Rita; she is with our crime lab. Isn't that right, Rita?"

My heart in my throat, I offered Mrs. Singleton my hand and she squeezed it. "I'm Rita Todacheene with the crime lab, ma'am. I am so sorry for your loss." Erma's ghost was sobbing at my side, her longing for her daughter palpable. I was relieved she didn't try to reach out and embrace the child—I couldn't handle any more heartbreak and anger from her.

Mrs. Singleton was still holding my hand, and squeezed it again. "Are you all still investigating what happened to my daughter?"

"Yes, ma'am." I glared at Garcia.

"There is no way my baby jumped off that bridge." Mrs. Singleton's voice rose. "Do you hear me?" Guests on the other side of the porch turned to stare.

"We understand, ma'am," Garcia muttered. "We didn't mean to upset you during this difficult time."

"Thank you, Mrs. Singleton." I shook her hand again. "Again, I'm so sorry for your loss."

I couldn't linger for Erma—I needed to get the hell out of there. But where could I go? Heart pounding, I turned toward Grandma's truck. I could feel Garcia's malevolence behind me, the heat of his fear drilling into my back. He caught up to me quickly. Vargas grabbed my arm and spun me toward him. Erma's ghost flickered in front of her mother's house, her little girl dancing in circles around her. Vargas's gun pressed into the bottom of my ribcage.

"Your big fucking mouth is about to get you into trouble. Get in the car."

Vargas's gun dug in as he guided me toward their car, pushing me headfirst into the backseat. He climbed in next to me as Garcia got into the driver's seat and pulled out, looking at me in the mirror. They were going to kill me.

"So where are the pictures?" Vargas's voice was a dull whisper.

"You can talk? I was beginning to wonder." I was going to die. Maybe humor might buy me a few minutes.

Vargas stabbed me again with his gun. I felt my ribs cramp. Maybe not.

"Not really a time to be a smartass, Rita." Garcia swerved into traffic.

"I left them at the station." I lied. I could feel my phone vibrating in my pocket. My hope that no one else noticed lasted about half a second.

"Answer it," Garcia ordered. "Put in on speakerphone."

"Hello, Rita here." I could feel that this phone call wasn't going to make any of this better.

"Rita, this is Lieutenant Declan, Internal Affairs." Declan cleared his throat. Garcia glared at me in the rearview mirror. "I received your email. I'm here with Sergeant Seivers. I was hoping to talk to you here at the station about these photos you turned over. Sergeant Seivers told me she was holding you here, but you left." Vargas pressed the barrel harder. "Rita? Did I lose you?"

"No. I'm here. I can come and speak with you later—I'm driving right now."

"Your photographs, Specialist Todacheene." He paused. "We need to talk to you about what you saw."

"I know," I said. Garcia was grinding his teeth, his jaw clenched. "I had some things to take care of, personal business. I can come by the precinct later today."

Garcia shook his head and narrowed his eyes as he watched me through the mirror.

"Are you okay?" Declan waited for me to reply, and when I didn't, he said, "Sergeant Seivers is concerned for your safety."

"I'm fine." I side-eyed Vargas and his gun.

"Okay, well, we're heading down to the courthouse to get a search warrant for Pino's Upholstery. We're hoping to seal that up by tonight, but we can talk tomorrow."

"Take her phone, Vargas." Garcia was livid.

Vargas stopped my call and chucked my phone on the seat next to Garcia, who rolled down his window and tossed it out into traffic. The street he turned onto looked familiar. When we slowed in front of the Apothecary, I recognized it at once from Erma's dream.

"Now, you're going to tell me everything you know. Starting with where my product is."

"Product?" I played dumb.

"About one million dollars' worth." Garcia pulled into the alley behind the delivery doors. "And you're going to help me find it. If we don't find that shit tonight, we're going back to that old lady's house and tearing the place apart until we find it."

Garcia got out of the car as Vargas jerked me out of the backseat with his thick hands. I knew that I should be scared about what was happening to me. Instead, I was angry. I wanted revenge and I wanted answers. Vargas jerked me through the back corridors of the old building, the walls below still decorated like the '20s and '30s, all brick and exposed pipe. I could hear Garcia breathing.

"Was it you that pushed Erma Singleton off the bridge last week?" I looked at Garcia.

Vargas pulled me closer and pressed the elevator button.

If Garcia was affected by my revelation that I knew how Erma had been murdered, he didn't let on. "With my bad back? Do you really think I could throw that fat cunt off a bridge?" Vargas and Garcia laughed. "Now Vargas here, he's young and strong. And he's a good man—does as he's told."

"I bet he does." I couldn't help but say it, but I should've known it would come with consequences. Vargas tapped my forehead with the butt of his gun. The sting was immediate—a straight line of blood rolled down my face.

Garcia reached into his breast pocket for his handkerchief. "Clean yourself up."

I dabbed at the blood, feeling the bump rising as we exited the elevator of the Hotel Parq Central. The hotel was a former hospital, first for TB patients, then railway workers, and finally a mental hospital for children. Remnants of the hospital were showcased in the long hallway leading to the Apothecary— old medical equipment, maps, and clothes from the era were propped up behind glass. I remembered hearing stories of ghosts in the building, voices whispering or an apparition wandering the halls. I could feel the heaviness of the place, the sick souls that remained inside its walls.

The bar was as bustling with the lunch crowd as it had been in my dream. We headed straight to the bartender, Vargas still gripping my arm.

"Can I help you?"

Garcia pulled his jacket back to show the badge on his waist-band. "Can you show me where the storage room is?"

The bartender looked at Garcia's badge and pointed to the back of the building. Garcia led us down the same hallway I had seen Erma take during my dream. The room was deep, rows of tall metal shelves packed with boxes and bar supplies. I hadn't seen exactly where Matias had put the bag, although I remembered it was toward the back of the room. But there was just an old medical sink in the corner.

"You're sure it's here?" Vargas was shoving aside boxes, his hold on me loosening in the heat of his search.

Garcia moved methodically along the rows, bending to peer into shadows. "Matias said it was."

"How do you know he told you the truth?" I piped up.

Garcia straightened up to level a look at me across the shelves.

"Because he knows what happens to people who lie to me. He knows I keep my promises."

I wondered if Erma had been one of his promises. I wondered if Garcia had threatened the rest of Matias's family too. "He's gonna kill you when he gets out."

"No, he won't." Garcia stopped right where I was standing and crouched to open the blue cupboard below the sink and remove the duffle bag. "He's dead. It's really easy to take care of that when they're in the *pinta*." Garcia brought his face close to mine. "You're fucked." He looked at Vargas. "Take her to the car. I'm taking whatever they left in the lockbox."

Vargas wrenched me down the hall toward the elevator.

"What do you need me for, Vargas?" I struggled to pull my arm away. "Let me go." Vargas just laughed. He was way too strong for me to fight.

I tried to think about what I could do to prevent my impending demise. As we turned down the hallway, I saw there was a couple waiting at the elevator bank. This was my moment, my chance to escape.

"Let go of my arm!" I shrieked over their conversation. "He's trying to hurt me!"

"Is there a problem?" The man broke away from his date to take a confrontational stance by Vargas. The elevator bell rang.

"There's no problem here," Vargas was saying, "This woman is under arrest." In that moment I heaved myself away from him with all my strength, wrenching my arm out of his grip. I ducked under the man's arm and into the elevator, desperately seeking the close door button and punching it with one shaking finger. I watched the man bodycheck Vargas, who was still shouting that he was a police officer. The last thing I saw was the woman's round eyes on me as the doors slid blessedly closed.

My heart pounding, I listened to the elevator bell ding past each floor. What were the odds that it didn't stop again before reaching the bottom? Or that Vargas didn't extract himself and beat me down the stairwell? Should I get off before the bottom? Or risk making a run for it? At least on the street there would be witnesses.

When the doors opened again on the ground floor, I didn't give myself time to feel grateful for my reprieve. I took off down Central Avenue, sprinting until I couldn't breathe.

With Ignacio Marcos and Matias Romero dead, Cedric Romero was the only one standing in the way of Garcia taking the entire cut. He stole Erma from her mom and her child, endangered me and all I ever cared about in my life—my grandma, Mr. Bitsilly, Mrs. Santillanes, Shanice, and Philip. It didn't matter if IAB was investigating Garcia, if Angie Seivers finally believed me— my photos were no protection against his revenge. How could I trust the law enforcement machine to stop and prosecute a dirty cop—or, as a lot of officers would see it, to turn on one of their own, who had risked his life going up against some of the most dangerous criminal entities in the United States? Even if Garcia went to jail, I would never be safe from his network of influence. Justice would never be enough. I was never going to escape this until Garcia was dead.

I had one last idea: I needed to get to Cedric Romero. He needed to know that Garcia was going to kill him, to erase the Marcos cartel from the entire equation. My legs ached, but I wasn't far from Pino's Upholstery.

As I rounded the corner on Broadway, a city bus screeched to a stop in front of me. I never in my life had been so happy to see the bus. I got on and sat in the first seat, dripping with sweat even in the winter air. I could feel everyone on the bus staring at me.

"Are you all right, miss?" The bus driver looked at me in his mirror. "Do we need to call anyone?" I felt a tickle on my brow as blood oozed from the bump on my forehead. I couldn't even speak. "You just hold on there, young lady, I can call dispatch."

"Just get me to Fourth Street." I wiped the blood away with my sleeve. "I can get help."

Cedric Romero was the last thing holding Garcia back from getting his big payday from the Sinaloa Cartel. I was riding the bus to Garcia's next murder.

CHAPTER THIRTY-FOUR

Pino's Upholstery was farther down Fourth Street, at the northern end of a long-forgotten neighborhood. The cinder block and stucco building stood wedged between houses on one side and the railroad tracks on the other. When the bus stopped at Fourth and Hannett, I headed toward the exit.

"Get some help, young lady," the bus driver said. "I'm still calling dispatch."

The doors hissed shut behind me. A few rusted cars from the '50s and '60s sat in the upholstery shop's parking lot, along with a few lowriders and chopped pickup trucks. I knocked on the heavy metal door until a man opened it, a gun tucked into the front of his pants.

"Are you Cedric Romero?" I asked.

"Who in the hell are you?" He put his hand on his pistol.

"A friend of Erma Singleton. I have some information."

Cedric didn't let me finish. He pulled the gun from his waist and waved me in. "Inside."

The old shop was smoky with marijuana. A few gangster-types

hung around the counter and weathered tables. Music blasted from a stereo.

"Turn that shit off," Cedric shouted, and the room immediately went silent. "What do you want?" he said to me.

"I know who killed your family."

Around the dingy room, dangerous men shifted in their chairs.

"Who the fuck are you? I thought you were friends with Erma. She's dead. You know that, right?"

"I swear I'm telling the truth. I work at the crime lab."

Cedric cocked his gun. "You're a fucking cop?"

I hadn't thought this through, clearly. "Please, just let me prove it to you."

"What are you going to prove to me?" Two of his goons had circled behind me.

"I can prove that it was Garcia who killed your uncle Ignacio."

Cedric let his pistol drop to his side. "That fat fuck wouldn't dare."

"Let me show you." I pointed to an old computer sitting dusty on the shop desk.

Cedric kept his gun on me as I signed into my Flickr account and pulled up my work files. He leaned over my shoulder. The photos loaded slowly, filling Cedric's face with hollow light.

The photos came up one by one, unfolding the series of events that took place at the Benavidez mansion. The twentieth image: his uncle falling. Then the twenty-sixth image: Garcia's face.

"I took these photographs of Garcia killing your uncle at the Benavidez mansion two nights ago. He is taking out everyone associated with this deal. He had Erma Singleton killed, too. And Judge Harrison Winters and his whole family." Cedric's gun hand began to shake with rage, and the muzzle was pointed right at me. But I wasn't afraid anymore.

There was an echo as the front door of the upholstery shop slammed shut. Garcia and Vargas stood at the entrance with their guns drawn. Cedric returned the action. His crew stood from their stools, their crusty couches, all with guns drawn.

"Garcia, you're gonna die," Cedric said.

"She doesn't know what she's talking about." Garcia aimed his gun at me. "We don't need her anymore." He pulled the trigger twice.

CHAPTER THIRTY-FIVE

f/5.6

WHILE I LAY on the floor of Pino's Upholstery, I could hear Mr. Bitsilly singing so hard and so loud that his voice resonated in my skin. His throat was becoming raspy, his handkerchief soaked with sweat. Grandma and Mrs. Santillanes prayed alongside his songs. They were ashen-faced. I watched it unfold like a fly on the wall, desperate to yell for help, to make myself heard. I could feel their fear pounding through my veins.

"Something is wrong," Mr. Bitsilly was saying. "Something is wrong with Rita." His nose began to bleed. He struggled to rise to his feet.

A knock at the door. "It's the neighbors. Rita's friends." Mrs. Santillanes opened the door for Philip and Shanice.

Shanice was shivering, her wet hair dripping on her shirt. "Have you seen Rita?" She noticed Mr. Bitsilly dabbing his mouth with a wet paper towel. "Is that blood?"

Deep in my mind, I watched Mr. Bitsilly step out of the apartment and through the yellow tape belting my doorway. He shuffled his feet through the pieces of my life. He sang as loud as he could and spread smoke and prayers into every inch of my space. Mrs. Santillanes followed him, gripping her rosary, praying in a whisper. Grandma prayed beside her. They stood together, the one source of warmth that now had them breathing clouds of mist into the cold air that filled my apartment. Philip and Shanice huddled together and watched the windows cloud into ice.

Edwin Bitsilly sang until he tasted blood in his mouth. He sang until we were staring at each other across the impossible void, until he could see my bleeding body lying next to frayed gray mops and a metal bucket. He pushed his voice into that room and his breath into me.

CHAPTER THIRTY-SIX

I woke up on the floor of Pino's Upholstery in excruciating pain. I could feel the pulsing hole in my thigh emptying onto the concrete and another wound on my side that went right through me. In my direct line of sight were Garcia and Cedric's feet. I tried my best to play dead under the bloody cascade of my hair.

"Cop, you need to drop your gun." The sounds of sirens rang from the freeway. "You're the one who let him go to jail and now he's dead. We've been paying for that drop for months. You were supposed to stop it."

That's when they started firing. Cedric dropped to the floor with a clean bullet hole to his face. I lay as still as I could, fighting the pain, willing myself not to flinch. Suddenly, Garcia was gurgling next to me, eyes open wide, his bloodied hands pulling at the neck of his collar. He was choking on his own blood. The ringing shots stopped; the room was filled with the smell of gunpowder and iron and dampened whispers.

My head throbbed. I pressed my hand against the gushing hole in my thigh, but the blood was coming out in pulses. I could feel myself fading.

This was it. This was my end. I was going to die on the floor surrounded by drug dealers, crooked cops, and cartel lieutenants.

As I drifted from life, my weightless, painless body hovered high above the room. I could see why people would surrender to death. That was the best thing, the painlessness. My leg, my head, and every part of my body felt soft. An untouchable warmth enveloped me. It was the smell of my grandmother's house, the sound of my mother's laughter, the sight of my cousin Gloria's smile. I willed my way toward that light and warmth. I was ready to not be a part of this world anymore.

My body jerked upward, the pain returning the instant I took a breath. I could hear and feel the EMTs working on me, their hands on my body, shining their lights in my eyes.

I don't know what I thought—maybe that if I kept my eyes closed, I wouldn't have to face the reality of being back in this world. When I finally opened my eyes, I could see all the dead men in that room, watching themselves drift from life just as I had moments before.

Garcia screamed at the men working on his chest. The more they pushed, the more blood gathered on the floor. Garcia was dead. He looked up from his corpse to find me staring at him from the gurney. He was in my face in an instant. "What makes you think you're going anywhere, you bitch?"

His cold arm reached inside of me. I could feel Garcia's grip on me, a vice of hate. I was beginning to drift away again.

That's when I saw Erma. She pulled Garcia's soul from me like a slab of tar. She lit up that upholstery shop so brightly that it burned Garcia into the white. Erma reached down and grabbed my hand as a flood of souls swarmed past her and into the light. When the last one had moved through, she let go. I wanted to go with her. I wanted to feel that warmth.

Instead, I felt metal on my chest and a jolt that shook through it like liquid light. Adrenaline. Going back into my body was a slap, a quick and magnetic pull.

I was alive. I was alive because Erma wanted me to be, because somewhere on this planet people were praying for me. Even if I didn't want to believe it.

CHAPTER THIRTY-SEVEN

f/2.8

I HAD BEEN in the hospital for four days before I opened my eyes again. Machines murmured and beeped in the room. The open window showed the world as it was, moving onward just as it had before. A sting and ache in my left leg brought me back to what had happened. I barely remembered it all, but I knew Garcia was dead.

I looked around the room, half expecting Erma to offer some of her witty banter or scream at me to get out of my bed. But there was no one but me.

No—I spoke too soon.

A nurse in cartoon-covered scrubs pushed open the door, calling out a cheerful "good morning" as she pulled back the blankets on my bed. "The leg is doing great. You're a lucky girl. Not everyone survives a shot to the leg like that. Just missed an artery." She wrote furiously on some paperwork. "I'll let your family know that you're awake. They've been here waiting for days. Your department chief asked me to call when you woke up, so I hope you don't mind if I let them know."

"No need." Angie was standing at the door.

"Angie." My voice was weak and raspy.

"Save it, Rita." She walked over to my bedside. "I don't know what to say. You tried to tell us."

"Please tell me he's gone." I could feel the fear in my throat even though I had seen his soul being sucked out of the world.

"He's gone, Rita." Angie squeezed my hand. "We reinstated you while you were out. You know, for the insurance." She laughed. "Remember what I told you. It's okay to quit. Don't think you have to come back to this if you don't want to."

I stayed silent.

"I'll leave that up to you." She smiled at me. "Lieutenant Declan is probably going to want to talk to you too. He's closing up the case." There was a long pause. "Your work had everything to do with that."

"It doesn't matter now," I admitted. Everyone was dead.

Grandma was already at the door with Mr. Bitsilly, and before I knew it, they were by my bedside, hugging me.

"We'll talk more later, Rita." Angie shook hands with Grandma and Mr. Bitsilly on her way out.

"Are you two okay? How long have you been here?"

"Just long enough," Mr. Bitsilly said. Grandma was quiet, tears in her eyes. "I hope that this is it. You've solved the case. The spirits are gone. It's time to stop. If—"

"I know, Mr. Bitsilly. If I let them in, they'll never leave me alone. Erma is gone. I was here to get her justice. And she got it." I smiled at them both. "She's on her journey now."

"Are you still seeing them?" Grandma broke her silence, a quiver in her voice.

"Not anymore, Grandma." I held her hand.

"Your two friends are good friends. They're helping clean

up your apartment." Grandma tried her best to tame my sticky, unwashed hair. "I was hoping you would come home."

"We were hoping you would stop doing this job. Stop letting this evil into your life." Mr. Bitsilly handed me my tádídíín bag. It had been tied to a string on my window shades, untouched for quite some time, and he knew it.

"We'll come by later and bring you a little something to eat." Grandma held my hand.

"Yes, don't eat this hospital junk," Mr. Bitsilly added. "It made me sicker than my last surgery."

CHAPTER THIRTY-EIGHT

Wide Open

IT'S HORRIBLE TO lie to the people you love. I had to tell Grandma and Mr. Bitsilly that the ghosts were gone. I had no other choice.

In my hospital room, a man sat reading a book with a title I couldn't make out. Every hour or so, his ghost would sigh and slam the book closed, then walk to the window and look out. The man did this over and over, all through the days and nights I was stuck there, like he didn't have the memory in the soles of his feet, the callouses of maintaining that journey for the rest of his days. He never noticed me or asked me for anything. I suspected that in his last moments, he had succumbed to some form of dementia. It made me wonder about death in a way I hadn't before. He was the first spirit I had seen that had taken his disease with him into the afterlife.

My second visitor came every other night and mopped the floors in my room. At first, I didn't think he was a ghost—he walked with a limp and worked so hard. Two or three weeks into my stay at the hospital, he noticed me staring at him from across the room. "I have nowhere else to be," he said, then turned to his bucket, the sound of his metal mop scraping on the floor. He'll probably be mopping well into eternity, or until they bring that building to the ground.

The third one liked to talk to me.

"Can you hear me?" The woman's voice was calming, a psychologist's tone.

I said nothing.

"Can you?"

I turned and looked right into her eyes, but I didn't say a word. I knew better.

"I knew it." She smiled at me, walked to the window, and jumped out of the glass. She did this nearly every night.

The ghosts were everywhere, just like they always were in hospitals. They lined the hallways, sat in waiting rooms and physical therapy rooms, lingered inside the women's bathrooms, and smoked on the benches outside the building. Saint Joseph's Hospital had become the bus station of the afterlife—the place where some souls came to move on to their destinations, while others lived on the floors of the station, waiting for the bus that would never come.

The doctors said six months on crutches was going to be my reality, a full year before my leg was fully functional. Therapy and doctor's appointments every day for a while. I was returning to the crime lab in a few weeks anyway on desk duty. With my injuries and my medical bills, I knew that it was better to stay put.

There was an optimism to moving forward. Even if my body was going to take its time to heal, my mind was awakened. The night I came home from the hospital, it was amazing to me just how many spirits lived in the hallways and apartments of my building. I counted five on my way up the stairs, walking in and out of walls. My senses were on full alert.

I sat in the darkness of my living room and absorbed the silence of home with my mother's Hasselblad on my lap. I would put new photos of home on the walls, take more photos of things that were alive—start a new way of life. Most of all, I needed to go home to Grandma and Mr. Bitsilly more often. I rested my head back on the couch and closed my eyes.

Sleep came quickly, as did the dreams. It was the first time in years that I dreamed about Gloria in a good and peaceful way. Her hand gripped mine as we ran as fast as we could toward the road north of Grandma's house. The light was perfect, the sunset setting Gloria's hair on fire. We ran and we laughed until our sides hurt, racing up the last hill by the sheep corral.

"Gloria." I breathed heavily. "You can't leave me like that again."

Gloria smiled, her hands on her hips. The final orange glow of the sun filled her face.

"I'm not going anywhere." She grabbed me around the shoulders and led me into Grandma's house. "You're going to need me."

Grandma always said to me that you never do things for people to get something in return. That is the white man's way of living. You do it because they need you. You do it because if you don't, no one else will.

ACKNOWLEDGMENTS

THANK YOU TO everyone who helped to make this book a reality.

Thank you to the IAIA Low Residency MFA Program and the SWAIA Discovery Fellowship for their early support of the book. Thank you also to my fellow writers for the discussions, the feedback and the friendship.

To my teachers and mentors: Eden Robinson, Amanda Boyden, Ramona Ausubel, Linda Hogan, Chip Livingston, Pam Houston and Writing by Writers—thank you for the red ink, the drafts and the passing on of dreams.

To all of my biggest supporters and champions: Joan Tewkesbury—thank you for moving me to fiction as it made all the difference in the world. Thank you for your support, Beverly Morris, and for always believing. Thank you, Nancy Stauffer Cahoon, for talking me through all of it and for supporting Indigenous storytelling.

Thank you to Juliet Grames, the best editor in the world, for being so patient and supportive. You literally waited years for me to come back. You're the best. Thank you as well to everyone at Soho. You have all been so welcoming.

Thank you to Mom and Joseph for cheerleading and being so proud of me.

Thank you to my son, Max, for reminding me, every day, to eat dinner . . .

And a gigantic thank you to my best friend, my husband, Kelly. Thank you for always being by my side. Here is to many more years of telling stories with you.